THE HOUSEWIFE ASSASSIN'S HORRORSCOPE

JOSIE BROWN

A BOOK BY

SIGNAL
PRESS

Praise for Josie Brown's Novels

"This is a super sexy and fun read that you shouldn't miss! A kick ass woman that can literally kick ass as well as cook and clean. Donna gives a whole new meaning to "taking out the trash."
—Mary Jacobs, *Book Hounds Reviews*

"*The Housewife Assassin's Handbook* by Josie Brown is a fun, sexy and intriguing mystery. Donna Stone is a great heroine —housewives can lead all sorts of double lives, but as an assassin? Who would have seen that one coming? It's a fast-paced read, the gadgets are awesome, and I could just picture Donna fighting off Russian gangsters and skinheads all the while having a pie at home cooling on the windowsill. As a housewife myself, this book was a fantastic escape that had me dreaming "if only" the whole way through. The book doesn't take itself too seriously, which makes for the perfect combination of mystery and humour."
—*Curled Up with a Good Book and a Cup of Tea*

"*The Housewife Assassin's Handbook* is a hilarious, laugh-out-loud read. Donna is a fantastic character–practical, witty, and kick-ass tough. There's plenty of action–both in and out of the bedroom… I especially love the housekeeping tips at the start of each chapter–each with its own deadly twist! This book is perfect for relaxing in the bath with after a long day. I can't wait to read the next in the series. Highly Recommended!"

"This was an addictive read–gritty but funny at the same time. I ended up reading it in just one evening and couldn't go to sleep until I knew what the outcome would be! It was action-packed and humorous from the start, and that continued throughout, I was pleased to discover that this is the first of a series and look forward to getting my hands on Book Two so I can see where life takes Donna and her family next!"

"The two halves of Donna's life make sense. As you follow her story, there's no point where you think of her as "Assassin Donna" vs. "Mummy Donna', her attitude to life is even throughout. I really like how well this is done. And as for Jack. I'll have one of those, please?"

Novels in The Housewife Assassin Series

The Housewife Assassin's Handbook

(Book 1)

The Housewife Assassin's Guide to Gracious Killing

(Book 2)

The Housewife Assassin's Killer Christmas Tips

(Book 3)

The Housewife Assassin's Relationship Survival Guide

(Book 4)

The Housewife Assassin's Vacation to Die For

(Book 5)

The Housewife Assassin's Recipes for Disaster

(Book 6)

The Housewife Assassin's Hollywood Scream Play

(Book 7)

The Housewife Assassin's Killer App

(Book 8)

The Housewife Assassin's Hostage Hosting Tips

(Book 9)

The Housewife Assassin's Garden of Deadly Delights

(Book 10)

The Housewife Assassin's Tips for

Weddings, Weapons, and Warfare

(Book 11)

The Housewife Assassin's Husband Hunting Hints

(Book 12)

The Housewife Assassin's Ghost Protocol

(Book 13)

The Housewife Assassin's Terrorist TV Guide

(Book 14)

The Housewife Assassin's Deadly Dossier

(Book 15: The Series Prequel)

The Housewife Assassin's Greatest Hits

(Book 16)

The Housewife Assassin's Fourth Estate Sale

(Book 17)

The Housewife Assassin's Horrorscope

(Book 18)

The Housewife Assassin's White House Keeping Seal of Approval

(Book 19)

1

What's Your Sign?

If your first exposure to this question took place in some bar, you're forgiven for rolling your eyes at this 1970s pick-up line.

However, if you are a serious student of astrology—the study of the movements and positions of stars and other celestial bodies—the question is relevant to the beginning and the end of your life's journey!

The science of astrology divines an individual's personality traits and foretells events in that person's life. Those who practice it believe we are each born under one of the twelve sun signs: Aries, Leo, Sagittarius, Taurus, Virgo, Capricorn, Gemini, Libra, Aquarius, Cancer, Scorpio, or Pisces.

For example, if you're a Cancer, your intuitive kindness means you hate any form of conflict. Ergo, when trapped by a player in a bar who insists on learning your zodiac sign, you'll "accidentally" spill your drink on yourself as an excuse to go to the ladies' room—but really, you'll slip out the back door.

However, if you're a Taurus, you are ALL about honesty. Completely. Totally. Without a doubt. So, when a guy asks about your sign but you're not interested in him, don't just tell him; show him! Your middle finger can make your point succinctly.

Finally, if you're a Leo, you are dignified, self-confident, and fearless. When approached by a lounge lizard, your first answer will take the form of a raised brow and a withering glare. Hopefully, that will send him scurrying off. If he persists, you respond in a voice that means business and with a phrase that can't be misinterpreted. Perhaps, "You're too ugly, and life's too short."

Finally, actions speak louder than words. One kick to the nutsack, and he'll get the message.

Come to think of it, these methods work whatever your sign!

"IT'S ANOTHER SUNNY DAY IN SOUTHERN CALIFORNIA! HERE IN DOWNTOWN L.A., TEMPERATURES HAVE ALREADY REACHED RECORD HIGHS—"

"Dude, tell us something we don't already know," my husband, Jack Craig, mumbles under his breath, "And without yelling it in my ear!"

Jack may be taking out his angst on the radio but really he, like me and everyone else within a two-mile radius, is peeved at Los Angeles' hellacious highway:

The 405.

It's been at a total standstill for the past hour, which means we're late for a very important date with our boss, Ryan Clancy, of Acme Industries.

He summoned us with a cryptic message:

Special showing of THE TRUMAN SHOW.

Nope, the movie reference isn't his way of announcing a Jim Carrey movie marathon at the black-op organization's offices. It's the code word for the U.S. National Defense Agency, our largest client.

The capped title in the text expresses the mission's urgency.

Only a few hours before, we'd returned from our latest mission: in London, where we'd successfully bid on a designer pocketbook containing a coded missive listing the identities of Chinese spies in the United States. We were then ordered to hang around for a second assignment: rendezvous with a CIA asset with intel on arms dealers supplying Middle-Eastern terrorist groups. Sadly, the asset was murdered just minutes before I got to her. But, by finding her killer, we fended off a massive political upheaval in the Middle East.

This week, anyway.

It doesn't help that our mission team's tech operative, Arnie Locklear, is also bombarding our cell phones with emojis depicting faces that are anything but smiling: his indication that Ryan is peeved at our tardiness. The first emoji's mouth was flatlined. The second one nursed an outright frown and eyebrows raised anxiously. The screen of Jack's phone is just within his peripheral vision. He sighs when the seventh and most recent pops up. This time Smiley's eyes are open wide, and its tiny hands are slapping its cheeks in terror.

Not good.

I text back:

The 405 is the Highway to Hell!

Will it appease Ryan? Doubtful, but it'll have to do.

"Donna, stand up and tell me what you see," Jack commands me.

Time to lighten the mood. "Aye, aye, Captain!" I raise my right hand to my brow in a mock salute before hoisting myself through our BMW i8 roadster's already opened soft-top roof.

It's January in Los Angeles, which means bikini weather. It's sunny and hot enough that most of the automobiles' windows are open. Music from the cars' radios fills the air around us, like a gin-tipsy band tuning up before a concert. Considering the variety of riffs colliding mid-air, you'd think most of the musicians are tone deaf and came to the wrong venue.

I scan the road. The traffic going in the opposite direction —southbound—is at least crawling along steadily, whereas all four of the northbound lanes are at a total standstill.

There is a dark haze in the air. It's not the usual SoCal smog. This is verified when my nose catches a whiff of smoke.

"Do you smell that?" I ask.

Jack sticks his head out the window. "Yeah." He looks off toward a hill specked with homes. "Over there—a fire!" Staring, he leans out. "It seems to be more than one house too."

Because we're not moving, our ears pick up the wail of sirens. Suddenly, in the opposite direction, a fire truck rolls by on the highway's safety shoulder.

"Let's find a news station to hear what's happening," I suggest.

As he punches the scan button on our car's radio, our ears are bombarded by a whirlwind of sounds—classic rock riffs, country whines, mariachi, some sports commentators trying to impress each other with L.A. Dodgers stats from days of yore—until he finds KNX 1070, an all-news station.

"—several dozen residential gas explosions in the Los Angeles Metroplex in the past few hours. Besides the Echo Park, Westwood, Glendale, and Monterrey Park neighborhoods, towns as far north as Santa Clarita, west to Pasadena, and Redondo Beach to the south have been affected as well. There are quite a few casualties because it's a Saturday and many folks are at home. Los Angeles's emergency services are stretched thin. Burn victims are filling hospital emergency departments. Evacuations in those towns are taking place now with no word as to when residents will be allowed back into these areas. California Electric & Gas is at a loss as to the cause—"

All of a sudden the cars ahead of us inch forward. Jack, anxious to get going, follows suit—

And I stumble backward.

But when he stops short to avoid hitting the car in front of us, I'm tossed forward again—

And find myself doubled up over the windshield.

As I inch myself off the glass, Jack exclaims sheepishly, "Jeez! So sorry, babe."

"Yeah, right," I mutter. Since his hand is too late to steady me, I slap it off my thigh.

"I'm just trying to pull down your skirt," he explains. "The van on our left is getting more than an eyeful!"

The draft on my backside is all the evidence I need that he's right. My eyes are drawn to the moving van beside us. Two guys stare back at me with leers on their lips as wide as their aging van.

In no time I've scrambled down into the passenger seat, only to find myself sitting on my pocketbook: not comfortable, what with the tiny bulge in its front pocket.

It holds an envelope containing a thumb drive. Evan Martin, my ward, is home this weekend from his studies at Cal Berkeley. He received it mysteriously: after the hit-and-run death of Jonathan Presley, a vice president at BlackTech, one the companies Evan inherited.

BlackTech has numerous contracts with the U.S. Defense Intelligence Agency. Evan has asked us to see if anything on the drive is confidential. If so, it may have played a role in Jonathan's demise. After we've been briefed on our current mission, I'll hand it over to our tech operative, Arnie Locklear.

"Forward, Jeeves," I sniff.

Jack takes the hint and hits the gas again.

At least now we're moving faster than a crawl—

Until an eighteen-wheeler stops dead center in the two middle lanes.

The cars behind it—ours included—screech to a halt.

"Just our luck," Jack mutters. He cranes his neck to see if he can inch into the lane closest to the shoulder. Unfortunately, the vehicles behind us have the same idea. Once again, we're stuck.

Then, suddenly, a bigger sound fills the air. It's as if some jazz orchestra has somehow found its way inside the massive eighteen-wheeler…

Well, what do you know: IT HAS.

The back panel doors of the truck fly open, revealing rows of musicians, playing as if their lives depend on it.

Despite the orchestra's loud, danceable ditty, I detect a

slight buzzing sound coming from overhead. I look up to see four drones. Who knows where they came from? Each has a camera strapped to its underbelly.

By now, the cars in the two blocked lanes are at a standstill. Immediately, the drivers and passengers, six deep behind it, leap out of their vehicles. All are dressed in bright primary-colored hipster haute couture.

They begin dancing.

Alone. In pairs. In chorus lines. They shake, shimmy, and shuffle off to Buffalo. They do flips off the hoods of their candy-colored cars, only to land in each other's arms.

Jack's expletive-laden exclamation is lost in the cacophony of music, now accompanied by the apparently miked dancers' singing.

Most of the drivers, held hostage on this hot blacktopped version of a Gene Kelly fantasy, are too stunned to even honk their horns. Others stagger out of their cars with bemused grins on their faces.

"It's not often that one stumbles across a pop-up film shoot," I declare.

"Unless you live in La La Land," Jack retorts. "This is all because some movie director never got a permit." He closes his eyes in disgust. "And during a public emergency, no less!"

"Even if he had applied, he'd never have gotten one," I point out. "So, I guess, now the rest of us have to sit awhile and enjoy the show."

"Like hell, we will." Jack scans the other vehicles but then grimaces when one catches his eye.

I follow his gaze. In one of the blocked lanes, a cherry-red

Marchi Mobile EleMMent Palazzo Superior motor coach sits behind one of the dancers' cars.

Several people stand on top of the motor coach, under an expansive canopied roof. Only one of them is sitting: a man, wearing a baseball cap. He's looking into a video monitor.

When he turns his head to scan the rows of cars behind him, we get a better look at him: mid-thirties, a scruffy beard, rainbow-tinted aviator glasses, and a tight white tee shirt that clings to his well-defined pecs.

"That's the Academy Award-winning director, Vance Melamed!" I exclaim.

"He's also the cause of this mess." Jack is out of the car in a flash. He moves with lightning speed, zigzagging between vehicles.

When he reaches a portable ladder on the rear of the motor coach, he climbs up. None of Vance's minions look up as Jack saunters over to Vance. They're too busy looking at their video monitors. But the moment Jack addresses Vance —with a placid smile on his face, though I'd bet his words are anything but that—two brawny, frowning guys go chest-to-chest with my husband.

At this point, Vance shouts loudly enough to drown out the orchestra. Phrases like "Who the hell do you think you are, telling me to stop my masterpiece…" and "My studio will sue you into the ground—" roll trippingly off his tongue.

In Hollywood, Vance may be a Master of the Universe, but Jack isn't buying it. He makes that quite clear to the director's bodyguards when, with one swift move, he puts one in a chokehold and then slams him into the other one. Both topple to the floor.

Vance's hissy fit only grows louder.

Oh, dear.

Somehow, I've got to get Jack's attention. I've also got to get us out of this traffic jam.

With that in mind, I glance around the car for something that can be used as a diversionary tactic. Since the i8 is sexier than my Mommy mobile, it is preferred by our children for afternoon pickups. Although nothing is in its tiny back seat, there may be something in the trunk that might do the trick.

I pop it open and hop out—

Bingo. Stashed there is the archery gear of our oldest child. Mary, seventeen, is decent enough with her bow and arrows to have made her school's team, which looks great on her college applications.

Here's hoping my aim is as good as hers.

I take the bow in my left hand. After pulling an arrow from its quiver, I position its pronged rubber base against the bowstring's nocking point. With my feet just as wide as my shoulders, I sight my target and take aim, slowly drawing the string back until it's taut—

Then I release the arrow.

It whizzes through the air toward its target.

Not to worry! Not at Vance, but at one of his camera drones.

The force of my bullseye hit slams the drone into a billboard before it crashes onto the highway's safety shoulder.

Hearing the racket, Vance exclaims, "What the…"

When he sees the smoking wreckage, he stumbles backward.

While he stares in shock, I put another drone out of its

misery. This one dive-bombs onto the hood of the motor coach.

As Vance scrambles down the ladder, he finally finds his voice and yells, "*CUT!*"

Not that the cast and crew aren't already clued into the realization that today's shoot has already been canceled.

Vance screams, "Who the hell shot down my cameras?"

Jack takes a wild guess and looks over at me.

Seeing the bow in my hand and the smile on my face, he nods appreciatively. In a flash, he's down the ladder and onto the street.

Not a moment too soon. A police cruiser manned by two uniformed officers crawls toward us via the highway's shoulder. But Jack is lost in the crowd of angry, bored drivers who have also hopped out of their cars to take a gander at Vance's hoopla.

While one of the cops tickets Vance for multiple traffic violations, the other policeman waves us through the bottleneck.

By the time we're a few exits away from the office, the traffic is flowing at a swift pace. Every now and then an emergency vehicle will scream past us, as do a couple of sports cars, which seem to be playing chicken in and out of all four lanes. When one cuts in front of the panel van two vehicles ahead of us, it stops short. The car behind it—a silver convertible Porsche Carrera S Cabriolet—slams into the van's rear bumper.

Jack screeches to a halt a few inches from the Porsche.

Just then the van's back doors fly open. Its cargo is people: six females, in their teens or twenties, who are bound and gagged.

A few stumble onto their bare feet and hop toward the open door. The first captive leaps onto the Porsche's hood with both feet, landing with a thunk before rolling off.

Angered, Porsche Guy jumps out of his car to berate the first captive and the others who, like lemmings, have also plopped onto his car before scrambling off and onto the asphalt.

Whereas other vehicles moving around us slow down, one swerves instead, barely avoiding hitting one of the women.

"Call the police," I command Jack. I'm out of the car in a flash, heading for the freed women.

By now many of the women have caught onto the fact that they are on a roadway. They tremble at the unknown dangers around them. When I reach them, I tear the electrical tape off their mouths and hands before herding them toward the Porsche. By the time I fling open the passenger door, I've been blessed numerous times in Russian. The women don't have to be asked twice to climb in.

Just then, a large, muscular, scowling man, his long light hair coiled tightly in a man bun, flies out the driver's side of the van. His identical twin leaps out the passenger side. Man Bun lunges at one of the fleeing captives, grabbing her by the hair. Twin Bun cold-cocks another prisoner before grabbing a third.

Porsche Guy is still yelling at the top of his lungs about the damage to his precious roadster when Man Bun pulls out a gun and points it at him—

But my punch to Man Bun's left kidney has him doubling over. With lightning speed, I wrench the arm holding the gun behind him and at the sort of angle that, when it cracks, Porsche Guy gasps.

Fearfully, his head turns in the direction of Man Bun's twin. He's relieved to see that Jack has grabbed Twin Bun from behind and slammed him into the van with such force that when his head hits it leaves a dent. By the time he slides to the asphalt, he has passed out.

A half-mile away on the shoulder lane, two police cars, sirens blaring, are quickly moving toward us.

"Great! Just what we need," Jack mutters. "I guess we should flip a coin as to who gets to call Ryan with the news that we'll be at least another hour, explaining to the cops how we cold-cocked a couple of human traffickers."

I sigh. "Not if I can help it. Head toward the car. I'll follow in a second."

Jack nods, then saunters off, as if he doesn't have a care in the world.

In the meantime, I snap my fingers in front of Porsche Guy's wide, wary eyes. "Apparently, these thugs kidnapped these women, possibly for slavery. So, here's your chance to be a hero. Tell the police what happened: that you unarmed them and kicked their asses—*all on your lonesome.* Otherwise"—I make it a point to drop my eyes onto his front license plate—"we'll find you."

Porsche Guy nods numbly.

A moment later, Jack and I are another mile down the road—

But we've got a tail: one of the cop cruisers is heading down the highway shoulder toward us.

"I guess the police didn't buy Porsche Guy's tale of derring-do," I grouse.

"Hey, it was worth a try." Jack guns the engine. One of the features of the BMW i8 is that it can do zero to sixty in under five seconds. Another eight seconds beyond this, Jack has somehow managed to zigzag two lanes over.

We're on the far side of an eighteen-wheeler as the black-and-white rolls past.

Jack's proud grin earns him an eye-roll.

"You're welcome," he retorts. "Now let's get to the office."

"We're coming up to our exit, and we're still in the far lane," I warn Jack.

He accelerates, propelling our car too close to the bumper of the mommy van in front of us before veering through an opening between two monster trucks to our right, and then into the far-right lane, which is wide open, at least for six car lengths.

Suddenly, we hear the blare of another patrol car's siren.

I look back. A police vehicle is dodging around the cars between us, but it's also gaining on us.

"Hold on," Jack declares.

I'm tempted to close my eyes but force myself to keep them open.

We fly up the off-ramp's two lanes. To get to the office, we should be in the right one. The line of cars waiting to turn in that direction is six long. So, instead, Jack takes the left lane—

And so does our police escort, but behind two cars. The officer tweaks his siren to warn them that he's got to jump the line.

By the time they realize he's there, it's too late. The light is now green, and Jack is off—

Turning right instead.

The car beside us, which legally owns the lane, veers to avoid sideswiping us. The driver's face would be quite pretty if it weren't contorted by angry indignation.

By the time the autos move out of the police cruiser's way, we've sped off—

But his siren clears a path for him and keeps us in his sights.

Dismayed, I murmur, "He's gaining on us."

"Do you love me?" Jack asks.

"With all my heart," I say warily.

His next question sends a chill up my spine: "Do you trust me?"

"Also with all my heart," I vow. "So don't do anything that makes me question my sanity."

Jack shakes his head. "Sorry, doll. No promises."

To prove it, he hits the gas.

We crest a hill—

And then Jack veers sharply to the right—

Landing us onto a narrow gap in a tall hedge.

We're a few hundred feet from a tunnel. With a push of a button on our car's dashboard, a radio signal emits the security code that opens its gate.

A half-mile later, the tunnel emerges inside Acme's underground garage.

Our car purrs to a stop in front of Ryan.

Scowling, he waits against a wall, his arms folded at his chest. "You'd better have one hell of a great excuse," he growls.

Jack and I exchange glances. Then, in unison, we offer: "Saturday traffic on the 405."

Ryan accepts our explanation with a resigned nod and a smirk. "What? No bullshit tales of evildoer shenanigans or earthshaking calamities? I must say, your honesty is refreshing. You should try it more often."

I frown. "Is that supposed to be a compliment? Are you saying you wouldn't have believed us if we said that, say, houses were exploding all over town?"

"Or, if we'd told you that the highway was at a standstill because they were shooting a movie scene on two lanes?" Jack adds.

"Or, that when a sports car slammed into a van, a bunch of captive slaves jumped out and we stopped to round them up?" I ask.

"Mr. and Mrs. Craig, I've always admired your very active imaginations," Ryan retorts. "And considering your new mission, the home explosion line is at least believable." He nods toward the elevator. "Ready to hear about it? The rest of the team is already waiting upstairs."

2

Mercury in Retrograde

[Donna's horoscope today]

Mercury is in retrograde!

Fair warning: no decisions should be made during the next three weeks. Otherwise, you'll wreak havoc in your life and those you love. Here are a few worst-case scenarios:

Example #1: Stay away from the shooting range. Even a crack shot can't avoid Mercury's gravitational pull on projectiles —especially when a colleague you remember less than fondly is within aim.

Example #2: Don't take on any new projects that may end in a raging inferno. Despite your expertise in pyrotechnics, the cosmic forces at work are ready, willing, and able to light a revenge-fueled fire under those who can do you the most harm. No need to see all you've worked so hard for go up in smoke!

Example #3: Don't let hurt feelings get in the way of making up with your beloved. Sure, the way he worded his latest

*thoughtless aside may have been petty and demeaning, but that's
no reason to poison the well of your relationship —*

*Especially when crushed cherry pits in his dirty martini will
do the trick just fine. Bottoms up!*

EVEN AS THE REST OF AMERICA ENJOYS A LAZY SATURDAY,
Acme's headquarters hums with the static urgency of a
world fraught with peril.

On our way to Ryan's situation room, we pass a sea of
cubicles filled with the handlers of Acme's legion of field
operatives, all murmuring into the microphones of the cush-
ioned headsets clasped firmly to their ears. Although the
conversations are *sotto voce*, from their postures, you can
deduce the operative's current circumstance. One handler
leans back in his chair, chuckling as he shoots the breeze
with an operative whose life he's saved on numerous occasions. The rigid back and furious typing of another handler
mimic her charge's dire situation. Another stands up,
shouting expletives before collapsing back down into his
chair. His face is damp with tears.

Apparently, Acme has lost an operative.

I bow my head at this horrible realization.

Ryan frowns. Like a seismograph, he is fine-tuned to his
staff's emotional quakes, fractures, and ruptures. "Go on in.
I'll be right behind you." He nods toward the situation room.

Before entering, I take a look back. The handler's head is
bowed. Ryan's hand is on his back. I can't hear what Ryan
says to him. It won't vanquish his grief, or lessen his guilt
over the loss of a life.

Together they head for the staircase that leads to Acme's rooftop garden.

Up there, one hopes that the ocean breeze will nudge away doubts of split-second life-and-death decisions. Benches, tucked deep in its tall hedges, give privacy to those who wish to shed a few tears. Paths meander around the garden's lush vegetation, but all lead to the center, where Acme has its memorial wall.

And now, yet another name will be added.

Can a few moments in stark sunshine warm away the chill of a life lost? Probably not. Still, it is a quiet, lush sanctuary for those whose nerves are pricked continuously by death, destruction, and the never-ending game of world domination with our enemies.

JET LAG IS A BITCH.

Apparently, not just for Jack and me but for the three other operatives who spent the past few days with us in London.

Arnie is passed out over two chairs. His erratic snores are almost loud enough to shake him off his precarious perch.

Emma Honeycutt—his wife, and also Acme's Communications Intelligence director—doesn't slow the breakneck speed of her typing even as she nudges his bum back onto the chair with her foot.

Abu Nagashahi, a field operative who acts as our team's lead cleaner, cutout, and driver, sits in a *padmasana* lotus pose. Is he meditating or merely sleeping?

Suddenly, he says softly, "Yep, Manny, that's right—

another two thousand shares of Apple stock. But dump half my Facebook…Yeah, the Russia hacking bugged me too…"

I know for a fact that Manny is his stockbroker. For the first time, I notice he's wearing an earbud. Abu is multitasking.

Jack grabs a tennis ball from a box on the room's credenza. With a practiced arm, he tosses it onto the floor at an angled trajectory so that it bounces off a wall and back to him, which he catches one-handed. He repeats the pattern again and again and again—

But then finally misses.

The ball hits Dominic Fleming—blond, British, and too handsome for his own good—on the side of his head. Today he's certainly not living up to his bad boy player reputation. His usually clean-shaven face now sports a rough scruff. There are dark hollows under his eyes, and his hair has a lopsided cowlick. I guess he didn't sleep a wink on the plane, or in the few hours we've been home.

Annoyed, Dominic looks up from the task at hand: texting. "Old boy, do you mind?" he declares stiffly. "I'm in the middle of a very delicate negotiation."

"Oh yeah? What's her name?" Emma rolls her chair beside him so that she can look over his shoulder.

She's not yet aware that Dominic just had his heart broken recently, by a suspect we'd run across on our recent mission in London. The woman, a casino owner appropriately named Lucky, turned out to be a wonderful asset. Unfortunately for Dominic, she's also engaged.

"I think we should give him some slack," I warn Emma.

She's having too much fun to take the hint. Seeing what's on his phone's screen, she gasps, "You're on *eHarmony*?"

"I hear it's an outstanding app to use when one's desire is to meet women with serious intentions," he retorts.

"The operative word there is 'serious'," Emma reminds him.

"I am *very* serious," Dominic insists. "Having already perused the talent on Match, OK Cupid, and Zoosk—"

"They aren't 'talent'," I point out. "The quest for a life partner isn't a Hollywood cattle call."

"That it isn't," He mutters disappointedly. "Although, in too many cases, 'cattle' is an apt metaphor."

Emma snickers. "If you're judging women solely on their looks or what you deem are acceptable physical attributes, it's no wonder you're striking out."

"Are we talking your American football?" Dominic asks.

"Baseball," Jack informs him as he smacks the wall again with the ball.

"My dear Mrs. Locklear, I'm doing anything but!" Dominic's face flushes. "If you must know, my responses have been quite deferential." He shrugs. "Perhaps, to a fault."

Abu puts a hand over the phone before adding, "What he means to say is that he's batting zero."

Befuddled, Dominic shakes his head. "Pardon? Did you mean that as a cricket reference?"

Jack catches the ball with a sigh. "Again—*baseball*."

Dominic's eyes get smaller as his scowl grows deeper. Still, he acknowledges this insight with a nod.

"Look, Dominic, be honest with yourself. The type of woman you're looking for is more likely on Tinder, Pure, and AdultFriendFinder," Emma reasons.

"Y–yes. I suppose." Dominic's stutter undercuts his

emphatic declaration, as does the longing in his eyes. Trying to shrug off his primal instincts, he sniffs, "In the past, that may have been the case. This time, however, I am not looking for yet another fast, tawdry one night stand!"

I can't believe my ears. But, okay, yeah: I'll go along with this new, improved and markedly more politically correct Dominic Fleming. "How about Happn? I'd think you'd be perfect for any woman who believes in 'love at first sight.'"

"I would second that motion," Dominic retorts. "But, while I may look like Prince Charming, those damsels find my responses to be anything but."

"What about The League?" Emma suggests over Arnie's buzz saw snore. "It should be right up your alley. You've got the whole snob thing down pat."

"Too well, it seems," Dominic admits. "Even for *its* female subscribers."

"And Wingman is certainly out." The words slip out before I have a chance to realize what I'm saying.

"What are you implying?" Dominic growls.

I wince. "To be honest, you're not exactly someone a real friend would set up with her bestie."

Dominic glowers at me.

Emma mutters, "So...I guess that leaves...Bumble?"

"Bumble?" Dominic cries as he rises half out of his chair. "Are you inferring that I'm some kind of social pariah?"

"That's not what Emma meant at all." I'm using my sing-song mommy voice. "Sometimes a more modest demeanor works better than a full court press."

Dominic's brow arches. "Baseball yet again?"

"Basketball!" Abu, Emma, Jack and I say in unison.

We're so loud that Arnie falls off his chair. Waking with a jolt, he mumbles, "What did I miss?"

"Nothing," Emma sighs. "Except that Dominic has lost his mojo."

Dominic sputters, "I have not!"

"I'll second that," Jack proclaims.

We turn to him, shocked—even Dominic.

"You just need a different M.O. You know, something a bit more subtle," Jack assures him.

"Really?" Dominic sounds doubtful.

"Believe it or not, Dom, some women like a guy who doesn't come off like a machismo narcissist who thinks he's a stud."

"My sexual prowess has been lauded the world over," Dominic bristles.

"That just says you do better in person than online," Jack points out. "But to meet these ladies, you have to impress them with your online profile first." he bounces the ball in his palm. "You know, I could help you with that. Massage a few words so that you get more times up to bat." Jack grins slyly. "Maybe even a few home runs."

"Baseball?" Dominic guesses.

"Bingo!" Jack assures him.

"Game time is over, children." Ryan's voice, coming from the doorway, puts us at attention. When he realizes that a Bingo game isn't actually happening, his grimace softens. "Grab a seat. The Director of Intelligence is on the line—and he's not a happy camper."

"So, what you're telling us, Director, is that the gas leak fires taking place this morning throughout Los Angeles were caused by Russian hacking of the California Electric & Gas company's utility grid?" Jack asks.

"Although other nation state-funded adversaries—China, North Korea, and Iran, to name a few—have had limited success, in this case, again, affirmative: Russia is the culprit." Through the conference table's speaker, Marcus Branham's voice is adamant. "Not just in L.A. This morning there were also attacks in Boston, Atlanta, Dallas, New York, Seattle, San Francisco, and Philadelphia. As we speak, DARPA's ACD—it's Active Cyber Defense program—is assessing all known U.S.-based Russian assets."

"Why focus on Russian actors here in the U.S.?" Emma asks. "As you know, sir, the hack would not have necessarily been made from this country. The Russians' infiltration of Estonia's utility grid is proof of that."

"The same was true of several Russian cyber attacks on our state-by-state election process," Arnie adds.

"Agreed," Branham admits. "Granted, those successful system hacks had been traced to outside the country. And yes, while U.S. utility companies are individually owned and operated, our nation's public utilities are part of a national grid, which makes such a hack from an enemy state easier to cause online havoc. But in this case, the coding changes that set off the energy surges didn't come from an overseas hack. Although it has the same fingerprints, it was done on U.S. soil."

"In other words, sabotage," I say.

"Exactly," Branham replies. "We intercepted chatter that

bears this out. For a few mere seconds, the perpetrator left a traceable footprint: a satellite call."

"Was the message intercepted as well?" Ryan asks.

"Yes. A voice said, simply, 'Zodiac is in place. Repeat: Zodiac is in place to coincide with Mercury in Retrograde.'"

"What does that mean, 'Mercury in Retrograde?'" Dominic asks.

"In astronomical terms, retrograde is an optical illusion," Emma explains. "At any given point in time, from Earth, another planet may look as if it's stopped its rotation around the sun—or even gone backward—when, in fact, no such thing has occurred. Astrologers assign fateful events to these times. For example, Mercury goes into retrograde three times a year, for about three weeks. During that time, one is advised to reconsider any change in plans; to take things slowly, or wait things out. You should never start a new venture, and so on."

"You know everything." Love weighs heavily in Arnie's voice.

Emma blushes.

"Was the voice on the satellite call male or female?" Jack asks.

"Unfortunately, an automatic dialogue replacement tool was used to mask the speaker's identification," Branham replies.

"A satellite phone's location can be triangulated via the Doppler-shift calculations from its host satellite," Arnie reasons.

"Another dead end for us, I'm afraid," Branham replies. "There are almost five thousand LEOs—that is, low Earth orbit satellites—circling the planet. On average, it takes one anywhere from seventy to one-hundred-and-ten minutes to make a complete orbital rotation. In many instances, the satellite might be out of range of an Earth station, during which time there is only a four-to-fifteen minute window for its GPS coordinates to be collected. In this case, we had less than that." He sighs. "The range is fairly substantial—ten to thirty kilometers."

"How can Acme be of service, Director?" Ryan asks.

"Glad you asked. POTUS insists that the operation be pitch black. Because Acme had great success for his predecessor, he asked that I reach out to you first. And, considering the satellite call was traced to somewhere within the Los Angeles metroplex, I agree with POTUS that you're the logical choice."

"We're honored," Ryan replies. He's always had a great poker face and an emotionless tone.

Mine: less so. When I put my finger in my mouth to mimic a gagging motion, he shakes his head at me. He knows I can't stand Bradley Edmonton.

Before Edmonton was vice president, for many years, he was a senator. Although just in his mid-forties, he sports a well-coiffed shock of white hair. This, along with a closetful of Saville Row suits and a block-long mansion in Georgetown, Edmonton has ably positioned himself as the consummate Washington insider. Despite his good ol' boy demeanor, he is pompous, shallow, and power hungry.

And as the Bachelor in Chief, there is no limit to the number of moneyed socialites who are vying for the role of First Lady.

"Honored, eh? I'll pass that along to POTUS," Branham

declares. "Ryan, I've already forwarded the sparse intel we have on Operation Flame."

Dominic frowns. "That's its official name?"

"It is now," Branham confirms. "It's POTUS's suggestion. And since it's his ballgame…"

As his voice trails off, Dominic mouths to Jack, *Baseball?*

Jack rewards him with a thumbs-up.

"I'll call the President immediately," Ryan assures him.

"No need. In fact, he's asked me to arrange for you, Jack, and Donna to meet with him in person—tomorrow afternoon, at sixteen-hundred hours—at former President Lee Chiffray's estate, Lion's Lair."

When our stunned silence hits the ten-second mark, Branham adds wryly, "Yes, it surprised me too, considering it's no secret that there's no love lost between those two gentlemen. However, the optics dictate that Edmonton treat Chiffray with some degree of deference. To that end, they'll be playing golf at Lion's Lair tomorrow before your meeting with him."

"Because people feel sorry that President Chiffray was the collateral damage in an assassination attempt?" Arnie muses in a soft murmur.

"Considering that Lee is the single largest donor to POTUS's party, I guess that he's here for some ass—I mean, ring-kissing," I whisper back.

"You hit it on the head, Mrs. Craig," Branham responds.

He heard that? Darn it!

While Branham chuckles at my supposition, Ryan slaps his forehead at my audacity.

"Good luck, ladies and gentlemen." There's a distinct click as Branham signs off.

RYAN TURNS TO EMMA. "THAT CRYPTIC MESSAGE ON THE satellite call may be our first clue. When is Mercury next in retrograde?"

Emma does a quick search on her laptop. "We're in it now, and for the next thirteen days."

"Then we have no time to lose," Ryan declares. "Arnie, take whatever coordinates were retrieved by the satellite phone and see if you can pinpoint the approximate location of the call. Emma, have your team scan NSA reports for any chatter on the blackouts that may be coming from Russian cells based stateside."

"Will do," she promises.

"The rest of you are on standby for the meeting with POTUS and for any needed legwork."

Abu, Dominic, Jack, and I nod.

As everyone rises and disperses, I make my way to Ryan. "Sir, an interesting thing was brought to our attention by our ward, Evan. It has to do with one of his companies, BlackTech."

Ryan thinks for a moment. "The firm's name sounds familiar."

"It should. Its largest client is the Defense Intelligence Agency."

Ryan's subtle nod demonstrates his sudden interest. "Go on."

"Earlier this week its chief engineer, Jonathan Presley was killed in a hit-and-run accident. Immediately afterward, Evan received this." I take the flash drive from my purse and hold it up to him. "It's from Presley. Upon his death, it was mailed to Evan anonymously. Evan feels it may contain sensitive information, and possibly a motive for Presley's murder."

"If what Evan suspects is true, I'm sure DI Branham will be grateful that we brought it to him." Ryan's smile is weak, but still, that counts for something. "I'm glad Evan was smart enough to save the envelope it came in. Do you know if he handled the thumb drive itself?"

I frown. "Yes, he did. So did I."

He shrugs. "Still, give it to Arnie. Maybe Forensics can pull up a partial fingerprint that pops up in IAFIS."

"The return address is a USPS box number," Jack informs him. "It matches the zip+4 code on the envelope."

"The post office is sure to have a couple of security cameras," Ryan replies. "Arnie will pull up footage from the past week so that we can see the last time Jonathan checked it, or for that matter, mailed something from it. But remember, Craigs: your first priority is Flame."

"Duly noted," I promise.

3

Bad Karma

In the Zodiac, each sign has a complementary relationship with a partner sign. And, for that matter, opposite zodiac signs also affect each other negatively.

It shouldn't surprise you that your best friend or a beloved is in the former category. Concurrently, don't blink twice should you discover that the frenemy who gets under your skin with predictable frequency is in the latter grouping.

Such events are the cause of "bad karma."

Word of caution: during such an altercation, should you find yourself within spitting distance, control any urge to hock a loogie in her direction. I say this not because it might turn into a hair-pulling contest (although it might) but because doing so is the typical reaction to the bad karma that the universe has already bestowed on both of you.

Your best bet: Control any urges that put you at odds with your opposites.

Otherwise, as Dorothy Parker famously said, "If you wear a short enough skirt, the party will come to you."

Yes, I know what you're thinking: "But, what if she starts it first?"

The short answer: This is why they say that Karma's a bitch.

WITH TRAFFIC ON THE 405 STILL MOVING SLOWER THAN molasses in February, it's dinnertime when we reach the city limits of Hilldale.

"We're both dead on our feet. As much as we'd like to catch a bite with the kids, let's hit the sack." Jack suggests.

"Works for me," I reply. "We'll have to table the Jonathan Presley affair until after we meet Edmonton tomorrow, anyway."

And, while Jack and I snuggled on the plane ride home, admittedly, neither of us had much time to sleep.

The faint buzz of my cell phone catches my attention. I stare down at it and sigh. "You may be headed to dreamland before me. Penelope and Aunt Phyllis have been bombarding me with texts!"

Jack groans. "Now what?"

As I scroll through them, I count twelve from Penelope Bing, a neighbor whose son, Cheever, is the same age as our son, Jeff. The boys are in the same class and are close friends. More to the point, Penelope is the perennial president of every parent-teacher association connected with any school her son attends.

Talk about a helicopter mom!

Now that the boys are in high school, she's there too. Rightly so, she's figured that, after eight years of non-stop volunteering, moms who might have been her competition are too burned out to volunteer for such time-consuming positions.

Still, by using the guilt-laden admonition "At this age, we have so little time with our children," she was able to strong-arm me into taking the thankless position of committee chair for Hilldale High School's Winter Prom, which takes place next weekend.

While in London during our last mission I outsourced the prom's logistics to my aunt, Phyllis, who usually stays with the kids when Jack and I are out of town. In hindsight, it wasn't the smartest move. According to Penelope, my aunt's decisions for everything—from its theme (*Game of Thrones*) to its decorations (a fire-breathing dragon chief among them) and party games (battle competitions with real swords, hatchets, and spiked clubs) and its entertainment (a Goth band of little people) are a disaster.

Not that I beg to differ. It's just that I haven't had time to go over these decisions with my aunt.

Well, surprise, surprise! Aunt Phyllis has left eight texts of her own. As I scroll through them, I groan.

"What's wrong now?" Jack asks.

"There's a definite pattern here, Aunt Phyllis's annoyance is rising at an equal level with Penelope's hysteria...Oh, and get this! Another thing they have in common: both question each other's sanity."

"No arguments there," he mutters as we turn onto our street. "Hey, do you think you can send them to their separate corners until tomorrow?"

"Doubtful. But I give you permission to try. Maybe if you ask nicely. Give 'em that curl-your-toes Jack Craig smile."

"Hardee-har-har," he mutters. Jack glances at our house, which is now in sight. Suddenly, he frowns.

Following his gaze, I see why: Penelope's Mercedes in our driveway. Right behind it is a van. A company name is painted on its side:

FANTASTIC FEASTS
AND HOW TO EAT THEM

Penelope and Aunt Phyllis stand nose-to-nose on opposite sides of a folding table filled with platters holding all sorts of culinary dishes: canapés, fruits and cheeses, several cakes, puddings, turkey legs—even a roasted pig complete with an apple in its mouth.

A woman—tall, slender, and sporting an apron and a chef's hat over her shoulder-length auburn hair—stands beside Aunt Phyllis. Her eyes shift from one of the women to the other, as if their heated discussion is a finals match at Wimbledon. Her eyes are damp, as if she's been crying.

Mary, Jeff, Trisha, Evan, Penelope's son Cheever Bing, and Jeff's other pal, Morton Smith, sit at another table. From the look of things, they've been feasting. Our family dogs, Rin Tin Tin and Lassie, stand beside them, on alert for any crumbs or scraps that may fall within chomping distance.

"No need to worry about making dinner tonight. The sampling was more than enough," I declare.

At that moment, the children's heads swivel toward Penelope, who's under the assumption that waving a turkey leg in my aunt's face will help make her point.

"Jeez, looks like a food fight is about to break out!" Jack exclaims.

"At least Aunt Phyllis seems to be keeping her cool!" I counter. "Look at the way she stands there, calmly, with her hands clasped behind her back."

Jack nods slowly, but I can tell he's unconvinced. "Yeah, I guess that's a good thing—unless she's found our gun vault *and she's holding a revolver.*"

Yikes.

By the time we pull into the driveway, Aunt Phyllis's hands are in front of her.

She holds an ancient saber.

Double yikes.

As Jack screeches to a halt, I leap out of the car. "Aunt Phyllis—*don't do it!*"

She stares at me as if I'm the one who's lost my mind. Shrugging, she raises the saber high over her head—

And without thinking, I blurt out the only thing that may stop her:

"TOO MANY WITNESSES!"

But it's too late. The saber comes down fast and hard, right on the neck—

Of the roasted pig.

Its head rolls onto the table, apple and all.

Aunt Phyllis beams with satisfaction.

Everyone stares at the sight.

Then all eyes go to me.

Oopsy.

I can kick myself for shouting out my worst fear. In hindsight, what were the odds that Aunt Phyllis would have actually swung the saber in Penelope's direction? Or, for that matter, connected with her carotid artery?

On the off-chance that Penelope would have bled out,

who could blame my dear sweet almost octogenarian Aunt Phyllis for being fed up with Penelope's nags and bullies and shouts?

And besides: even if Phyllis had murdered Penelope, she's the last person to end up as anyone's cellmate bitch. Instead, she'd be running the joint in a week, maybe two.

Still, I'm glad to see it wasn't her intention to do bodily harm. Think of how it may have ruined my aunt's life! Ever the social butterfly, she is quite aware that the mere mention of one's incarceration flattens even the most scintillating cocktail conversation. Am I right?

As if reading my mind, Aunt Phyllis clucks her tongue at me. "Donna, sweet niece, I was just demonstrating to Penelope how sprinkling a few of the prom's props among the catering staff could enhance our thrilling *Game of Thrones* theme."

"That was cool!" Cheever crows.

"Until someone loses a finger," Penelope argues. Suddenly, she looks sharply at me. "What did you mean when you said 'too many witnesses'?"

I widen my wince into a benign smile. "Um...who, me? What...?"

She's not buying it. She strains the Botox in her forehead as she hisses, "You know 'what'!"

Before I can make up something that sounds plausible, Morton asks, "Hey, will the serving wench cut off the porker's head before or after the fire eaters?"

"*What?*" Penelope shouts. "Neither, you little idiot!" She glares at Aunt Phyllis. "Despite the support of the cheering squad you've assembled, I still won't approve of anything that might catch fire, blow up the school, or do bodily harm to students, staff, or volunteers!"

"Party poop," Aunt Phyllis grouses. She nods in my direction. "Of course, since Donna is running this show, she's got final say-so on all prom logistics."

"Says who?" Penelope replies coolly. "As its chairperson, I'm the last word on every PTA-sponsored event."

I was thinking just the same thing.

"Not according to this agreement you signed, at Donna's behest when you twisted her arm to take on the task"—Aunt Phyllis pulls a folded paper from her jacket pocket—"despite her protests that her professional commitments took precedent."

"But...when did I...?

Aunt Phyllis's eyes catch mine. She winks.

With just the slightest nod, I show her, *Yeah, okay, I'll play along.*

"A written agreement? Why...I don't remember any such thing!" Penelope snatches it out of her hand. Reading it closely, her face changes from smug skepticism to dumbfounded bafflement to boiling rage. "This says...But I'd never...*It's a forgery!*"

"It isn't," my aunt assures her. "Go ahead and admit it! That's your scrawl, lady."

"Ha! Not until it's been verified," Penelope sniffs.

Phyllis looks around innocently. "Well, let's see...I assume your son has seen your signature on enough suspension notices to recognize it. Will he do as a witness?"

As Penelope shrugs, a smug smile rises on her over-Collagen-filled lips. "I suppose so."

When Aunt Phyllis whistles at Cheever, he, along with Lassie and Rin Tin Tin, look up on full alert.

"Get over here, boy!" Aunt Phyllis waves him over.

Cheever points to his chest, as if surprised that he's being drawn into this face-off.

Frankly, so am I. Surely, he'll side with his mother.

Still, he trots over. He takes the paper from his mother. Very slowly, he looks it over. Then he holds it up to the sun like a detective in a lousy movie looking for a watermark. Next, he places it flat on the table. Curling the fingers of his right hand in an enclosed circle, he lowers his head to view the signature through them.

Finally, he sighs. "Sorry, Ma. It's yours, alright."

"But...it can't be! This is a lie! A travesty! As far as I'm concerned, it means nothing!" She grabs it off the table. She holds it up triumphantly between her fingers, ready to rip it apart—

But I jerk it out of her hands. "The prom is next weekend," I remind her. "If you don't honor this, you'll have to inform the students that it's being called off."

"No, I won't! That would be your job," she sneers. "Once again, you'll have disappointed the people of Hilldale."

"Not if you rip this up. If you do, it's on you—and at quite a cost to the PTA too, considering all the deposits that have already been paid out. The props, decorations, roving entertainers, the band"—I point to the caterer—"and the food."

She nods vigorously.

I hold out the agreement. "So, what's it going to be, Penelope?"

Speechless, she turns to the kids.

Their stares beg her: *PLEASE! DON'T!*

Her eyes shift to her son. Cheever, frowning, crosses his arms at his chest. Evidently, he thinks that her cruel decision will be yet one more opportunity for the other kids to hate his guts.

Heck, even without her help, he's already given them plenty of reasons.

Realizing this, she steps back as if it's radioactive. Finally, she growls, "Have it your way!" Glaring at me, she adds, "But if your consigliere here has put you even one penny over budget—"

Aunt Phyllis's smile fades.

As does the caterer's happy face.

Ouch.

The kids are no dummies. They skedaddle, plates in hand. Not to miss a crumb, the dogs follow at their feet.

Jack is right behind them, the coward.

"I would imagine that there's a little bit of leeway...right?"—I hold up a hand, thumb and index finger separated by an inch.

Okay, maybe a couple of inches.

Penelope rolls her eyes. "This feast is over budget...but at least it's tolerable."

"Too bad. It's already paid for," Aunt Phyllis exclaims.

Reminded of that, the caterer tosses her cap in the air like a graduate freed from her studies. She practically runs to her van.

Penelope's hand sweeps toward my house. "I'd hate for the neighbors to learn of all the ways you've gouged the school. Shall we go inside, ladies?"

My aunt's walk of shame is a mere twelve feet: from the front foyer to our formal dining room table, where brochures, receipts, decoration samples, floor plan diagrams for the serving tables, and guest seating are piled up.

Impressive indeed.

But one long look at a whiteboard sitting on the easel beside my midcentury mahogany sideboard is all it takes for any awe of her diligence to sink like a boulder in a lake of red ink.

Scrawled in Phyllis's frenetic writing, the event's numerous expenses—catering, balloons, decorations, props, band, side entertainment, and on and on—total twice the allotted budget.

Triple yikes!

Penelope smacks the board with an open hand. "Do you see what I'm dealing with? While you're off gallivanting, I've been trying to reign in this spendthrift nincompoop!"

"Let's be civil, shall we?" Phyllis sniffs.

Penelope nods grudgingly, but only because my aunt is still holding the saber.

"Well, it is a bit disconcerting," I admit. "Perhaps there are areas in which we can dial back some of these costs."

"But the kids will be disappointed!" Aunt Phyllis protests. Ticket sales are through the roof! It will be the most successful prom in Hilldale High School history!"

"Oh well, then—that's great!" I point out. "If the ticket costs are covering a lot of the expense—"

"Um...not really." Aunt Phyllis grimaces. "Okay, yeah—

there will be a significant loss even after the current ticket sales are added in."

Penelope taps a French-manicured index finger on one of the line items:

MUGGALOS - TALON

"This item alone costs ten thousand dollars!" Her double take is accompanied by a frown. "What the heck is it, anyway?"

"The musical entertainment," Phyllis replies.

"That much money—*for a band*?"

"It's not just *any* band," my aunt retorts. "It's the hottest group in the indie-pop world! Talon has a cult following."

"*They're a cult?* And you've invited them on campus?" Penelope whips around, growling, "See? What did I tell you? Spendthrift lunatic!"

"Nincompoop—" I correct her.

Aunt Phyllis arches a brow.

"—Of which my aunt is neither." With a pleading glance, I pry the saber from Phyllis' hand.

"If you remember, Penelope, the last time you butted your nose into my position as prom committee chair, you insisted that we hire a band handled by one of your old boyfriends. His contribution—at a very steep price, I might add—wasn't Taylor Swift as he'd promised but *a female impersonator*."

"You have to admit, if one didn't know better, one couldn't tell the difference," Penelope sniffs.

I roll my eyes. "The Adam's apple was a glaring giveaway."

Aunt Phyllis snorts. "And I got the real deal at the same price? Get outta here!"

I pull out two chairs, side by side. "Okay, ladies—enough already! It's time for a little teamwork."

Slowly, they take their seats. I drop into another chair on Aunt Phyllis's other side. That way I don't get caught in the crossfire of their angry glares. "Now, let's be creative!" I declare brightly. "Considering the expansive amount of fun and games to be had, why don't we consider ways in which the students can help out?"

Penelope frowns. "By that, do you mean pay for the privilege of attending their own prom?"

"Phyllis has already created the template to make it a once-in-a-lifetime experience! If the event is leaps and bounds above the mundane gym dance, I'm sure the students won't mind chipping in. We'll take it out of them a few dollars at a time. For example, we can charge for the, er, battle competitions. We'll crown the player with the highest tournament score."

"Great idea," Phyllis declares.

Penelope nods grudgingly.

"And why don't we charge for desserts?" I suggest.

"But we must keep the main courses free," Penelope insists.

"Deal," I reply. I turn to my aunt. "If this band is as popular as you say, perhaps we can charge for reserved seating."

"That alone should make our nut!" Phyllis exclaims.

Penelope shivers. "When pigs fly!"

I flinch, but manage to ignore Penelope's sarcasm.

Instead, I ask: "Aunt Phyllis, tell me about this, um, fire-eating dragon."

She gives me a thumbs-up. "I've got one of the set designers from *Game of Thrones* working on it, so it'll be an exact duplicate of the one used in the show! Speaking of a way to monetize this shindig: why don't we charge for the honor of turning on its flame?"

Even Penelope is intrigued. "You mean, like, hold an auction?"

Phyllis nods vigorously. "We'll make it something that only the female students can do, but of course their dates can bid for them too. That way, one lucky lady will be crowned Hilldale High's 'Daenerys Targaryen'—just like the character in G.O.T."

"Well, now, I like that," Penelope purrs.

"You do?" Phyllis and I exclaim in unison.

"Sure! Because Cheever—I mean, the male student who helps his date win the crown—will make it a memorable experience! And, not just for the lucky girl, but for everyone."

Despite Penelope's numerous attempts to help her son along on the path to popularity, invariably she fails.

In her defense, it doesn't help that he's a bully. Like mother, like son.

Penelope stands up. "Now that I've righted this ship of fools, my work here is done." She saunters to the foyer. As she snaps her fingers, she bellows, "Cheever, dear—is that your fourth turkey leg? *Put it down!* Calories in, pounds on!" She lifts her eyes heavenward. "If only he had my svelte gene!"

"Well, he's certainly got your bitchy one," Aunt Phyllis mutters under her breath.

I nudge her into silence.

I wait until the door shuts behind them before asking my aunt the big question: "By the way, since I never requested a written agreement to chair the prom committee, how did you get Penelope to sign one?"

Phyllis grins. "I didn't—but Cheever did."

I lean back in my chair, surprised. "Why would he do that?"

"Get real, Donna! Does Cheever ever do anything for anyone but himself?"

She has a point.

I shudder, but I have to ask: "So, what did you have to do in return?"

"Hire the Muggalos's favorite band. He's obsessed with the lead singer, some guy named Talon." Aunt Phyllis shrugs. "His followers paint their faces like a bunch of wild banshees. Some even shave their heads into mohawks. I guess, 'to each his own.'" She leans in and whispers, "Word has it that the FBI has them on its cult list."

I shake my head in wonder. "I'm sure Penelope has no idea about his fanboy crush."

Phyllis giggles. "She'll figure it out on prom night."

"Why do you say that?"

"It's going to be her little prince's very public coming out party—as a Muggalo!"

I sigh. Yet one more reason for Penelope to hate me.

It's only late afternoon. Still, I stumble off to bed.

4

Zodiac

The analysis of planetary movements is called the "Zodiac." Those who study it—astrologers—believe it affects our behavior and future events.

Taking its name from the Greek word "zodiakos," the word literally translates into "circle of animals."

You'll note that, like the constellation of stars continually moving in the cosmos above us, many of the zodiac's sun signs are in fact named after beasts:

Aries (Mar 21st to Apr 19th) Ram.

Taurus (April 20th to May 20th) Bull.

Gemini (May 21st to June 20th) Twins; yes, they are humans; hopefully, not toddlers.

Cancer (Jun 21st to Jul 22nd) Crab.

Leo (July 23rd to August 22nd) Lion.

Virgo (August 23rd to September 22nd) Female Virgin; again, human—but much more impetuous than twin toddlers.

Libra (September 23rd to October 22nd) Scales, which are neither beast nor fowl, but somehow fairer than the rest.

Scorpio (October 23rd to November 21st) Scorpion.

Sagittarius (November 22nd to December 21st) Male Archer, which gives Virgo someone to pine over.

Capricorn (December 22nd to January 19th) Goat.

Aquarius (January 20th to February 18th) Water Bearer, mostly depicted as female.

Pisces (February 19th to March 20th) Fish.

If you're born within the dates of a particular sun sign, you supposedly demonstrate some of the characteristics of your spirit animal. For example, someone who is Taurus may be stubborn and bold.

A Scorpio's instinct is to wound deeply.

A Gemini demonstrates dual personality. A best-case scenario: she sees both sides of a situation. Worst case: she's wishy-washy, or she flip-flops on issues.

Right now, you may be thinking: "Well, I'm a Gemini, and I stand firm on my beliefs! In fact, on most issues, I'm quite bullheaded."

Gotcha. No problem. You see, astrologers have come up with numerous ways to cover their bets! Not only do you have a sun sign, but a moon sign, too. And if you're "on the cusp" of a sign's dates, your actions may also reflect characteristics of the neighboring sign.

In other words, nothing is written in stone, let alone in the stars.

IN THE DAWN'S EARLY MORN, WHEN I'M TOO TIRED TO REMEMBER when my head hit the pillow, Jack knows how to bring me back to life.

It is a delicious form of torture: gentle kisses on eyelids shut tight against visions of all the things that could have gone wrong on missions past.

He doesn't stop there. A light-as-air lick on one nipple followed by a gentle stroke on the other. My quickly beating heart, still connected to repressed memories of death and destruction, finally slows down as both nipples rise to attention, two sentries dispatched with an essential coded message: *Alert! Alert! Pleasure at hand...*

It's fair warning. He follows this sensual wake-up call with a kiss.

My mouth opens eagerly, as if, had he not offered it, the heaviness of my dread would have stifled all desire for his love.

To take my mind off my anxieties, I trace the curve of his tricep with a finger. Its journey doesn't stop until it has followed the main artery in his arm —the brachial—all the way to his palm.

Instinctively, he tenses at my touch. I don't blame him. Had it been with a knife he'd be bleeding out by now.

I put his middle finger in my mouth. As I suck on it, his grin tells me his mind is now relaxed, but when I look down, I see that his cock has stiffened.

As I mount him, his pupils dilate in anticipation. One of his hands rests on my hip but the other cups the closest breast, as if he knows he'll need to hold on for dear life.

When I contract around him, I feel tension once again building in him. I know better than to assume it's just unadulterated lust or the primal elation over a conquest. *If only it were a mindless joy!* Its fierceness proves it's anything but. Jack knows all too well that the best bouts of passion aren't during times of innocence or leisure. They occur in times when too much is at stake.

My clenches, met with his grunts, push him deeper inside me. Our bodies sting from the frenzied slaps taking place as I rise and fall onto him, again and again—

Until we climax: me, submerged in a wave of elation; he, exploding, then convulsing, and finally shivering inside me.

Passion is a unique pain. Not, *per se,* physical agony but the ultimate emotional scar: a memory of joy as fleeting as all of human life.

So then, why test life's boundaries when what you have taking place right now is the human ideal?

It is why I'm driven, at this moment to ask the man I love with all my heart: "Should we still be doing this?"

Even to my ears, my voice sounds husky and haunted.

Jack, who has been stroking my cheek gently, freezes as he considers my question. "By 'this,' do you mean having sex?"

I stifle a laugh. "No, silly. I mean…Acme."

His head sinks into his pillow. When he finally speaks, I can barely hear his voice from deep in a cloud of Polish goose down encased in one thousand-thread count Supima sateen cotton:

"I'll quit anytime you say."

"But the Quorum is still out there, somewhere. Licking its wounds," I argue—more with myself than with him.

"And it will always be there too, in one form or another."

I know he's right.

Seeing the sadness in my gaze, he cups my face in his hands. "So, what will it be?"

Good question. And frankly, it shouldn't be hard to answer.

If we get out now, we can still enjoy our children before they're adults. Instead of traipsing around the world, we'll be here for them through the most difficult trials of their youth. We'll be around to revel in their adult experiences: degrees earned, professions chosen, successes achieved. We will meet their life partners. We will dote on our grand-children.

Jack and I can grow old together.

But if we choose to stay in the game, there may be a mission from which one, or both of us, never returns.

Family or country?

It can't always be both.

Before I can answer my phone buzzes. Caller ID shows that it's Arnie. I grimace at this interruption, but I'm relieved that I don't have to answer Jack just yet.

"Talk to me," I mutter to him.

"Well, good morning to you too," he retorts.

"You sound cross."

"You'd be grumpy if you'd been up all night after hacking an encrypted thumb drive and a week's worth of surveillance footage." He pauses. "Not to mention missing your lemon pancakes."

"Okay, I can take a hint. Sure, okay. You're invited over for breakfast."

Arnie must have me on speakerphone because Emma shouts, "Can Nick and I come too?"

I laugh. "The more, the merrier."

"Panty-cakes!" their three-year-old Nicky, squeals. At the same time, the front doorbell chimes. "Donna, let us in—puh-weeze!" the little boy wails.

I leap out of bed. "Arnie, you mean to tell me that you're already at my front door?"

"Yes, but only because I thought you'd want to see the intel I've pulled up on Jonathan Presley's thumb drive! Trust me, it's worth a stack of hotcakes...or two...maybe three... with bacon?"

I sigh. "Jack will be right down to let you in." I click off.

Despite having slung the pillow over his head, I hear Jack's muffled plea: "Why me?"

"Because if I'm going to play short order cook and do it without burning down the house, I'll need a shower first to wake up."

As I head to the bathroom, Jack grumbles, "I was looking forward to joining you."

We have a long day ahead of us. Ergo, now is not the time to have that discussion, let alone the more serious one.

I'll figure out a way to make it up to him later, when we don't have company, and we're not busy saving the world.

"—AAN...*WAWAAH*! DENN I SAHHH DUH WHUMIN!" ARNIE jabbed his knife in the air with a flourish.

"Talking with your mouth full is bad manners," I admonish him. I nod at Nicky, whom I've just served a Mickey Mouse-shaped pancake (blueberry eyes, a strawberry nose and a banana sliced lengthwise as its mouth).

The little boy looks at his dad expectantly.

Arnie freezes with his mouth open. Finally, he closes it. After taking a gulp, he sheepishly adds, "Oh...yeah. Sorry."

"Now, repeat—without letting your food get in your way." To make my point. I move his plate out of reach.

While tapping away on her computer, Emma gives me a thumbs-up.

Frankly, I'm doing Arnie a favor. By stopping now, he'll avoid the inevitable bellyache that comes with finishing off a stack of pancakes the height of the leaning tower of Pisa.

I'm also doing my kids a favor. Although they're still asleep, I hope he'll leave enough syrup for their pancakes.

Arnie repeats, "I said, 'And, *voila*! Then I saw the woman!'"

"Wha womam?" Jack garbles out before swallowing.

"E tú, Bruté?" I murmur, nodding toward Nicky.

Jack rolls his eyes, but gulps before adding, "Show us, Arnie."

I sit down next to Jack while Arnie turns his iPad toward us.

"Jonathan Presley's hit-and-run fatality happened in Irvine, California; on Thursday, a little after one o'clock," Arnie explains. He then clicks his screen open to a video clip. The color footage is grainy, but you can still make out a clerk behind a desk—a man in his twenties, helping an elderly man with a shipping box.

"I take it Evan's envelope originated from there," I murmur.

Arnie nods. "It's also where Jonathan Presley's private mailbox is located: the post office for Avalon, California."

"On Catalina Island?" Jack muses. "Interesting, considering that Jonathan lived and worked in Irvine. Talk about off the beaten path."

"For good reason, apparently," I reply. "Especially if you send or receive mail that you wish to hide from the rest of the world."

"There are three mainland ferries to Catalina," Emma tells us. "You can reach it from San Pedro, Long Beach, or Dana Point."

"And it would be a toss-up as to whether he'd leave from Long Beach to the north, or Dana Point to the south," I reply.

"Or by private boat, which could be out of anywhere in between," Jack points out. "Huntington Beach, Newport Beach, Balboa Island..."

Arnie winces. "I could pull sec-cam footage from the various ferry companies. Maybe he came by private yacht."

"If you're wondering, I can assure you Jonathan didn't have a second home on Catalina," Emma declares. "At least, not under his own name."

As the video fast-forwards, people move in and out of the small mail facility at lightning speed. Finally, Arnie pauses the footage. "It's just before four-thirty. Now, watch the front door."

The footage moves at normal speed. There are only three people in the store besides the postal worker. A person—mid-height and slight, wearing dark glasses, sneakers, and a long, bulky zip-front jacket with the hood up—enters and goes toward the post boxes that fill one wall of the building. He squats in front of the lower, larger boxes on the far side.

"It's Jonathan's box," Arnie affirms.

Like me, Jack has been closely scrutinizing our person-of-interest. He sighs. "I can't tell for certain if it's a man or a woman, let alone what age."

"A woman," Emma replies.

Jack frowns. "How can you tell?"

"Arnie, zoom in," she insists. After he does so, she turns to Jack. "Now, look at the nails."

I lean in to get a better look. "French tips!"

She nods.

Arnie blushes. "Some men like manicures too."

"Guys who go in for more than a buff and clear polish are few and far between," I counter. "It's a greater chance that it's a woman."

This person pulls out the mail—mostly mass mail flyers. The person shreds all the mail before stuffing it in the trash receptacle next to an empty counter. Then, from her jacket pocket, she pulls out a small envelope similar to the one Evan received and walks it to the postal worker, who takes it and hand-stamps it before setting it in a sorting bin.

Jonathan's surrogate then leaves the post office.

Jack nods slowly. "Was there any exterior surveillance footage?"

"I thought you'd never ask," Arnie replies. "But you won't like what you see."

Another click takes us out onto the street. The person walks a few blocks before turning into a posh boutique hotel: the Vista del Mar. People are streaming in and out.

"There's got to be interior cameras," I say.

"There are—but only in the common areas."

"Did this maybe-woman go up in the elevator?" Jack asks.

"Yes—with several other people. I've been culling the

hotel's sec-cam footage from that moment through the next seventy-two hours. Even with facial recognition software I've had no match. The person we saw never came back down," Arnie insists.

"At least, not in the same get-up or with her face exposed to the camera," Emma adds.

"In other words, somehow our person of interest made a quick change then took off," Jack mutters.

"And all of this was done with the supposition that someone would do exactly what we're doing," I reply. "That is, tracing any evidence that Jonathan may have wanted to get the thumb drive in someone's hands in case of his untimely demise."

"Which brings us to what is on the thumb drive." For once in his life, Arnie sounds deadly serious.

5

Lilith

In mythology, before there was Eve, there was Lilith. Like Adam, his first wife was formed from earthen clay rather than from his rib.

The first couple's parting was less than amicable. Affairs will do that to a relationship. In this case, Lilith ran off with the archangel Samael.

In astrology, Lilith is the name of the "Black Moon," a supposed invisible satellite of the Earth which is also considered the third leg in the Sun-Moon-Earth energy vortex.

There is also an asteroid called Lilith, as well as a "demon star."

No doubt about it: astrologically, Lilith has been slut-shamed!

ARNIE PULLS UP ANOTHER FILE: TEXT, AS OPPOSED TO VIDEO OR a photo. "Although Jonathan sent the thumb drive containing this letter to Evan, by its salutation it was obviously intended for his father."

"So, he wrote it before Robert died," I murmur.

Evan's father died two years ago. At the time, Evan's mother, Congresswoman Catherine Martin, was running for the presidency. They were the ultimate power couple: she was a savvy Washington insider and her party's golden girl, whereas he was a recognized visionary and self-made billionaire whose engineering knowledge allowed him to build a conglomerate of tech companies. His fortune underwrote her political campaigns.

That is, until he realized that she loved power more than she loved him.

Although I was a few years younger, I'd known both in high school. They were the catalyst for my shameful reputation, a scenario that Catherine had set up out of her jealousy over Robert's infatuation with me.

Years later, he admitted to me that he could have endured a loveless marriage if she'd at least been willing to serve her country instead of the donor eager to buy her the presidency—at a price the country could ill afford: treason.

Her backer was the Quorum, the terrorist cell I've fought since I learned the role it played in my first husband's supposed death.

In truth, Carl defected. As for Robert, Catherine had him assassinated before he could tell the world their endgame.

Carl pulled the trigger.

So that we can read it for ourselves, Arnie airdrops Jonathan's letter to Robert into our phones:

Dear Robert,

If you're reading this, it's because I've been murdered.

Knowing you as I do, I have no doubt that your first instinct is to mourn me as a friend as well as a sincere and trusted colleague in the creation and the success of BlackTech.

My biggest regret is that I was neither.

I was a traitor: not just to you, but also to our country.

I confess to the theft of Operation Horoscope. I personally gave it to our worst enemy.

As you remember, you gave BlackTech's most important project its name. You may also remember that I laughed when you insisted on calling it that. For me, your choice was both ironic and prophetic; not just for the devastation it will wreak on the world should it somehow fall into the wrong hands, but because it speaks to my treasonous journey.

Robert, you know I went to school at Stanford. While there, I took an elective course—astrology.

The purpose of the course was not only to learn about the history of astrology, but to test its theories as a predictor of human behavior and world events.

In essence, is fate predetermined?

We were told, half in jest or so we thought, that we were the course's guinea pigs. Quite seriously, we were warned that seeking each other out during or after class would result in our immediate expulsion, which would mean we'd lose the opportunity to graduate with our class: the perfect incentive to keep curiosity at bay.

There were only twelve students in the class, both men and women. On the first day, we were told we had been chosen because each of us was born under a different sun sign. Mine is Gemini.

As part of the course, neither my classmates nor I were to be called by our given names. Instead, we wore robes to cover our clothes and masks that represented our Zodiac sign. The mask contained a device that disguised our voices.

According to the instructor, the purpose of this was so that we'd be honest with ourselves and with each other throughout the course's tasks: ethical scenarios in which our actions and responses would be compared to the traits often attributed to our sun signs.

During class, we only spoke when our assignment required it. We arrived and departed the class one-by-one, changing in an anteroom before one of the other students were allowed to do so as well.

The requisite for anonymity worked. Entering the class in disguise took away all inhibitions. It inspired us to speak and act freely during our theoretical trials. We expressed our true feelings on every topic broached to us.

We exposed our deepest, darkest secrets.

Did we trust each other? Not necessarily. But the thought that any of the others could do me harm disappeared the moment I became Gemini. And by the way my classmates talked—freely, with such strident convictions—I realized they felt the same way.

A month into the class, as I was leaving an off-campus coffee shop, I was approached by a woman. She divulged that she too took the astrology class. Her sun sign is Taurus.

The woman admitted that she'd recognized me by my left sneaker. While painting my dorm room, I'd spilled dark blue paint on it.

Outside of class, Taurus and I began meeting covertly after class. At first, we were just friends who shared a secret. We discussed in greater detail the issues that had been brought up in class and the answers we'd given—

Things like what were our saddest memories? And why did we feel they had stayed with us?

Who in our lives had caused us the most pain?

Who would we always love? How had this person earned our adoration, our devotion?

Under what circumstance could we bring ourselves to cheat?

How easy was it for us to lie?

Had we ever stolen? If so, how had we justified it?

Could we kill another? If so, under what circumstance?

Without a classroom setting, these conversations became less strident. After a few wines, they became more passionate.

Honesty was never an issue. I trusted her completely.

I guess it's why eventually we became lovers.

The sex was incredible. And, admittedly, it was quite a high to feel as if we'd bested our professor in his experiment.

He too did his best to stay an enigma. Doing so allowed us to assume anything we wanted about him. On the other hand, like us, our classmates were open books.

Still, like mine, her curiosity was piqued about our anonymous classmates. But when I asked her if she'd been successful in unmasking any of the others, she told me no. Like me, she needed the grade to graduate and wouldn't take a second risk at losing it.

When the class was over, we stayed lovers. I learned her real name—Lilith—and she learned mine.

At first, we kept our relationship clandestine. Then, realizing there was no real reason to hide our feelings in public, we stopped doing so.

Ironically, when it was no longer forbidden, it was no longer special. Within a month, Lilith and I drifted apart.

Several years later, I saw her again. By then, I was Vice President of engineering at BlackTech.

It was at one of the U.S. Military's Future Forces Forum conferences. You were there too, Robert. We'd just gotten our first Defense Department contract for BlackTech and were riding high.

I'd run into her in the lobby. She told me she worked as a Congressional aide. As it happens, her boss sat on the Intelligence and the Homeland Security committees—both instrumental for the success of BlackTech products.

I bought her a drink.

It didn't end there.

She was now married—unhappily, she told me. So, once again, we had a reason to be covert in our love affair.

Pillow talk was inevitable. Maybe I'd hoped to impress her about how well BlackTech was doing. And, as I was its chief engineer, I wanted her to know I was integral in its success.

She was sold. She made sure I was invited to some invitation-only fundraiser that allowed her boss to be thanked by his many donors for pushing their agendas. Her casual introduction to him was laced with all the right hot-button words. He quickly made the leap that approving another BlackTech contract could make him even wealthier, should his blind trust purchase our stock before additional contracts were announced.

I was flabbergasted. Yes, I wanted BlackTech to have the contract, but I also wanted it to happen with clean hands. Our project merited it.

That project was Horoscope.

I'm sorry, Robert, that I never said a word about it to you. Even if I had, it would have been too late.

After the contract was awarded, Lilith called me. "Let's celebrate," she said.

I tried to come up with an excuse, but she wouldn't hear of it.

When we met, she was angry that I refused to make love to her. "This may loosen you up," she said. She handed me a folder. It contained verification of an offshore bank account that had been established in my name.

I was astounded—not just at the amount of what she called my bonus, but that it had been set up by "her employer."

"The congressman?" I asked.

She laughed. "Don't be stupid! He's just a means to an end. My real employer deals in death and destruction. And now BlackTech—that is, you—are our newest supplier. Unless you prefer to be tried for treason."

I knew she was right. I was trapped.

Because Horoscope is software and its implementation relies on the completion of other vendors' components, I'd prayed that, in the ensuing decade, the project would somehow be scrapped; that some new technology would make it obsolete. But thus far, despite the usual red tape and delays, our government gets closer and closer to launching it.

After years of radio silence, last month Lilith arranged to see me again. How I dreaded the meeting! But she made it quite clear that I couldn't say no.

Our conversation was brief: "My employer would like you to make a tiny change in Operation Horoscope's code."

Tiny? It was hardly that! It would unleash hell on earth.

I refused.

She insisted. She begged. She threatened. Still, I refused.

A few days later she let me know that I was off the hook. "We found another way to alter the code," she declared triumphantly.

My heart sank in my chest. "Why are you telling me this?"

"You are our safeguard. If the modification is discovered before the project's launch, you'll be asked to correct it. That must never happen," she warned me.

I said nothing. Finally, I walked out.

Lilith and those she works for have no reason to trust me. And the moment Operation Horoscope is launched, they'll have no further use for me.

It's why you're now reading this letter.

Robert, have no doubt: I was killed by those who will benefit from Operation Horoscope's devastation.

If they've succeeded, God help our country!

And God forgive me.

Robert, I'm asking for your forgiveness as well.

—Jonathan Presley

"WHAT EXACTLY IS OPERATION HOROSCOPE?" I ASK.

"Good question," Emma admits. "I've done a search of the U.S. Defense Department's project database. From what I can tell, it's never been formally announced to the public, and it doesn't show up on any Eyes-Only memoranda."

"But, from what Jonathan wrote here, it goes back at least a decade," I counter. "This letter was written when Robert was still alive. He died two years ago. Jonathan's death indicates that Lilith's employer no longer saw value in keeping him alive. If Operation Horoscope's activation is imminent, Jonathan was a loose end that had to be snipped."

"If so, then the congressman who Lilith worked for may still be in office," Jack points out.

"Lilith may still be there too," I reply. "If she's the asset for a foreign state, they will have kept her in that power position for as long as possible."

"I'll run a check on all U.S. Representatives who are still in Congress for a decade or longer. I'll focus on those who sat on the Intelligence and the Homeland Security committees," Emma offers.

"Run one on Congressional aides too," I suggest. "Lilith isn't that common a name. Even if he eventually left office, she may still be there working for someone else."

"We need to find out what Operation Horoscope means," Arnie points out. "Perhaps they changed the name since this letter was written."

"Branham will know," Jack replies. "We'll ask him when we see him this afternoon."

"We should call Ryan before the meeting, just in case he'd prefer to backchannel this to Branham," I suggest.

"You mean, instead of springing it on him in front of Edmonton?" Arnie asks.

Emma rolls her eyes. "Move to the head of the class."

"At least, not until we're able to get into BlackTech's secure database," Arnie adds. "No doubt it's kept onsite—probably on an Apache server protected by a Faraday shield."

"In other words, we won't be able to hack it from the outside," I reply.

Jack laughs. "We won't need to. If we need an eye or finger scan, we have its chief executive sleeping in the bonus room over our garage."

"He'll hate me for not letting him sleep in," I warn him.

"That's okay. Better Evan should grouse about that than

have his company face severe consequences for Jonathan's treason," Jack counters.

"You're right!" I exclaim. "And now, knowing that there's been a security breach, the CIA may be able to use it as an opportunity for counterintelligence."

"I hope Branham sees it your way," Jack mutters as I head up the stairs.

6

Part of Fortune

The astrological term "Arabic Parts" refers to the sensitive points on one's astrological chart. These are calculated using specific formulas whereby two planets, or points, are added together. When this happens, a third planet (or point) is subtracted from that result. On your chart, the "part of fortune," —also called "Fortuna"— is where a person is thought to possess natural talent.

Before you ask, let me assure you that a "natural talent" does include your innate ability to

- Find your way through a city you've never before visited

- Make the Vulcan salute

- Be double-jointed

-Do that little thing with your tongue that drove your high school boyfriend to distraction.

I TAP TWICE ON EVAN'S BEDROOM DOOR.

No response, so I tap harder.

Still nothing.

Time's a wasting, so I look in:

The bed is empty.

Hmmmm.

I walk down the hall to the other bedrooms. I come to Jeff's room first. The door is unlocked. I open it a crack, to see him sound asleep. He lies on his back. Because he runs hot, he's tossed off all his bedding. Silently, I close the door.

I don't have to pause beside the guest room, where Aunt Phyllis sleeps. Her snores rock the walls, so I know Evan is not in there with her, enjoying an early morning chat.

Like Jeff's door, Trisha's is unlocked. I sneak a peek. My angel child sleeps with a smile on her lips.

Besides the master suite, that leaves one other door: Mary's.

It's locked.

No problem. I slip into my bedroom, where, in a secret compartment in my vanity table, I've hidden a lockpick set. I pull out the one I think works best.

Okay, yeah, maybe I already know which ones open specific doors in our house. *I never claimed to be Houdini.*

I walk back to Mary's door and debate if I should knock.

Of course, I knock—*really softly.*

And then I open the door really quickly.

Mary sits up abruptly. She holds her blanket next to her neck, as if she's Little Red Riding Hood and I'm the Big Bad Wolf.

Nope. He is that large lump in the bed beside her.

To hide my anger, I force my lips into a smile and sweetly

exclaim, "Good morning, dear! Glad to see that you're already...up!"

The word sticks in my throat. I didn't mean it as a double entendré, but Mary must have taken it that way. Her face turns the color of an overripe beefsteak tomato.

"I'm making pancakes downstairs. Care to join us?" As I flop down on the lumpy side of her bed, the lump gives a yelp—

Which Mary tries to cover up by launching into a coughing jag. When she finishes this Academy Award-winning performance, she, adds, "I'm...not feeling too well."

"Gee, I hope you're not coming down with something contagious!" I reach over to feel her forehead with one hand—

While yanking back the cover with the other.

The bad news: I now know Evan's whereabouts.

The good news: he and Mary are still dressed.

Sort of.

That is, if his boxer briefs and her thong panties and a midriff-cut teeshirt count as clothing.

He doesn't have to be asked to get out of my daughter's bed. His leap would give Superman's speeding bullet trajectory a run for its money.

"Mom, please, it's not what it looks like!" Mary's plaintive plea demands that I believe her as opposed to what I see with my own eyes.

I scan her face, then his, then back to her again. "Convince me."

The fact that they're both chattering at the same time makes it difficult to hear either clearly. What I make out is

Mary saying "—finally wanted to hear about...about the girl in the selfie—"

"I already told you! She's not just—just *some girl*! She's also my Poli-Sci project partner—"

"Okay! Whatever! Your 'PROJECT PARTNER'." Mary further emphasizes his remark with air quotes. "Who dares to laugh at me—"

"You're twisting my words!" Evan exclaims. "That's not what I said at all!"

"You didn't have to! I knew what you meant!"

"Why do you think you can read my mind?" Angrily, he raises both hands skyward. "See? This is what I'm talking about! You're...you're..."

"You mean when you called me, hot-headed—like my mother?" Mary points at me *"Do you know how...how hurtful that is?"*

"Ha! Well, I'm glad you heard at least one thing I've said these past eight hours—"

"Evan compared you to me?" For some reason, I'm actually flattered—

Wait...*what?* He said I'm...

HOT-HEADED?

Noting the look on my face, Mary and Evan's mouths shut in unison.

At that moment I remember I'm still holding the lock-pick: tiny, but functional as a weapon.

Evan's eyes shift to the window. Would a drop from the second story kill him any quicker than a jab with something tiny and sharp to his chest?

Probably not.

But, hey, I'm a reasonable person. "Evan Martin, give me

one reason to let you walk out of here without the need to reach an emergency room before you bleed out." He can't read my mind, but there's enough light filtering through Mary's window to allow me to admire the pick.

"Um...because..." Finally, he stutters, "Hey, I was only quoting Jack!"

Seeing my frown, it dawns on Evan that he's failed the test.

Just at that moment, Jack's head pops through the door. "Hey, does anyone else want pancakes before we go?"

I smile as I pocket the pick. "Nope, sorry, Jack! Evan doesn't have time for hot-heads. *Oops!* I meant hot-cakes." I point to Evan. "You're coming with us—*now.*"

Is it cruel of me to take him on an empty stomach and keep him in the dark as to where we're going? Nah. He'll learn soon enough.

In the meantime, I'm keeping the lockpick handy.

"Donna, on the record: last night Mary and I didn't... we didn't..." Evan's voice dies off.

Evan, Jack, Arnie, and I are almost at BlackTech. Jack is driving, I'm sitting shotgun, while Evan and Arnie sit in the back seat.

The drive hasn't been easy. With all the detours caused by gas pipe fires between Hilldale and Irvine, what used to be a half-hour trip has taken us over two hours. We anticipate we'll face similar traffic on the way home.

During the ride, I haven't said a word. Not about Evan and Mary's sleeping arrangements. Not about our trek to

BlackTech. Certainly not about my anger and hurt that my trust has been violated.

Not that I'd get a word in edgewise while Jack and Arnie filled Evan in on what they'll need to take off his company's database: anything that explains Operation Horoscope, every bit of code that might have gone into it; even Jonathan's correspondence files.

I left my visor down to watch Evan's reactions. He listened, stone-faced. But apparently, his mind was somewhere else.

My guess: still in Mary's bedroom.

To find out if I'm right, I turn around to stare at him. "So, I catch you and my daughter in her bed—both in your underwear—and you insist nothing happened? Truly refreshing! Tell me something Evan: Why not?"

"I...I don't know what you mean," he stutters.

"What I mean is that you're a couple of hot and horny-for-each-other teenagers. The whole night you lie side by side, practically naked. So"—I take a deep breath—"Why not?"

"Well...because..." Evan looks down into his lap. "I said no."

"*You* said no?"

Is he implying that Mary was ready, willing, and able?

The blood leaves his face. He's reading my mind.

Arnie's eyes grow big. This is one soap opera he'd prefer to tune out.

"I don't think now is the time for family drama," Jack interjects.

"You're right," I say sweetly. "No need for anyone to get *hot-headed*."

"That's quickly becoming your new favorite term," Jack retorts.

"No, it's Evan's." I swing around to face Jack. "Seems he learned it from you."

Jack winces when he sees my eyes narrow.

Arnie is sweating bullets, like a child who hates it when his parents argue. Anxiously, he points to the BlackTech's block-long campus. "Hey, folks—look! We're here!"

Jack swings the car into the driveway and up to the security gate.

As far as I'm concerned, Evan is off the hook—for now.

As for Mary? She and I will have an interesting conversation when I get home.

"EVAN! SO GREAT TO SEE YOU!" TINA CUTHBERT, JONATHAN'S assistant, meets us in the lobby. She wraps Evan in a motherly hug and then extends her hand to Jack, Arnie, and me. "What brings you here on this beautiful Sunday?"

Already coached by Jack, Evan keeps the conversation short and bittersweet: "I came as soon as I heard about Jonathan's death. You know, he was a very dear friend of my dad's—his first hire, in fact. BlackTech would not have existed without him."

"He was the company's heart and soul." Tina's face crumples with grief. "He's irreplaceable."

"I know. But I'll do my best to find someone who can fill his shoes." Evan waits for her to wipe away a tear then adds, "Tina, we'd like to be shown to Jonathan's office."

She nods sadly. "Understandable." She shifts uncomfortably on her feet. "As always, he locked it when he went out to lunch. No one's been in it since. Not that we could enter it in any event. His office security needs image recognition."

"Or mine," Evan reminds her.

Tina's curious gaze roams over our bland faces. "Gotcha. Do you remember the way?"

Evan nods. "Engineering building, top floor, last office on the west-facing side."

"By the way. The memorial service for Jonathan is next Friday, at two o'clock. If you're in town, I'll send you the details."

He nods. "I'd like that."

So will Ryan. Jack and I will accompany him. It might be worth having an Acme drone flit about, honing in on the faces of the attendees. Odds are his killers are long gone and won't show. But hey, you never know.

Tina waves us off without any suggestion of accompanying us. I guess Jonathan's penchant for secrecy is reason enough not to ask questions.

JONATHAN'S OFFICE IS ON THE OTHER SIDE OF A METAL WALL AT the end of a large office pit. Because it's a Sunday, there are only a few engineers at their stations. Their eyes are fixated on their large screens as their fingers roam their keyboards like frenzied jazz pianists.

Evan's eye and hand scans unlock its single metal door.

We step inside to discover that all four walls are metal. There is only one narrow window, but its shade is also a metal panel that can be raised with the push of a button.

The room—a vault, really—is as austere as a monk's sanctuary. The metal desk is a solid cube except for a single cutout to accommodate the legs of the person sitting in the desk's chair.

There is only one item on the desk: a copy of Carl Sagan's astronomy tome, *Cosmos*.

Interesting.

"There's no computer here," Evan points out.

Jack walks around to the chair. "The whole desk is his computer," he explains.

"I'm guessing it's also the server," Arnie adds. Making his point, he walks around the desk to sit in the chair. The part of the desk facing it has a slight indentation about sixteen inches square. He points out four small metal buttons on the side of the indentation closest to the chair.

Fascinated, we move behind him.

Arnie looks up at Evan. "Do I have your permission to see what these do?"

Evan nods.

Arnie pushes the one furthest on the left. A keyboard rises through the indentation, as does a screen, which is dark except for a prompt bar.

"Neat," Arnie murmurs, "Except that it wants another security protocol." He looks up at Evan. "Want to give it a shot?"

They swap places. As the screen reads Evan's face the keyboard's pad is large enough to do the same to his hand.

Retaking the seat, Arnie puts a thumb drive into one of the USB slots on the keyboard. "First I'll search for 'Operation Horoscope.'"

"No arguments here," Jack assures him.

Nothing comes up.

"But how could that be?" Jack wonders.

Arnie shrugs. "Worst case scenario: his well-deserved paranoia might have made him write in a self-destruct trigger."

"You mean, like, if he doesn't open the file after a certain time period, it would just evaporate?" I ask.

"Something like that," Arnie replies. "Hey, look at the upside: if he were still alive, it might have needed some sort of password. Had we inputted the wrong one, the same thing might have happened." He rolls his hands into fists. When he opens them again, he exclaims, "*BOOM!*"

"Maybe he left it at his house," Jack reasons. "Pull up his personnel file. We can stop there on the way home."

"Or, maybe he left it with the person who sent Evan the thumb drive in the first place," I suggest. "Arnie, are you sure there wasn't anything else on that drive?"

"Nothing," he assures me.

Evan snaps his fingers. "Something as important as Operation Horoscope would have also been on my dad's old computer, right?"

"Perhaps an older version of the project," Jack reminds him "I would imagine modifications would have been made in the past couple of years."

"Where is your father's computer now?" I ask.

Evan grimaces as he glances over at me. Hesitantly, he mutters, "At home in my room."

I guess he's wondering if he still has a home.

When I put my hand on his shoulder, an uncertain smile replaces his grimace.

He doesn't need to worry. On the other hand, Mary has

some explaining to do.

"Let's download his online correspondence," Jack says. "It may lead us to Lilith, or at least help us identify his post office courier."

Arnie taps a few keys. "I'm in his BlackTech address book. How far back should I go?"

Jack thinks for a moment. "Operation Horoscope was the company's second military contract, so, I guess you may as well go all the way back."

It takes a few minutes. Finally, Arnie murmurs, "Done."

"Is there a personal email account, or text tied to a mobile number?" I ask.

Arnie clicks around. "Yes, on both accounts. I'll download those as well." A minute later he adds, "Jonathan used Protonmail for his private email provider. It's a high-grade PGP end-to-end encryption service. We'll need to know the email address and his password. If we guess wrong, any attempt to open an email without it may cause the email to self-destruct. In fact, Jonathan may have already set specific emails to self-destruct after a certain date."

"Sheesh," I mutter. "Well, we can't just guess the email address!"

"We don't have to," Evan exclaims. "I have it. He wrote to me when Dad died." He swipes through his phone's contacts. "rocketman@pmail.com."

"What are the odds that 'rocketman' also refers to the project?" Jack asks.

"Wouldn't that be a lucky break!" Arnie replies. "Hey, so, does anyone want to take a guess at the password?"

No one speaks.

I glance around the room. There's not even a picture on

the metal walls.

Only the book on the desk.

Finally, a thought hits me: "What sign was he again?"

"Gemini," Jack replies.

When I flip open the book, a sterling silver pendant falls onto the desk.

I pick it up. The tiny oval is stamped with an image: the zodiac sign for Gemini. I slip it into my pocket.

I open the book to its index and I search the word Gemini. Finding its primary reference, I turn to the page with its pertinent information, scanning it until I see what I'm looking for. "Try that word followed by the number 85."

Arnie nods. "With the first letter capped?"

"Yeah, okay," I reply.

Our tech-op cracks his knuckles. Then with his fingers dangling over the keyboard—

He pauses. "No, wait! We should cap the 'n' instead."

"Why?" Evan asks.

"Because capping the first letter is too commonplace. And besides, the 'n' is the only letter that 'Gemini' has in common with the name 'Jonathan Presley.'"

I shrug. "Interesting rationale. Sure why not? I mean, what have we got to lose?"

"Everything," Jack mutters.

Yikes. He's right.

Jack sighs. "Go for it."

Arnie cracks his knuckles, then types it in…

He gives a gleeful yelp: "We're in!"

Each email is listed by the sender's name.

One pops out: Lilith.

I know Jack sees it too because he whispers: "Bingo!"

7

Masculine Signs

Some sun signs are considered "masculine," whereas others are considered "feminine." This is not to say that women are the only people born under a feminine sign, and vice versa. Although both men and women have masculine and feminine sides to their personalities, in this case, "masculine" and "feminine" refer to the type of energy most likely to be emanating from someone born under these signs.

For example:

Aries, Gemini, Leo, Libra, Sagittarius, and Aquarius are considered masculine signs. The good news: those born under these signs are found to be assertive and self-assured. They are more aggressive in standing up for what they believe. They are people of action.

The bad news: Many are extroverts to the point of being combative and obnoxious. If they hurt another's feelings, they justify it somehow. Perhaps the person "deserved it" or needs to "toughen up."

Feminine signs are Taurus, Cancer, Virgo, Scorpio,

Capricorn, and Pisces. The positive traits: they are team players, enjoy socializing, and are sensitive to the needs of others. They think before they act.

Sadly, there are negative aspects too: those born under these signs have a tendency to micromanage the actions of others. Also, any slight cuts deeply.

If your sign falls into a gender category that doesn't sound at all like you, no need to worry! Just because you don't recognize the bad things that come with your gender sign doesn't mean others haven't felt it.

Rest assured: somewhere along the line, you dealt it.

WE REACH HILLDALE WITH NO TIME TO SPARE FOR OUR MEETING with President Edmonton at Lee Chiffray's palatial estate: Lion's Lair was built on the crest of the hill that gave the town its name.

Mary is waiting on the front porch. She has Nicky in her lap. Emma sits beside her. When our car turns into the driveway, Mary hands Nicky to Emma, leaps up, and runs down the steps.

By the time she reaches us, Arnie and Evan are already out of the car. But before Jack and I drive away, she taps on my window. "We need to talk."

I shrug. "Agreed. Unfortunately, I'm late for a meeting. We'll talk when I get back."

"Evan may be gone by then! He's got to leave for the airport in half an hour if he's going to catch his flight back to the Bay Area—"

"Evan and I have already talked," I reply stiffly. "Frankly,

I didn't like what he had to say."

"But—"

"Mary, we have to go now. I can't be late for a meeting with the president." I roll up the window.

Mary stands there as Jack rolls the car out of the driveway. Her glare is starred with tears.

Jack sighs mightily—his signal that I might have handled things differently.

Maybe he's right. Then again, he's never been a mother whose daughter is contemplating sex for the first time—perhaps for a very wrong reason:

To hold onto a guy.

Even if he's someone as wonderful as Evan.

SECURITY AT LION'S LAIR IS HEAVIER THAN I'VE SEEN IT IN A while: that is to say, since Lee chose to leave the presidency as opposed to being impeached for collusion with Russia.

Lee was set up by a long-time Russian asset: Randall Hart, owner of the worldwide news broadcast conglomerate Hartland Media. Randall had help on the inside. The First Lady, Babette Breck Chiffray, was the Quorum's last leader standing—

Until she was incinerated in the presidential motorcade. She was riding in the vehicle meant for her husband.

Ironically, she'd rigged it to blow, so I guess it's proof that karma's a bitch.

Edmonton's Secret Service detail motions us to a parking spot on the far side of the circular driveway.

On the front portico, we go through the pat-down

protocol before being allowed into the foyer, where Lee's assistant, Eve, awaits us. When I shake her hand, she clasps mine with both of hers. Always a loyal Girl Friday, she was heartbroken when Lee resigned. She never doubted his innocence. Nor did she trust Babette. I've no doubt that Eve realized Lee resigned as opposed to calling out his wife as the real traitor.

I gave Lee the evidence he needed. Still, he blamed himself for being stupid enough to fall for her in the first place.

It's the country's loss. Lee's immense wealth made him immune to being bought by special interests.

In contrast, Bradley Edmonton is the ultimate political animal. When he was the party's Senate Majority Leader, only bills favoring the party's political donors and had the needed fifty-one votes to pass made it to the floor. Otherwise, they were buried in committee.

When Lee's first vice president resigned after his wife's tragic death, Lee was forced by his party to select Bradley Edmonton to replace him.

In other words, both resignations benefited Bradley greatly.

Eve escorts us into the anteroom outside Lee's home office, where Ryan is already waiting. He's talking to another man: late twenties, tall and slim, with a mop of blond hair. His deep-set eyes squint when he listens intently, as he does now to Ryan.

Our boss nods in my direction. "Jack and Donna Craig, this is Mario Martinez, President Edmonton's Chief of Staff."

Mario shakes my hand first. His grip is firm. His smile is warm.

As Eve takes her place behind her desk, Mario walks over to discuss a directive from POTUS. This gives Ryan a second to lean over and murmur, "Emma tells me you've had an interesting morning."

Jack smiles.

"Branham may be interested in it," Ryan whispers back.

In other words, Ix-Nay on mentioning it to OTUS-Pay.

We nod ever so slightly to signal we've heard him loud and clear.

After tapping her earbud, Eve declares, "The presidents will see you now."

Plural.

It still breaks my heart that Lee had to resign.

THEY ARE LAUGHING AS WE ENTER.

Not just Lee, DIO Branham, and Edmonton, but also a woman I can't identify, though she looks familiar.

Lee and his guests are no longer in golfing attire, but they are comfortable enough. The men wear khakis and button-down shirts. Lee's shirt, blue broadcloth, is rolled up at the sleeves.

The woman's ash blond hair falls just above her shoulders. She wears navy slacks. They hug her slim physique like a glove, as does her cream-colored tucked-in silk blouse. Its top two buttons are open, revealing a cream tank top with navy pinstripes.

It also reveals a delicate web of wrinkles and a few tiny sunspots—the only giveaways that she is older than I would have previously suspected: maybe mid-thirties, considering the smooth skin of her face. Now I'd guess her to be over forty.

Lee has allowed Edmonton to sit at the desk. He and Branham share one of the two large sofas flanking the desk, whereas the woman has taken one of the two chairs opposite it.

"Come on in, folks," Edmonton declares, although he doesn't move out from behind the desk. Instead, he waves us into the room. "So glad you could join us while we recover from Lee's spectacular golf game—albeit on a course he designed himself."

This elicits another round of chuckles as Lee and Branham stand.

Since I've entered first, I'm the first to shake Edmonton's hand, then Branham's. Lee foregoes decorum, leaning in to peck my cheek instead.

From the grin rising on Edmonton's lips, this familiarity is not lost on him.

Nor does it escape the woman's attention. She scrutinizes me that much closer. But by the time I proffer my hand, she's lifted her lips into an inscrutable smile.

Edmonton declares, "Congresswoman Elle Grisham, this is Donna Craig, Ryan Clancy, and Jack Craig."

The crispness in his tone signals her that she need not know more.

As Ryan and Jack exchange handshakes with her and the others, I rack my brain as to which state she represents. Somewhere in the Midwest...Missouri? No. Kansas, maybe?

As if reading my mind, Edmonton adds, "Congresswoman Grisham hails from the great state of Iowa. She serves on the Permanent Select Committee on Intelligence.

She is also the ranking member on the Homeland Security Committee."

She rolls her eyes at the "ranking member" moniker before shifting a sympathetic glance at Lee. His political scandal caused his party to lose both houses of Congress in the recent mid-term elections.

Congresswoman Grisham rises. "I'll take my leave now, gentleman—and Mrs. Craig." She winks at Lee. "Since you have home course advantage, I look forward to picking your brain over dinner as to how I can lower my handicap on your course, should I be invited back."

"Anyone kind enough to gift me a golf club that once belonged to Bobby Jones has an open invitation." Lee points to the present, now placed on the shelf behind his desk.

Edmonton waits until she walks out and closes the door behind her before retaking his seat. Only then do the rest of us follow suit. I opt for the couch opposite Branham and Lee. Ryan does the same. Jack takes the seat vacated by Congresswoman Grisham.

With a nod, Edmonton cedes the floor to Branham.

"Ryan, I gave you and your team a brief description of what you'll be facing on, er, Operation Flame." Branham winces at the name. "As we've known for quite some time, our energy infrastructure has become a primary target for hostile cyber-actors. In the past two years, more than a million probes into our nation's utility systems have been detected and deterred. They have come from every government hostile to our national security: the Russians, the Chinese, the North Koreans, the Iranians—"

"And folks, as bad as the attacks were here in Los Angeles, the perpetrators did even more damage in other cities,"

Edmonton interjects. "Already in Houston, there are short-ages of potable water, which means the city is unable to treat sewage. There's been a significant out-migration of resi-dents." He frowns. "The hit on commerce will be devas-tating—and inestimable."

"Our utilities aren't prepared to withstand these attacks," Lee adds. "They are also exhausting our country's fuel reserves. Even before this, last season's hurricanes and flooding put our critical infrastructure at crisis mode. The same first responders—police, firefighters, the National Guard—are up against a relentless onslaught."

Lee shifts his gaze to Edmonton. Within weeks of taking office, Edmonton loosened EPA restrictions on the fossil fuel companies—not surprising, considering how much their lobbying firms have donated to him during his years in the Senate.

Edmonton shrugs off Lee's glare. "This time, the Russians have gone too far. This attack on our largest cities is an act of war," he declares coldly.

"I guess this is our new reality," I murmur.

"Not necessarily, Mrs. Craig," Edmonton counters. "As we speak, Homeland Security has presented our nation's utility companies with a security mandate that will assure our grid is protected from further outside interference."

Branham opens his mouth to say something but then stops himself. Finally, he divulges, "In this case, the attacks were triggered locally."

Edmonton frowns. "This is new intel?"

Branham nods slowly.

"Thanks for the heads up," Edmonton's flippancy

doesn't hide his anger at Branham's apparent reluctance to mention that one of the saboteurs' calls was intercepted.

"Acme's mission is to expose any embedded saboteurs?" Jack reasons.

Branham nods.

"Why not make this an FBI investigation?" Ryan asks.

"Suppose a 'saboteur' is some high ranking utility official who was being blackmailed—or worse yet paid off by an enemy state?" Lee asks. "Politically speaking, the optics would be awful. The public's trust in the current system will be eroded beyond repair. And since the public utility lobbies grease enough Congressional palms to keep any competition at bay, it's best that no intelligence agencies lead the mission."

He doesn't have to say what we're all thinking: Should any resolution involve an extermination or two, POTUS can claim clean hands.

"Your point is well taken," Edmonton declares dryly. His way of dismissing us is to glance down at his watch. "Thank you, gentleman—and Mrs. Craig."

As we rise, Ryan murmurs to Branham, "Sir, perhaps you'd care to walk us out?"

Edmonton glances up sharply. "No need for a huddle, Mr. Clancy. You're among friends here."

Ryan keeps his poker face in place, but Branham is barely able to stifle his frown. If I were to guess, I'd say he'd prefer to filter any and all intel before it reaches Edmonton's ears, especially any chatter coming from outside sources.

Acme is as far outside as it gets.

Catching my gaze, Lee's lids fall to half-mast. He doesn't fool me. His benign smile indicates that he's enjoying

Edmonton's peevishness—a small consolation, considering that Lee's downfall was the best thing that ever happened to DC's most notorious political animal.

Ryan sits again, a signal that Jack and I should do the same.

"Gentlemen, we've come across intel that a U.S. military operation may have been jeopardized—something called Operation Horoscope."

"I've never heard of it," Edmonton declares. He glares at Branham, daring him to admit to another exclusion.

Branham furrows his brow. "That's impossible! Operation Horoscope was shelved a couple of years back…" He glances at Lee for confirmation.

"And for a good reason," Lee adds. "I killed it my first month in office. It was a boondoggle that cost the American taxpayer far too much for far too long."

Edmonton frowns. "A military operation?"

Lee nods. "A leftover from the Administration before mine."

"A dinosaur," Edmonton scoffs.

Ryan nods. "No problem. Then as far as Acme is concerned, it's dead and buried."

"Lilith too?" The question slips out before I can stop it.

Edmonton looks up sharply. "What did you say?"

"I…nothing, really."

Foot. In. Mouth…

His icy blue eyes drill into me: "Indulge me." Hidden deep in the velvet recesses of his tone is a menace that pierces like a dagger.

"It's just…Well, you see, the chatter we intercepted mentioned a person who…" I hope my squinting gives the impression that I'm having a hard time remembering what was said, as opposed to the fact that I'm lying through my teeth. "…That is, a Russian asset who may have been embedded for quite some time."

Edmonton leans back slowly. "What does—*did* this Russian asset have to do with Operation Horoscope?"

"Apparently, she compromised it somehow," Ryan explains. "Unfortunately, the chatter wasn't specific."

Edmonton lets that sink in. Finally, he swings around to Lee. "What was Operation Horoscope, exactly?"

Lee closes his eyes for a moment to think, then says. "If I remember it was a missile program." He turns to Branham. "Am I right?"

Branham shakes his head. "Sorry, sir. I only joined your administration in its second year. Before that, I was the CIA Bureau Director in London. If this Operation Horoscope was classified Eyes Only, I might not have been cleared for it." He turns to Edmonton. "If you're interested, I can do some digging."

Edmonton shrugs. "Not important. I'm sure President Chiffray had a good reason to kill the project." He smirks, as if making a joke at his host's expense.

Lee doesn't seem at all annoyed. So, why am I?

"However the thought that there may be some mole in my administration is worrisome." Edmonton tents his fingers as he thinks. "Lilith…So, the supposed mole is a woman?" He looks over at me to confirm this.

"The chatter indicated as much," Ryan declares. "I wish there was more I could tell you."

But there is.

Like the fact that the "chatter" was a letter to Evan. And

that it specifically mentioned an act of treason by a government contractor.

Worse still, Horoscope may still be in play.

So, why don't Branham and Ryan want Edmonton to know any of this?

Jack's eye catches mine. He purses his lips: his way of telling me to hold my powder.

My way of feigning nonchalance is to look down at my nails.

Goodness, I could use a mani-pedi.

Lee stands. "The staff will be summoning us to dinner soon. Ryan, Craigs, I'll walk you out."

Branham's cell phone is buzzing. He pulls it out of his pocket. "If I'm to catch my flight back to DC, I should take off too." He looks over at Edmonton, "Unless you have anything else for me, sir."

President Edmonton shakes his head. "No. You're excused."

We make it to the door when POTUS says, "Mr. Craig, would you mind staying behind? There is a separate matter I'd like to discuss with you."

Jack shows his surprise at this request with a mere blink.

"Not to worry. I'll drive Donna home," Ryan assures him.

By the time Jack closes the door behind us, I'm about to burst. Still, I hold my cool until Lee, Branham, Ryan, and I are in the elevator before I hiss, "What the hell just happened in there?"

"I'll explain when we get into the car," Ryan promises.

"You can still give me a lift to the airport, right?" Branham asks him. When Ryan nods, Branham adds, "Great. I'll grab my bags and meet you at your car." He smiles at Lee. "Although, as lousy as my golf game was today, I might as well just leave my clubs here. Feel free to toss them in the trash."

Lee chuckles. "You just need a little practice. Edmonton never misses a weekend on some course. Try cozying up to him on the links. It may just save your job."

"Not if he finds out Horoscope is still in play."

"He already knows it," Lee retorts.

"Jeez, guys!" I mutter. "Okay, now you're just driving me crazy!"

"Short ride," Ryan murmurs.

That earns him a pinch.

He pats my arm. He knows he's the one who has a lot of explaining to do.

IT TAKES BRANHAM ALL OF FIVE MINUTES BEFORE HE JOINS US AT the car.

He could have taken an extra ten. Lee seems in no hurry to get back to his guests. Besides, Jack is still in with POTUS. "I don't want to barge in on any bromance going on between those two," he teases.

"Edmonton isn't exactly Jack's type," I assure him. "So, should we take bets on what they're discussing?"

"My guess: Lilith," Ryan says.

I roll my eyes. "Are you implying that he'll break with your code of silence on that subject?"

Ryan shakes his head. "Nope. Jack is smart enough to say as little as possible—and just listen."

"I'm only surprised that Edmonton didn't ask you to stay behind instead," Lee teases.

"She'd be the wrong choice for what he has in mind," Branham replies.

Curiouser and curiouser. "Oh yeah? And why is that?"

"This conversation is for the drive home," Ryan declares.

That's my cue to get into the car. Lee opens the back seat door. Before I slide in, he kisses my forehead. "Drop by later in the week if you have time."

I groan loudly. "If only! Besides a workload that seems to be growing by the minute, I'm chairing the high school prom."

Lee hides his disappointment with a shrug. "If you need an extra chaperone, let me know."

"Depending on what Edmonton has in mind for Jack, I may take you up on that," I warn him.

I wave as we drive away.

8

Oh, Joy!

Some zodiac signs have "joy places" — that is, a planet where it enjoys complete harmony and provides the most beneficial effect.

According to the noted astrologer William Lilly, the joy planets coincide with the following signs:

Saturn (Libra)

Jupiter (Sagittarius)

Mars (Scorpio)

Sun (Leo)

Venus (Taurus)

Mercury (Virgo)

Moon (Cancer)

Ironically, joy places are rarely referred to in modern astrology. The reason: we now find an incredible amount of joy on Earth — especially during Nordstrom's Semi-Annual Sale.

WE ARE DOWN THE HILL IN NO TIME.

Ryan waits until we're on my street before pulling over. But before he says anything, I turn to Branham: "What exactly was—is Horoscope?"

Barnham snorts. "Despite what Lee would have Edmonton believe, it wasn't some sort of super missile. It's much worse—especially if its plans fell into enemy hands."

I cringe. "How much worse?"

"Remember Reagan's Star Wars program?" Ryan asks.

"You mean, what Putin now calls his 'Death Star'?" I say sarcastically.

"That's it," he replies. "Along with every other weaponized satellite program fantasy since Sputnik went into space."

"But doesn't the Outer Space Treaty ban its signatories from putting weapons of mass destruction into orbit?" I exclaim.

"It does—in theory," Branham explains. "And yet, China, Russia, and the US still see it as a viable goal. Go figure."

"So, Horoscope is the latest iteration of a satellite that can blow up a city from space?" I ask.

Both men nod.

I still can't believe my ears. "And, we are—or we were— that close to achieving its launch?"

"We weren't. At least, not when Lee killed the project," Branham replies. He turns to Ryan. "By the way, how did the chatter come your way?"

"From Horoscope's creator, albeit posthumously," Ryan explains. "Donna's ward, Evan Martin, received a letter meant for his father. It was written a couple of years ago— before Robert's death. It came from Jonathan Presley, the Chief Engineering Officer of BlackTech, which developed the satellite's targeting software. Evan inherited BlackTech from Robert. In the letter, Presley admitted he'd made a software change at the behest of the Russians."

"Ah yes, Robert's boy." Branham shrugs. "If Evan is anything like his father, it must have broken his heart to hear of Presley's deception."

"It did," I assure him. "According to the letter, Presley claims he was turned while at Stanford, by a female Russian agent in an astrology class. She went on to become a Congressional aide. We're sifting through Congressional HR files now to see if anyone fitting the meager description we have still roams the halls of Congress."

"That would have been nearly two decades ago. In any event, I'll pass Acme the dead file so that your people can comb through it." Branham rolls his eyes. "For once Edmonton is right about something: There may be a powerful mole among us."

"One bit of good news," Ryan says. "We retrieved surveillance of the letter's mailer. We assume it was a friend of Presley's. From what we can tell it may have been a woman."

"Have you been able to ID her?" Branham asks. "She may be more than just a courier."

"The trail is cold," Ryan admits.

"If we hit the pause button on Horoscope, why would Jonathan think otherwise?" I ask.

"Great question," Branham sighs, "unless the Russians have their own version and it's ready to launch."

Shite.

Double shite if it accidentally disintegrates an ally's capitol.

Or even worse, ours.

Well, it certainly means all hands on deck—which brings me to Jack. "Sir, what did you mean when you said that Jack was right for whatever POTUS has in mind?"

He shrugs. "Edmonton is worried that Lilith may still be in play."

"What does that have to do with Jack?"

"If I'm right, he'll ask Jack to find her," Branham explains.

"I don't get it. How is he supposed to do that?"

"Edmonton may already have an inkling of who she is," Ryan replies.

"So, why aren't you two being briefed on this too?"

"Isn't it obvious?" Branham asks. "He doesn't trust us."

Now I'm baffled. "But…he trusts Jack?"

Ryan frowns. "He will if Jack doesn't break his trust by revealing the mission to either of us—or you, for that matter." Ryan leans in. "Will he?"

"Of course not," I retort.

But that doesn't mean I won't try to get it out of him.

Suddenly, Ryan is laughing.

"What's so funny?" I ask crossly.

"You should see your face," he crows. "Hey, do me a favor—"

"Let me guess: if he tells me anything, I'm to pass it along to you," I say stiffly.

"Yes," Branham replies. Only he's not laughing.

A long-embedded Russian operative will have a keen survival instinct. If she even suspects Jack is on to her, she'll strike first.

I know because if it were me, I'd do the same.

Noting my concern, Ryan adds, "Don't worry, Donna. Jack's a big boy. He can handle himself."

That doesn't comfort me.

"In the meantime, you'll be the mission leader on operations Flame and Horoscope," he adds. "We'll work out logistics tomorrow with the rest of the team."

I nod and get out of the car.

In the half block to the house, my game face is in place.

That's a good thing: Mary is still waiting on the porch.

It was only an hour since we left for Lion's Lair. And yet, it seems like a year.

In other words, it's time my daughter and I had a much-needed talk.

About life in general; and love in particular.

BEFORE MARY GETS UP, BEFORE SHE CAN SAY A WORD, I SIT down beside her on the porch swing. "We had an agreement, you and me: to always be honest with each other."

She nods warily.

"So tell me the truth now: Did you ask Evan to make love to you?"

Like tiny quakes, emotions shift on the supple planes on Mary's face. When she finds her voice, they stop: "Yes."

I let that sink in. Then: "Why now?"

Mary purses her lips. "I...I just thought it was time."

I nod as I take this in. "Is it because you're concerned that he'll be attracted to other women while he's at college?"

"That...yes, that has something to do with it." Her relief at saying it out loud shows itself with a shrug. "No need to worry, Mother. Evan was too much of a gentleman to say yes to my desperate attempt to hold onto him."

"Do you still believe Evan loves you?"

"I...I don't know what to believe!" A tear rolls down Mary's face. "When he lived here in Hilldale, we discussed everything. We spent all our time together. We were..." Her voice fades away.

"Inseparable. Of one mind. In love."

Her eyes open wide, as if seeing me for the very first time. "Yes," she finally whispers.

I hold her close. "When we are separated from the ones we love, we're more susceptible to the fear of loss. It doesn't mean they love us any less. When they are away from us, we must remember *why* we love them. We trust them because they've earned our trust. We love them because they have proven their love and adoration for us. If they no longer feel trusted no matter what they do or say, what is left for them to do other than walk away?"

Mary nods. "You're lucky you have Dad," she whispers.

"Luck had something to do with it, yes. It put us in each other's paths. But he had to earn my love. He had to win my trust. Especially after..."

"After Carl," she says.

She's never called him that before. She has matured enough to look at him objectively.

Thank you, God.

"And I had to earn his too," I add.

She nods. Hesitantly, she adds: "Mom, now be honest with me."

I brace myself. Will she ask me if I've ever doubted Jack's

love? Or, if I still get jealous when he's given an assignment where sex is involved?

Or, if I worry if he'll ever leave me?

I'd answer honestly: Yes, we had to work through our doubts. Yes, it pierces my heart to imagine him kissing—let alone making love to, another woman.

And yes, I worry about him leaving me—

Because doing so would mean he'd died. We love each other too much now to part any other way.

Mary takes a deep breath: "Do you think I've ruined things with Evan?"

Thankfully, she takes my relieved sigh as a sign of serious contemplation. "After what we've discussed, do you still feel he's fallen out of love with you?"

She shakes her head. "I was afraid he had. It made me angry—*at him*. Now, I'm just angry at myself for doubting him."

"Well, then, that's what you should write to him."

"I'll do it right now." An errant thought darkens her hope. "Mom, do you think there will come a time when he no longer loves me?"

Ah, love! Like a spider's web, it is complex, unique, fragile—and no two are alike.

I've never known of a web that lasted forever. Perhaps that's where it differs from love.

In this case, hope conflicts with honesty. My vow to my daughter leaves me no choice but to choose the latter. "I don't know, Mary. But if there comes a time when one of you no longer feels the same way about the other, you'll both survive."

She nods sadly. Kissing my cheek, she heads inside.

Nothing is sweeter than your child's gratitude.

I head for the kitchen. Aunt Phyllis has already started dinner. I hope I have time to salvage whatever is burning in the oven.

JACK ENTERS THE HOUSE JUST AS WE'RE ABOUT TO SIT DOWN to eat.

He smiles genially and kisses my forehead.

I grin back and motion toward the well-charred roast. "Care to carve?"

"Sure," he declares.

As he does the honors, I spoon mashed sweet potatoes and roasted Brussels sprouts onto each plate before passing it forward. I feel him watching me out of the corner of his eye. When I look over at him, his eyes move to Mary.

She's all smiles again and teasing her brother about his reticence toward asking out his *crush du jour*: Felicity, a cute redhead in his Algebra II class. Trisha is debating with Aunt Phyllis why the latest television incarnation of *MacGyver* is so much better than the '80s version.

You'd think Jack would be relieved that all is serene in the Craig household. So, why is he frowning? Is he disappointed that I didn't corner him the minute he stepped into the house and drill him about his conversation with Edmonton?

Well, surprise! I'm saving that yummy morsel as my dessert.

In bed.

"Go ahead and ask." Jack grants permission after helping me with the dishes.

And helping Trisha with her science project.

And after a rousing romp of lovemaking, as I lay cradled in his arms.

"Ask what?" I say casually.

He rolls me over so that we're face to face. When he doesn't find what he expects—craven curiosity—he scowls.

This is so much fun.

Still, he can't help taunting: "I know you want to know why Edmonton asked me to stay behind."

"Some secret mission, I suppose? Let's see…Oh! I know: he wants you to find Lilith!"

"Go to the head of the class." Disappointed, he rolls over so that his back is to me.

I hang over him so that he has to face me. "Does he suspect who she is—or at least where you might find her?"

"That's confidential," he replies smugly.

I punch his arm.

"*Ow!*" He yelps.

As I fall back behind him, I mutter, "You asked for it."

"I have to follow orders. I'm not supposed to tell anyone anything about the mission."

"Not even Ryan?"

"I called him, yes—to relay POTUS's request."

"I suppose he agreed."

"He has no choice." There's an edge to Jack's voice.

"Does Branham know?"

"I was instructed by POTUS to tell Ryan, but that it was to go no further."

Interesting. Thus far, Branham has been on the mark about Edmonton.

But if Edmonton has some inkling as to the identity or whereabouts of Lilith, why wouldn't he want to share it with his Director of Intelligence?

"I take it you'll be undercover."

"Affirmative."

"Will Acme have eyes and ears on you?"

Jack thinks for a moment. "You know, that wasn't something I discussed with Edmonton. But I don't see why not."

Perhaps Edmonton isn't aware of Acme's technical fail-safe. Not that I'll point this out to Jack.

"Will you be away from home?"

A long beat: "Some nights."

I say nothing.

Eventually, I whisper, "Be careful. I don't want to test the theory that I could live without you."

I say this because I don't trust Edmonton. He is the antithesis of Lee, who was good at laying his cards on the table.

Most days, anyway.

Jack doesn't move as I head for the shower. I guess I've given him something to think about: the rest of our lives.

All the more reason to survive this mission.

9

Pisces

Those born between February 19th and March 20th are under the sun sign known as Pisces, or "the fish."

You'll note such emotional traits as intuitive and compassionate—both of which make them great listeners and give the rest of us shoulders to lean on.

They also need to feel a connection to their partners. (More on this below.)

As with every sign, Pisces has its share of negative traits as well. For example:

Negative Trait #1: No need to see red when he calls you a "nag." He just hates to be criticized!

Negative Trait #2: If he tries to sell you on the notion that his foray to a strip bar was only to "return a wallet to the girl who lost it," (despite the fact it was his wallet), you can write it off to Pisces' "wild imagination."

The same can be said for his excuse that he offered this grateful lady his shoulder to cry on, but she elected to massage his crotch instead.

Another thing he'll imagine: stars, as you hit him over the head with a frying pan.

"So, here's how it goes, folks!" This morning, Ryan's bellowing has a particularly anxious edge to it. "Emma, you and Abu comb through Presley's data files. See what you pull up regarding Horoscope. Also, cross-reference any congressman still in office from the past twenty years. If one has an aide named Lilith, we may be able to catch an embedded Russian operative red-handed."

"On it, chief," they say in unison. Realizing this, they hit a high-five.

"Hey, don't forget: Evan gave me Robert's computer. No need to hack it, since he gave me the password." I blush. "It's sH1Ves2135551515."

When Evan read it to me, I almost fainted. Robert created an alpha-numeric code using my maiden name and the telephone number belonging to my parents.

I no longer think Catherine was the love of his life, but I'll never share this with Evan—or Jack, for that matter.

"Abu and Emma: once you finish with Presley's data, you can swing over to Robert Martin's. In the meantime, Donna and Arnie are to head over to California Gas & Electric's facility in Temecula. You'll be posing as two California Public Utility Commission auditors."

I nod. When Arnie tries to high-five me, I tickle his underarm instead. He snorts raucously.

Ryan looks up and curses Zeus. When he calms down, I ask, "What are we looking for?"

"In a nutshell: anything out of the ordinary. Donna, just keep asking questions until they're stumped on the answers. In the meantime, Arnie will hack into their system and do some skullduggery of his own."

"Look, I hate pleading ignorance, but the truth is, what I know about electrical grids wouldn't light up a single LED. Can you be more specific?"

Ryan sighs. "Although many states are 'vertically structured'—meaning that all aspects of the grid are managed by the same company—our country has three main transmission networks. ERCOT, or the Electric Reliability Council of Texas; Eastern Interconnection; and Western Interconnection. These networks are regulated by FERC, the Federal Energy Regulatory Commission."

"Only three? Wow! Each must cover a lot of ground," I murmur.

Ryan nods. "There's an economic reason for this. A larger grid is the most efficient way to deal with blackouts. When an unexpected one occurs, operators can pull energy from other generators within the same grid that are working below capacity. Doing so also allows electricity to be sold at the lowest price, which protects consumers from price fluctuations."

"But there is a downside," Arnie points out. "For example, a blackout can affect several states simultaneously."

"Just like this weekend's gas surges devastated neighborhoods all over the region," I murmur.

"Exactly," Ryan replies. "While you're questioning the managers on how the transmission networks can be sabotaged, Arnie will run a software analysis to assess any discrepancies in the distribution system's operational code."

"Got it."

Ryan now turns to Dominic. "Fly up to Stanford. Get a list of the other students in Jonathan's class. Even if the number of men and women were even, that gives us six names, max, to narrow down to 'Lilith.'"

"What would you suggest I use as a cover?" Dominic asks.

"Since all universities appreciate free publicity, tell them you're a reporter for *Bloomberg* and that you're writing one of those 'Where Are They Now?' pieces."

Dominic's brow furrows. "Do you mean Bloomsbury, the literary salon?"

Ryan hits his forehead with the palm of his hand. "No. I mean the business magazine. Trust me on this."

Dominic looks around, puzzled. "By the way, will the illustrious Mr. Craig be joining us this fine morn?"

"He's on a solo assignment," Ryan replies.

"Ah! Well, I hope I don't prove to be a disappointing alternate," Dominic sniffs.

Chances are that will be the case unless I nip his whiny attitude in the bud post haste.

I use a backhanded slap—always an effective maneuver.

Stunned, Dominic reels backward. Rubbing the sting, he sniffs, "I *beg your pardon!*"

"As you should!" I exclaim. "Dude, dig it: Russia is blowing up gas lines all over the country, and that's just the *entr'acte*! For a finale, they may try to incinerate a major metropolis!"

"I think what she's trying to say is that now may not be the best time for a pity party," Emma points out.

Dominic nods solemnly. "I see your point."

"Battle stations, people!" Ryan waves us off.

JANET BENDER KNOCKS TIMIDLY ON HER BOSS'S DOOR BEFORE peeking in.

"*Jeez Louise*, Janet! Didn't they teach you any manners in Redding?" Spencer Winston shouts. "Next time, wait until I invite you in! What if I'd been, you know, partaking in some hand-to-gland combat? Then the next thing you know, I get one of those calls from HR that you've reported Mr. McGoo and me for MeTooing you, or something!"

By the ruby shade of Janet's cheeks, I'd guess he was doing precisely that. And, from what I've read in Spencer's personnel file, his MeToo violations have stacked up to the point that he might have considered the surge a welcomed diversion.

Janet faces away from him, back toward Arnie and me. "But Mr. Spencer—I just wanted to tell you that there are two PUC auditors here to see you!" She points shaking a finger in my direction.

"Dammit! I thought those people have already been through here!" Spencer's gruff response is accompanied by some drawer slamming and muffled shuffling.

When he makes it to the door, his eyes, like heat-seeking missiles, hone in on my breasts.

To break the spell, I snap my fingers in his face.

"Well, hello to you too!" I reply brightly. "My colleague and I just have a few follow-up questions about this weekend's grid surge." I nod toward his office. "Shall we?"

I saunter past him.

Intrigued, he follows.

After he's all the way in, I close the door behind us.

Realizing Arnie hasn't followed us in, Spencer is doubly intrigued. "Isn't the nerdy guy joining us? Not that I'm into threesomes or anything. Well, not the kind where I might cross swords, if you get my drift." He raises his brows three times with a dexterity that would have made Groucho Marx proud.

"My colleague had to run to the little boys' room," I coo in my baby girl voice.

Not really. Arnie is making a beeline to an empty cubicle. It's all he needs to hack the system, download all of CA Gas & Electric's WHAT THE FUCK JUST HAPPENED memos on the incident, and run a malware diagnostic. He'll then look for anomalies in the grid's code that may have set off the surges.

Spencer offers me the only guest chair in his office. But instead of sitting behind his desk, he stands directly in front of me and leans in. I guess he wants to make sure I notice the bulge straining against the zipper of his too-tight chinos.

So yeah, I look at something that resembles a sleeping anaconda.

Less mesmerized than appalled, I glance around the room. The décor consists of a *Sports Illustrated Swim Suit Edition* calendar and some pictures of Spencer on a beach vacation. Some of the women lounging with him are topless. In it, Spencer leers at the camera. His right hand is bent into the Hawaiian shaka sign.

And yep, the anaconda is there too—stuffed in his Speedo banana hammock.

"Like what you see?" he asks.

I guess I'm staring again at the elephant—er, snake—in the room. Even in 2D, it gives me the shivers. "So, tell me, Mr. Winston—"

"Please, call me *Spence*." When he shifts his haunches on the desk, the anaconda seems to come alive. "And what should I call you?"

A cab.

Instead, I purr, "Dixie."

"I like Southern girls."

"I'll just bet they like you too." I lick my lips in the hope that it keeps me from upchucking. "So listen, um… *Spence*. Is there anything you can tell me about the events leading up to the surge? You know, any deviations in the system, any strange emails that may have come in, any—"

He places his hands on each of my breasts. "Are these real?"

More so than that snake in your britches.

There's only one way to prove it. When my knee hits his nuts, he doubles over.

On the other hand, I'm groaning from the sharp pain in my knee, which, apparently, slammed against some sort of steel codpiece in Spencer's pants.

I bite my tongue to keep from moaning because it may actually turn Spencer on.

This time when Janet knocks on the door, there isn't a waiting period. Maybe she really does want to catch him in the act. She'll have to settle for watching him roll on the floor in agony.

She's accompanied by Arnie and two security guards.

"What the hell do you want?" Spencer shouts.

"These gentlemen are here to arrest you." She's no longer cowering. In fact, she's jubilant.

As the security guards lift Spencer off the ground, he sputters, "What the...*for what*? How did you know I touched her boobs?"

"Apparently, you, Mr. Winston, were the source of the malware campaign," Arnie explains. Suddenly, his mouth drops open. "You touched *her* boobs?" He stares at me, then back to Spencer. "Man, you are *so* lucky you're just on the floor! You could be *dead*."

Time to change the subject. "What other trouble has Romeo here gotten himself into?"

"The malware entered through his computer," Arnie explains.

"But—but it couldn't have been me!" Spencer whines. "Look, I'm no fool. I've been very cautious *not* to open emails—not even from the usual industry groups!"

"It didn't come through a mirror of the typical PUC employee watering hole sites," Arnie explains "It was allowed into the system when you opened PartyCentral."

"The hook-up app?" I can't believe my ears. Okay, considering this guy's MO, maybe I can.

"The very one." Arnie turns to Spencer. "Aren't you registered under the name, 'American Pharaoh'?"

Noting the stares from the security guards, Spencer shrugs. "Okay, yeah, I like to give the ladies a heads-up on what they can expect."

Janet and I shudder in unison.

"From what I can tell, you're on the site practically your whole shift," Arnie declares. "This week alone you've accessed it over a hundred times from your office computer."

A security guard rolls his eyes. "I've heard enough," He mutters. He and his buddy goose-step Spencer out the door.

Janet turns to us. "What should I do about Mr. Winston's computer?"

"Don't touch it," Arnie advises.

"At least, not without wearing latex gloves," I add.

I follow him out the door.

ARNIE BEATS ME TO THE CAR, BUT ONLY BECAUSE HE WANTS TO slide across its roof, ala *Starsky and Hutch*.

He lands on his ass.

I hold out my hand. "Give me the keys. I'm driving."

Arnie knows better than to argue with me. He climbs into the passenger seat. But before I start the engine, he exclaims, "Donna wait! Something just occurred to me."

I raise a brow. "Don't leave me in suspense."

"The way the Russians went about the surge-mageddon —this shotgun approach to creating disasters? Well, it wasn't simply started with that Spencer guy's dating app password. Which, interestingly enough, is 'PussyGalore69'."

"No surprise there." I look heavenward. "So, what you're saying is that Spencer didn't launch the malware?"

"The short answer is no. Granted, McHandsy downloaded the trojan that got the malware into CA Gas & Electric's grid. With all of his unsecured Internet use, it was easy enough to set him up to be the fall guy. But the real mastermind had the equivalent of a backstage pass."

"Come again?"

Exasperated, Arnie sighs loudly. "Whoever set off this system-wide surge-gasm is high enough up the engineering ladder to merit an ID card that gets him beyond the grid's multi-factor authentication system."

"Ah! You think there's a bigger game afoot," I reply.

Arnie nods. "Well said, Watson! No, wait—*I'm* Watson… but I did come up with the theory, so I guess that does make me Sherlock—"

"Shut up. You're driving me crazy." I start the engine. "So, where are we going?"

"Marina del Rey."

"What's there?" I ask.

"Thunderbolt Cloud Services. It's a private server and secure cloud company. All the utility companies use it because it provides the services needed to share and maintain the grid: operations, maintenance, personnel, energy management, you name it."

"But since we already know how the malware got in and we know the code that needs to be pulled out, why stop at Thunderbolt now?" I ask.

"The number of utilities affected—and the fact that they were hit all at once—took coordination from some sort of command center."

"Ergo, Thunderbolt. Sound deduction!" This time it's me who raises a hand for a high five.

And it's Arnie who tickles me under the arm.

Bad move. He realizes this when my hands go to his throat. "I suggest you stick to the traditional high-five return. Agreed?"

He nods because no one can talk while they're choking.

And we're off.

"You're with the PUC? An audit? Well, in that case, you'll need to talk to our CEO, Carlton Miller." Thunderbolt's receptionist sounds as harried as she looks. Her phone console blinks like a store's window display during a Christmas sale.

Thunderbolt is only fourteen stories, but it's the tallest building in the bedroom community of Marina del Rey. The elevator banks are busy. Employees flow in and out. All have worried scowls on their faces. The lobby is filled with anxious utility executives who wince as they read their phone screens.

Something's not right here.

"Unfortunately, Mr. Miller is...well, he's on the roof," the receptionist adds. "He's in the middle of his meditation hour." She frowns at the thought.

I don't blame her. *The world is on fire, and this dude has the nerve to take a time-out?*

"We'll wait," I assure her. "Hey, can you point me to the girl's room?"

She hands me a keycard. But because she's already fielding calls, she can only nod toward the small hallway where I'll find the powder room.

Next to it is the fire exit.

I take it straight up to the roof.

CARLTON MILLER IS INDEED MEDITATING.

His eyes are closed, giving me time to study him. He's in his early forties. It's a relatively cool day for LA in January, and yet his completely shaved pate is sweating profusely. It may be why he's stripped off his shirt, too.

I notice he's wearing a pendant around his neck. By getting closer, I can make out its design:

The zodiac sign for Pisces.

The pendant is sterling silver, just like the one Jonathan left in the book on his desk.

A tiny tray sits to his left. It holds slivers of something—maybe mushrooms? And a vaping pipe. The necessary accoutrements to mask one's guilt.

Carlton opens his eyes. My presence is finally felt.

Before he can ask me who I am, I come to the point: "You did it for Lilith, didn't you?"

His stare is a cauldron of emotions: shock, guilt, shame, grief, and finally, resignation.

"That's how it started, yes. But, hey, even after I realized her game, the money was too good to turn down." Carlton points at the ground beneath him. "It built this. I owed her that."

"You're a software engineer, right? Okay, so yeah—maybe she pointed out that public utilities were a growth industry ready to be cultivated in your field. But Carlton, you were the one with the right skillset, not her. *You* made Thunderbolt! And *you* chose to sell out your country."

He dropped his head. "I...I had no choice! She put me in front of some foundation that paid off my student loans...and my other debts. I didn't know the Russians were behind it!"

"What other debts?" I ask.

He shrugs. "I like to travel. And I like hallucinogenics." He nods toward the tray.

"It doesn't take a billionaire's bank account to do either of those things," I point out.

"And...I like to gamble."

That's where they had him over the barrel.

"You gambled, all right—and lost. The death toll is over two hundred!"

"It's two hundred and eighty-four, to be exact. Or, it was before I headed up here." He looks up at the clouds, as if that is where he'll find the souls he's damned for all eternity.

"You know, you weren't the only one she recruited from the horoscope class."

"You're telling me!" His pain heightens his snarl. "There was Tommy and Lawrence...and Howard too. They all fell for her!"

"How do you know this?"

Carlton drops his gaze to look at me. "It's what I do, bitch! I hack—right?"

"You hacked her emails."

He nods. "Yeah. *Looooove.*" His hands reach up over his head, as if swatting it away. "I had it bad."

"What are their last names?"

Carlton giggles raucously. "What does it matter? They're all dead!"

"Dead?" My heart sinks. "How?"

"Lawrence—he was Capricorn—liked to skydive, so I guess that made it easy for them." He snickers. "Howie— 'Aries'—choked on something..." He paused to consider this. "That one had to have been harder to pull off."

"You think they killed them?"

He nods.

"What about the third guy, Tommy?"

Carlton shakes his head. "Ah, 'Libra,' the heart of the class! Disappeared into thin air! Believe me, I've tried to find him." Carlton drops his head again. "I can only imagine what they did to him, and why. And now they'll kill me too."

"I can help you, Carlton! If you give us what we need, we'll get you into Witness Protection—"

His giggles propel him to his feet. "No, no, no! You don't get it! She's the all-knowing, the all-powerful wizard! She will find me. She will kill me!" He stops cold. "There is one way around her—*just one.*" He nods to me. "Thank you for sharing my clarity."

With that, he runs to the ledge and jumps.

Cars on Mindanao Way screech to a halt. The shrill screams of startled pedestrians punctuating the air are even louder than steel slamming into steel.

By the time the ambulances show up, Arnie and I are in our car.

We are drained. I call Ryan. "You caught that?"

"Yeah. Not to worry. Marina del Rey is covered by the LA County Sheriff's Department. I'll clear your involvement with them." Ryan sighs. "Great work, both of you. Now go home and get a full night's rest."

Even when the clock is ticking, a good boss knows when to back off.

10

Negative Forces

[Donna's horoscope today]

The negative forces facing you at every turn are now fierce enough to raise your skirt high above your hips, knock you off your Loubies, and make this your worst hair day ever.

Not to worry—you are not alone! Quickly align yourself with fearless allies who vow to shield you from the dark tsunami that swirls around you.

Oh, sure, these furious headwinds may leave your pals a little worse for wear. But considering their lack of fashion sense, any rearrangement of their retro boho garbs will actually be an improvement! Later, they may thank you for it.

JACK DID NOT COME HOME LAST NIGHT.

Now, as I enter Acme, I contemplate the best way to

suggest (okay, to *beg*) Ryan to keep me abreast of Jack's mission.

If Edmonton has some clue as to who Lilith is, why not share it with us so that we can initiate trailing surveillance?

And if that's all Jack is doing, it's a waste of his talents. Even Edmonton knows this—

Unless he needs Jack's confirmation of her bad-actor status to justify her extermination.

If Ryan admits this, I'll leave well enough alone. The last thing I need him to tell me is that somehow Lilith discovered Jack's real purpose and set a trap that took his life.

Killing is not fun. It is not a game. Even when sanctioned by your government, even when you're driven to avenge an atrocity, it never fails to chip away at your soul.

Take it from one who knows.

"—And then I discovered the malware. He downloaded it via his PartyCentral app, of all places! Ha! That's when I knew we had the dude dead to rights!" I've walked into Ryan's situation room to find Arnie regaling Abu, Emma, and Dominic with our tales of derring-do while we wait for the arrival of our fearless leader.

Dominic's face turns a ghostly pallor. "But...I'm on..."

His voice fades as he reaches for his phone, taps one of its many apps and hits the delete button. Glaring at Emma, he mutters, "Thanks for the suggestion."

She waves away his pout. "Hush! Arnie is just now getting to the good part!"

It should be interesting to see what Emma considers "the

good part." I hope it's not some macabre description of Carlton's body after falling fourteen stories onto a wide boulevard of moving traffic.

Arnie exclaims, "After grabbing the creep's assistant and a couple of security guards, I walk in just in time to see Donna manhandling said creep—"

"That's interesting." We turn to see Ryan standing in the doorway.

"It was self-defense. He 'woman-handled' me first!" I retort.

He frowns at me. "How?"

I shrug. "In the, er, *chestical* area."

Ryan flinches. "And how did you, er, retaliate?"

Before I can answer, Arnie crows, "Let's just put it this way: he's now singing soprano!"

While the others laugh until they cry, our boss glares in my direction—

But there's a hint of a grin on his lips. Finally, he growls "Enough, people! Never forget: *the clock is ticking!*"

He's right. We all know it.

It's why we don't get the chance to laugh too often.

EMMA IS FIRST UP: "I'VE GOT GOOD NEWS AND BAD. THE BAD news is that Jonathan must have scrubbed all traces of Horoscope from his computer."

Ryan closes his eyes, as if it's all a bad dream. When he finally opens them, he says, "Hit us with the good news."

"For some reason, he read his horoscope every day since he left college—always from a website called 'Signs of the

Times.' He archived them on his computer. My guess: word codes were used."

"Then there has to be a cipher key," Ryan replies.

"I'm still searching for it through Jonathan's files," Emma admits. "In the meantime, I've got the ComInt team working on another way to decipher it."

Ryan turns to Abu. "Any luck with the mention of Horoscope on Robert Martin's computer?"

Abu frowns. "I only wish he had used the word, 'Horoscope!' Interestingly enough, Robert's files don't have names, just alphanumeric labels. I'm going through them one-by-one. I started back fifteen years ago."

"What are you using as search criteria?" I ask.

Abu shrugs. "It's a short list. The words missile and satellite, which is in at least half of the files. I've also got Jonathan Presley's first and last names on the list. But because of his role as chief engineer, he's mentioned in practically all the files."

Ryan nods. "I know it's arduous work. Just keep at it, and thanks." He ignores Arnie's hand-waving, barking, "Dominic, you're up."

Our resident Brit shrugs. "Frankly, Chief, I've also hit a brick wall. There is no trace of an astrology class taught at Stanford during Jonathan's senior year."

"But how could that be?" I ask.

"The school thought it strange as well," Dominic admits. "In fact, I had the archivist pull up Jonathan's class schedule for his senior year. He needed five during that last semester to graduate. Sadly, none of the courses was astrology."

"Let me see it," Emma insists. "We live in California.

Esoteric names are used all the time here to sell boring classes as something that might be fun or interesting."

With a drawn-out sigh, Dominic hands her the schedule printout.

I look over Emma's shoulder and scan it for any class name that could pass as an elective...

Darn it, Dominic is right! Five courses are listed. Three are specific to the Computer Science curriculum: Theory, Biocomputation, and Information. The only elective course was Film Noir.

Jonathan's only other course was a corporate internship.

In other words, no astrology class. Was his letter to Robert a hoax of some sort?

Resigned to the inevitable, reluctantly Ryan nods at Arnie. "Okay, fill us in on Operation Flame."

"Finally!" Arnie exclaims. "Okay, so, yeah: we were *very* productive yesterday!"

He looks over at me for validation.

I give him a thumbs-up.

"First off, I located the malware that set off the nation-wide grid surges." He pumps his fist.

I shake my head.

"Then, it hit me: even if Donna's bud, McHandsy—"

"Please don't call him 'my bud,'" I mutter.

Arnie's fig leaf to me is a bow. "Right. My bad. As I was saying, then it came to me: considering the scope of the surge, it had to come from a centralized location. Hence, Thunderbolt—the company that provides operational services to all of our nation's utility companies!" Arnie licks his index finger and taps air with it.

"Don't get cocky," I warn him.

He frowns. "Yeah, okay. So then, Donna hears that the CEO is on the roof, and she goes rogue—but in a *good* way." He bows to me. "I cede the floor."

"Arnie's deductions led us to the bad actors who initiated Operation Flame," I begin. "And he's right: Flame was a diversion for a bigger crisis: Operation Horoscope."

Dominic's brow furrows. "The two are connected? How so?"

"As you already know, Carlton Miller admitted to espionage. Like Presley, he met Lilith at Stanford—like Jonathan, in an astrology class. Carlton was Pisces. And, like Presley, he had an affair with Lilith. He was jealous enough to hack her emails. He learned that she was also having affairs with at least three other men in the class, also engineers. He gave me their first names only: Lawrence was the Capricorn in the class, Howard was Aries, and Tommy was Libra. According to Carlton, the first two have had confirmed deaths. He claimed that Tommy died too, although a body was never found."

"Considering who we're dealing with, that doesn't surprise me," Ryan mutters.

He walks over to the room's whiteboard and writes their names on it, along with the others we've identified:

Lilith - Taurus (Presumed Alive)

   Jonathan Presley - Gemini (Deceased; confirmed)

   Carlton Miller - Pisces (Deceased; confirmed)

   Lawrence - Capricorn (Deceased; confirmed)

   Howard - Aries (Deceased; confirmed)

   Tommy - Libra (Deceased; to be confirmed)

   Leo?

Cancer?

Aquarius?

Virgo?

Sagittarius?

Scorpio?

"Do we know what role these last three confirmed names played in Horoscope if any?" Abu asks.

"If Carlton knew, he didn't say. But he insisted Lilith was behind their deaths." I shrug. "Considering how high he was, it's hard to say if anything he told me has any veracity."

"Emma, run those names and iterations of them in Stanford's alumni database: same graduation year as Presley, and also engineering, science, or computer majors. We'll need their class schedules and anything else that will help us piece together this puzzle in a more timely fashion."

She nods.

"We still haven't identified the last six classmates," Dominic points out.

Ryan grimaces. "And until we do, we'll all be combing through Robert and Jonathan's computers in the hope that we locate some intel on Horoscope's sabotage. Arnie, I want you and Dominic to work with Abu on Robert Martin's data."

"O…kay." Arnie grimaces.

I don't blame him for being disappointed that he's being pulled back onto a desk. He enjoys being in the field. His versatility makes him a wonderful asset. I'll thank him for his quick thinking with a chicken potpie. He once hinted it was his favorite casserole.

"Donna and Emma will do the same with Presley's data," Ryan commands.

Dammit! Depending on how long he keeps me desk-ridden, I may have to drown my sorrows in a potpie too.

As the others head out the door, I raise my hand. "Boss, can we have a word in private?"

Ryan nods.

Emma closes the door behind us.

"Jack mentioned he cleared his mission with you, so I assume you already know that his assignment is to find and exterminate Lilith."

Ryan gives me the slightest of nods.

"Just how long is Jack going to be on special assignment to POTUS?" I ask.

As if warding off evil, Ryan crosses his arms at his chest. My question has put him on the defensive. "I think you already know the answer to that: either until POTUS releases him or he accomplishes the mission."

"Maybe it would go faster if he had a little help." I smile sweetly.

"If you're asking to be released to tag team with your husband on POTUS's boondoggle, my answer is a loud and emphatic 'like hell that will ever happen.' We're short-handed enough as is! You know that."

I nod to let him know I'm duly chastised, yadda yadda, whatever. "Okay, yeah, you're right. I should stay put. I guess his radio silence has me worried." I shrug. "But I'm relieved that you've got eyes and ears on him."

He looks me in the eye. "Who says I do?"

"When I suggested to Jack that it might be a good idea,

he agreed." Here's hoping my poker face is as good as Ryan's.

Without blinking, he declares, "I will neither confirm nor deny your supposition."

I take that as an affirmative.

But I also get the point that he's not giving me permission to see what's happening with Jack.

Angrily, I turn to leave. I'm halfway to the door when he says, "Donna, you're going to have to trust me on this one. Wait for the post-mission report."

Like hell, I will.

WHAT THE HECK? WE'VE SPENT THE PAST THREE HOURS slogging through Presley's files, and Emma still has a smile on her face! Crossly, I ask, "What are you so happy about?"

"Oh...nothing." She blushes. "Okay, well, to tell you the truth, I'm so proud of Arnie!"

"You should be," I admit. "He was really thinking on his feet out there. In fact, I've thought of the perfect way to thank him: I'm making him a potpie."

"He'll love that!" She giggles. "I, um, thanked him too."

"Not with a potpie, I'll wager."

"Hardly!" Her eyes sparkle. "But he appreciated it all the same," she adds happily. "He came home so—so *energized!*"

"I hear ya. Fieldwork is the ultimate aphrodisiac. Nothing kicks up the ol' adrenaline like running for your life." At that moment, a thought occurs to me. I drop my lips into a pout. "It's why I miss Jack so much when he's on a solo mission." I look down into my lap, as if bereft.

Emma grabs my hand. "Oh—Donna! I'm so sorry! Believe me, I'd be worried all the time about Arnie if I wasn't the one with eyes and ears on him when he's in the field."

I nod slowly. "Jack is up against a dangerous operative. If anything happened to him and I had to wait to hear about it…" I let my voice trail off before tossing in a few sniffles.

Emma frowns. "You know if it were up to me I'd let you see what's going on. But Ryan gave me strict orders."

I nod as I wipe away a tear. I had to bite my tongue to get it. But hey, it works every time.

Five minutes of my silence is all Emma can stand. She taps me on the shoulder. "I've got to go powder my nose. Do me a favor and *stay away from my computer screen*." She gives me a wink as she saunters off.

RYAN IS RIGHT. I DON'T LIKE WHAT I SEE.

Jack has just walked into some coffee shop. Because its security footage is intercut with his video lens feed, I feel as if I'm watching a movie.

Anyone else would consider it a rom-com. For me, it's a horror flick.

I barely recognize him because his hair is streaked gray and combed straight back. He wears wire-rimmed glasses. Whereas his clothes—suits, jeans, or tuxedos—are usually custom-made to fit his body like a glove, what he wears now hangs loosely on him: khakis and a blue button-down shirt under a sweater vest. It ages him by at least ten years, maybe more.

A woman, sitting at a corner table, waves to him. Forty-ish, she wears the years quite well. Her hair is pulled back into a bun. Her glasses, large-framed, sit at the edge of her nose. Her breasts are full, but the arm raised to catch his attention doesn't sag.

So this is Lilith.

She is pretty, but she's not the *femme fatale* I imagined. Maybe that is part of her charm.

After walking over, he gives her a peck on her cheek. Sweet.

Not.

Flirtatious phrases are bandied around. Jack teases her for keeping him, now apparently one of her students, after class.

She says she hopes he makes it worth her while. "My time is very valuable. I can't waste it on someone not willing to make the grade." This taunt comes with a wink.

"If you've got a syllabus I can study, I promise you I won't disappoint." His right hand, resting casually on the table, is close enough for his pinky to stroke hers.

Her eyes flutter appreciatively.

As he leans in for a kiss, she doesn't pull back.

When they part, she's smiling. With a playful shrug, she whispers seductively, "I'm sure I have an extra syllabus in my apartment if you care to follow me there."

As they walk out, Jack puts his arm around her.

WHEN THE VIDEO PICKS UP AGAIN, THE POINT-OF-VIEW IS specifically through Jack's eyes.

When his face is inches from hers, I know he's kissing her.

When he shoves her against a wall, her bun loosens, and her hair falls in coils around her shoulders.

During the frenzied motions that come with a desire to disrobe as quickly as possible, Jack's eyes synchronize with his hands. Because her dress unzips at the back, he must turn her over so that she faces the wall. In the process, she drops her purse. Feeling the zipper journey downward, she arches her back.

When Jack strips Lilith of her dress, she places her hands up against the wall. Anticipation lifts her onto her toes.

As his mouth and hands move over her naked body, Lilith's lusty moans are a great tipoff that he's hitting all the right pressure points.

"Please," she moans, "*Now...*"

He's ready to give it to her all right. He places his thumb on the tiny syringe in his right hand. My guess: It contains enough aconite to stop her heart.

All it takes is one jab—

But there's a knock at the door.

Really, someone is pounding on it.

Jack hides the syringe behind his back. At the same time that Lilith lurches away from the wall to grab the dress that has fallen to the floor.

As she wriggles back into it, Jack whispers, "Don't answer it!"

"You don't understand! I have to!" She is still wrestling with the zipper as she hurries to the door.

She doesn't open it all the way, so Jack can't see who is there. Their voices are too muffled to hear what's being said.

When she heads back to Jack, she has left the door open just a crack. Ashamed, she says, "I'm sorry. You'll have to go."

"But..." His exasperation is real.

She puts a finger on his lips to silence him. "It's...a family emergency. I'll see you in class on Friday, okay?"

She seals this commitment with a long kiss.

When they pull away, she nudges him toward the kitchen. "Do me a favor and go out this way, okay?"

Without another word, Jack does as she asks.

The kitchen door leads out onto an alley. It circles back around to the street in front of Lilith's apartment. But by the time he runs back around to her front door, it's already shut.

Her guest is now inside with her.

Jack curses this change of events. Finally, he says, "Emma, Lilith's building has surveillance. Keep your eye on the one closest to her so that we see who went in. Maybe we can catch them on the way out too."

"Are you going to stick around?" I hear Emma ask.

"Yeah—at least for a couple of hours. Who knows? Maybe I left her horny enough to let me back in."

At that second the video goes black.

What the...

A finger has tapped the computer's OFF button.

Ryan's finger.

His face looks as if it's carved in granite. "Out. *Now.*"

"But I—"

"Yes, I saw what you did—*disobeyed a direct order.*" His growl is low but firm. "For that, you're suspended until further notice."

"But...we're undermanned as is! You'll need me to—"

"You're right Donna. I do need you." Suddenly, Ryan smiles. "You'll work from home. Emma will send you a password that will get you into the files that need to be scanned—*and only those files*. You'll be locked out of everything else." He waves toward the door. "Have a splendid week."

11

Rulership

[Donna's horoscope today]

Great news! Your ruling planet is moving into its domicile!

What does this mean for you? All great things—

As long as you ignore any of those disturbing tendencies that usually set you back.

For example: You are such a worrywart! What is UP with that, sister? Don't you know? If you let the bothersome things go, good karma will flow!

This includes any and all emotional attachments. Remember out of sight, out of mind. (That goes double for your missing mister!)

Heed these words, and your success will be out of this world!

"Mom...*MOM! AGGGHHHH!* Mrs. Bing is on the phone —*again!*" Trisha has every right to be annoyed. It's the third call Penelope has made today. And since Trisha is not yet allowed her own cell phone, the house phone is her lifeline to the outside world—in this case, Janie Chiffray and the latest local heartthrob sighting.

"She's supposed to be talking directly to Aunt Phyllis," I shout back. "Hand the phone to *her*."

"Aunt Phyllis is not here," Trisha yells.

"Yes, she is," I retort. "She's in the backyard—fourth bush on the right!"

I hate working from home. The only advantage is that, with a click of a button, I can access all of our home's security cameras, not to mention every Sec-Cam in Hilldale. (The only real perk in being on our community's neighborhood watch program.)

It's now Thursday. In the past couple of days, I've discovered all of Aunt Phyllis's hiding places. It's been a much-needed distraction from looking through file after file for any hint as to Horoscope's function.

I fully get that Aunt Phyllis hates dealing with a micromanager who second-guesses every decision. At the same time, I see Penelope's point: Phyllis had no right to put the PTA in the red.

Granted, prom ticket sales are breaking all records. The kids are excited about the theme, the food, the games—

And then news got out to the Muggalos that Talon is the house band. To accommodate the demand, Jeff designed a raised thrust stage., and we can provide VIP seating on three sides.

By Saturday morning, fingers crossed, the PTA will not only be in the black but have made a tidy profit. Aunt Phyllis will be in the clear.

More importantly, so will I.

No doubt, my banishment from the office has caused me to be sorely missed there. Still, it surprises me that Arnie is the only one who's reached out. Granted, it was to inquire when he could expect his chicken potpie, but still...

I guess the rest of my team is too busy scanning these darn files.

Trisha has tracked down my aunt. Our camera has no audio, but I can tell that Phyllis is none too happy that I found her yet again. The giveaway? Her body language: She glares up at the security camera and gives me a middle finger salute.

JEFF KNOCKS ON THE DOOR. "YOU MISSED DINNER," HE SAYS. He's holding a covered dish.

"You're a sweetie." I beckon him forward.

He grimaces. "Don't thank me until you've tasted it."

When I uncover it, I see his point: Phyllis figured out a way to burn soup and salad.

I sigh and shake my head.

Jeff looks over my shoulder. "What are you working on?"

"I'm doing keyword searches through a bunch of files. It's tedious as all get-out."

He leans over to read a few of the ones opened on my laptop screen. "Wow! Some of these files are humongous!"

"That's why it's taking so long."

Jeff clicks a file I've yet to open. The title:

RULERSHIP

"That's a funny word! It has a sci-fi vibe," he points out.

It dawns on me: "No, really, it's a term used by astrologers when discussing zodiac signs—something about planets and which signs they affect the most strongly…"

Just as I say this, an idea springs to mind. I open the file.

It shows two columns. One is filled with astrological terms—sun signs, planets, words like "cusp," "domicile," "degrees," "nodes," "exaltation," and on and on.

The other column holds mathematical equations, scientific terms, and software code.

It's the key code to Operation Horoscope.

Apparently, Jonathan hid it in his horoscopes.

I jump up from the desk and kiss Jeff over and over and over.

My son pretends to fight me off—but only for a few seconds. "Hey, shouldn't you save all that loving for Dad?" Then it hits him: "How long will he be gone, anyway?"

"I…don't know." I turn away from him so that he doesn't see my frustration.

"Hey, Mom, I hate to ask but…would you mind if we order pizza? No one really touched the soup and salad."

"Sure, go for it."

"I guess we should order three since you're eating too and Evan is home again."

"He is?" Oh, dear. I hope Mary didn't go into another emotional tailspin while I've been in here working…

"He's attending a memorial tomorrow, so he came home a day early for prom."

I'd forgotten about Jonathan's funeral.

"Three pizzas are fine," I reply.

"You never know—maybe Dad will show up in time," Jeff adds hopefully.

I wait until he shuts the door before calling Ryan with the good news about the cipher.

I pray it puts me back in his good graces.

THERE MAY WELL BE SEVERAL HUNDRED PEOPLE AT JONATHAN'S memorial service. Held in the Segerstrom Center for the Arts, this modern, multi-level concert hall is a fitting venue for a tech engineer-slash-ground floor billionaire who loved classical music and donated to many orchestras, both local and far-flung.

A small orchestra plays now at the base of the concert hall's massive floating circular staircase.

It's a beautiful setting, but the Segerstrom's size—several stories within the circular atrium—makes it a nightmare for the thirty or so Acme operatives who must scan all the faces in the crowd for any Russian assets already posted in the Interpol facial recognition database.

I too must mingle.

I don't have to worry about Evan. BlackTech's employees are ubiquitous and eager to draw him into conversation. Those who remember Evan as a toddler playing with his LEGO bricks on the floor next to his father's desk now stand in awe of the tall, handsome young man he's become. They start by patting him on the back, then toss out a memory they hope he shares with them. Eventually, though, worry creeps into their voices. Evan grimaces at their questions:

Will the company be sold? Are there to be layoffs? And, most importantly, who will now be their fearless leader?

He stutters through his answers.

Maybe he needs saving after all. I start up the staircase to make my way to him when I feel a hand on my arm:

It's Lee.

Surprised, I smile. "What brings you here?"

"I see it as emotional support for Evan. You know, his father was a close friend of mine too. Plus, I'd met Jonathan on several occasions—most recently, and sadly for him, when I canceled Operation Horoscope."

"Frankly, from the letter he left with Evan, I'd say he was quite relieved—until he got wind that somehow it's still a go." I shrug. "I guess his death proves it."

"You know, that's what bothers me. I ordered the paperwork that killed it. Hell, I signed it! The thought that, somehow, all trace of it has been erased from the Pentagon's databases..."

Lee doesn't finish his sentence. His frustration shows itself in his clenched fists.

I know just how to change the subject. "We've had a breakthrough or two since we last met. Regarding Operation Flame, Acme ID'ed the malware that breached the grid. Interestingly enough, the perpetrator may also be connected to Operation Horoscope."

"You're on your A Game, Mrs. Craig! But I'd expect nothing less."

Thinking about my all too recent suspension, I blush. "It's always a team effort."

Lee laughs heartily. "Speaking of your team, where is that dutiful husband of yours?"

I look skyward. "Still on special assignment for POTUS."

He laughs. "Should be interesting to see who Edmonton's mole hunt turns up."

Well, speak of the devil.

Lilith is here—

With Jack.

Like all of us, Lilith is dressed somberly. Her black cocktail frock is unadorned but elegant. Her hair, upswept, accentuates her almond eyes.

Jack is in a dark suit. It's a size larger than he typically owns, giving him the illusion of aging stockiness.

Because Lilith is looking down at the crowd in the center foyer, she doesn't see Jack's eyes lock with mine. His nod is imperceptible.

Lilith recognizes someone too because a frown rises on her lips.

She is looking at Lee.

She nudges Jack. I read her lips: *Can you take me home now?*

He answers her with a peck on the cheek before taking her in hand and—

Lee is saying something to me? "—called into chaperone duty?"

"I'm sorry...what did you say?"

Amused that he caught me off-guard, Lee follows my eyes upward. "I asked if my services would be needed at the prom—you know, to tackle the hellions spiking the punch."

I laugh. "Your offer is tremendously appreciated. But considering everything that can and will go wrong, it's best that you stay as far away as possible. No need to sully your reputation."

"Not to worry. The impeachment took care of that." By his grimace, he's only half joking.

"There is one thing you can do. Since the rest of the family will be at the high school, can Trisha hang with Janie?"

"No problem there." He sighs. "You know, all those two discuss these days is boys. Okay, and soccer. But mostly boys."

I pat his shoulder. "Get used to it—until she finds the right one."

Hearing this, Lee's eyes sweep over me. He's always wanted our friendship to be more than just that. Still, he's accepted the parameters I've put on it.

My heart belongs solely to Jack.

I'm glad Jack opted for the elevator. All we need is for Lee to see him heading our way and burn him to the target.

"I saw Jack." We are driving home when Evan springs this on me.

"I did too," I admit.

"Don't worry. I didn't say anything to him."

"Good. For obvious reasons, I didn't either."

He lets that sit for a while. Eventually, Evan asks: "Who was the woman with him?"

"That information is only given out on a need-to-know basis." My tone is light enough. Still, he knows me well enough to grasp that I'm serious.

We drive in silence for a few minutes. Finally, he asks: "How do you two do it?"

"Which part?" I ask.

Evan looks out the window. "Everything! But I guess the hardest part is when you have to pretend not to know each other." He hesitates: "And—the killing."

"The first is easy. It's make-believe. The second is the conundrum. It's not fun. It's not easy. It's hard to forget. Harder to forgive."

"But somehow you do."

"We have to." *Or else we wouldn't be able to live with ourselves.*

We couldn't live with each other either.

Evan and I don't speak again until we reach Hilldale. Then he says, "You know, should anything happen, I'll always be there for Mary."

He really didn't have to tell me that.

And I know he'll be there for Jeff and Trisha too.

He is family.

A SLIVER OF SUNLIGHT SLIPS THROUGH THE DRAPES, REVEALING Jack in silhouette.

"You're home," I whisper. "So, it's done?"

He doesn't answer. Instead, he strips down, walks over to the bed, and climbs in next to me.

I don't know if his mouth is hungry for mine because he missed me or because he is so desperate to forget what he did tonight. Foreplay is not on the agenda. Random acts of love aren't possible after deliberate acts of war.

Tonight, I am his salvation. As such, I yield to his touch: strokes, probes, slaps, prods, and the ultimate pierce.

Sex isn't always about pleasure. Sometimes it's about easing the throbbing pain in the recess of one's heart.

Can I absolve him of his guilt? No. It will haunt him as long as he lives.

I can only love him despite it.

AFTERWARD, WHEN OUR HEADS CLEAR AND OUR HEARTBEATS slow, I ask, "What went wrong?"

Jack doesn't move, but he sighs. "It just...it just didn't feel right."

"What do you mean?"

He shifts so that he's on his side facing me. "Granted, some of the craft was there. When it came to surveillance, she was always on high alert. Although she hid it, she conceal-carried. And she had a great rapport with her students. I could imagine her being successful at turning a few. But..." Jack shrugs, perturbed.

"Of course Edmonton showed you her dossier."

"Yes. And it read like a master spy's." He shrugs. "Still, I didn't expect her to fall for my patter so easily."

"If she's been embedded for a few decades, maybe she responded out of loneliness. And hey, you're not hard on the eyes—even in your 'old man' getup."

He chuckles gently. "I guess, what I'm trying to say is...*she was too easy.*"

"Give yourself a little credit. Maybe the truth is that she was too *horny.*"

He shakes his head. He's not buying it.

"Here's the sixty-four thousand dollar question: did she try to recruit you too?"

"Not at all. And my cover made me an ideal candidate: I spoke several languages, I was retired and loved to travel. I would have made an ideal asset. And she knew I hated the current administration."

"Based on that, half the country could be recruited," I mutter. "Hon, seriously: my guess? *You were too damned desirable.*"

"What do you mean by that?"

"She could have really liked you and didn't want to draw you into the dirty part of her life." I wrap his fingers in mine. "I guess we'll really never know. Well, at least Edmonton will be happy."

"For whatever that's worth."

Possibly nothing.

We'll find out soon enough.

12

Fire Signs

Aries, Leo, and Sagittarius are the Zodiac signs that embody qualities found in the element Fire. This includes a willful nature, energy, passion, and a mercurial temperament.

For example:

Your bestie is an Aries. You notice that she has a habit of picking up the wrong guys, all who have fallen in love with her passion. (Others—certainly not you!—might characterize her ardor as sluttishness. But I digress...)

As it turns out, her ex-boyfriends have had a propensity for cheating on her. Her heart has been broken more times than a supposedly sixteen-year-old hooker's cherry. Her way of dealing with it is to start this dead-end wrong-guy wrong-love cycle all over again.

What's a best friend to do?

PUT OUT THE FLAME.

Firefighters are always on alert, ready to douse the next nasty blaze. Sadly, the same has to be true of a fire sign's bestie.

So, tell her the truth. Let it sink in. Recognize that other mistakes will be made. Offer a shoulder to cry on. Don't judge. On the upside, she does exactly the same for you.

DESPITE THE CHAOTIC EVENING AHEAD OF ME, I DUTIFULLY GO into the office to join the rest of my team.

Jack and I take our seats next to Dominic, who is swiping his Tinder app: left, left, left…

Before finally pausing, nodding, and swiping right. Satisfied, he leans into me and whispers, "By the way, Old Girl, in my quest for love eternal, I've taken your advice to heart."

I give him a fist-bump. "Super! When does your vow of silence begin?"

He frowns. "I don't think that's what you meant. At least, I didn't take it that way. Instead, I am 'opening my kimono,' as they say—and as widely as possible."

Emma claps her hands. "Like at Chippendale's! Want to give us a sneak peek now?"

Dominic scowls. "I was speaking metaphorically."

Emma's mouth purses into a pout. "Again, you disappoint me."

"Still, this new philosophy works for the right woman— or perhaps I should say, 'women!' It's gone over swimmingly!" He leans back, triumphant.

"Refresh my memory," I say. "Exactly what did I say to you?"

"To be less self-centered. To consider the feelings of those I meet. To judge others by their actions, not their words. To look beyond the superficial and the physical."

His eyes cloud over. "To do everything I can to forget Lucky."

He's not kidding.

I'm not either when I reply, "And you will, Dom —eventually."

As Dominic turns back to his phone, Jack takes my hand and kisses it.

It is at this very moment that our fearless leader chooses to make his entrance. Noting our very public display of affection, Ryan declares, "As predicted, all's well that ends well."

I wait until he turns back to answer a question from Abu before sticking out my tongue at him.

Jack sighs at my impertinence.

It's great to have him back.

"Arnie's deductions led to finding the bad actors who initiated Operation Flame," Ryan begins. "But what we've discovered—again, thanks to Arnie—is that Flame was a diversion for a bigger crisis: Operation Horoscope."

Eyes open wide at this revelation.

"Dominic discovered Lawrence and Howard's last names and majors: Dougherty and Freedman, respectively. Lawrence's specialty was cybersecurity. Howard's was data mining—both of which fit perfectly with Lilith's agenda."

Nods and grimaces are exchanged.

"And another team win: Donna discovered Jonathan's key code for Horoscope," Ryan adds.

I grin as my co-workers give me a round of applause.

"Now, Emma, fill us in on what the cipher has revealed," Ryan requests.

"From what we can tell, Jonathan relayed the project's design to his handler, little by little, via postings of what he wrote as his own horoscope," Emma explains.

"Where did the postings appear?" Jack asks.

"On the Internet," Emma replies. "Twitter, in fact. Jonathan used the handle, 'OurHorrorscope.'" All one word and spelled like the scary word, 'horror.'"

"Talk about dark humor," I mutter.

"Is it an open or closed account?" Abu asks.

"Open, and it had tens of thousands of followers. As I speak, ComInt is running all of their at-signs through a veri-fication process to see how many came from Putin's bot farm."

"What a great way to give Lilith anonymity," I declare.

Emma nods. "Plucking her handle may be a moot point. Now that Jonathan is no longer among the living, Lilith may have scrubbed her account anyway."

"Lilith is no longer an issue either." Ryan's declaration is blunt.

All eyes go to him before shifting to Jack. He taps away on his laptop, seemingly oblivious.

"Bravo," Dominic mutters under his breath.

"So, what exactly is Horoscope?" I ask.

"It's Putin's wet dream!" Arnie exclaims. " Horoscope was supposed to be a DEW—directed energy weapon—that shoots Earthbound targets from space."

Jack's eyes open wide. "You mean, some sort of space laser gun?"

Arnie nods. "Yep. In this case, mounted to a satellite circling Earth."

"DEWs have been in the works for some time now," Dominic points out.

"You're right," Arnie says. "The Air Force was developing MARAUDER, a plasma rail gun. Before that, it worked on something called Shiva Star, a pulse-powered device. A decade ago, we partnered with the Israelis on THEL–a Technical High Energy Laser. While it was successful in shooting down artillery rockets, its size, weight, and budget—$300 million—made it unsustainable. More recently, the U.S. Army invested in FELs: free electron laser weaponry. Trucks and helicopters have been equipped with laser prototypes, but success has been limited to a distance of about a mile."

"If the Russians want to steal Horoscope, the Chinese must be interested too," I point out.

Arnie chuckles. "At this point, they're hedging their bets. You see, the mirrored surfaces of the targets keep the laser on track. The Chinese feel it's more cost-effective to come up with a special coating and slap it on anything worth saving."

"There is an upside to our country's R&D investment: a laser's targeting is precise, and the cost-of-use would be quite low, just a dollar a shot," Ryan explains.

"But there are negatives too," Arnie interjects. "Lasers are expensive to develop. And because a laser is, essentially, highly controlled beams of light, its kryptonite is anything that may make it 'bloom'—that is, diffuse its power and aim. Once it hits our atmosphere, that could be dust, fog, or smoke."

"Another downside: currently, it would be a single-use weapon," Ryan adds.

"So, the target had better be specific as well as accurate," Jack reasons.

"A satellite's ideal distance from the surface of the earth is 22,369 miles. From there, a weapons-grade laser would need mega-wattage capability," Abu points out. "Typically, a satellite's rechargeable batteries are solar-powered. But the amount of power needed to incinerate a building—say, the size of the Capitol—"

"Bite your tongue," Ryan mutters.

"—Would have to be hundreds of thousands of gigawatts," Arnie concedes. "That's the beauty part! Apparently, Jonathan's solution is fiber optics. He envisioned weaving together strands of the stuff, just like we do for telephone service. That way, the laser's power source is small and lightweight. It would also provide an unlimited magazine. And as energy and battery technologies become more efficient, the next step is every little boy's dream—"

"You mean *yours*," Emma declares dryly.

Arnie shrugs. "Okay, yeah—mine too." He points his finger at me. "A handheld laser blaster!" He pumps his finger in my direction.

I bend it all the way back from his hand.

"*Owwww!*" he groans.

"Back to reality, folks." Ryan is not amused. "Jonathan's death tipped us off that the Russians have been successful in creating Horoscope. But we still don't know when or how it will be launched, let alone its target."

"ComInt is hoping these details show up in one of

Jonathan's horoscope postings, but it's a long shot," Emma replies.

"Keep cracking the whip," Ryan commands her. "We also have Lilith's computer and cell. Arnie, you, Dominic, and Abu will hack it for any viable intel."

They nod.

"How about us?" Jack nods toward me.

"You're getting the day off," Ryan growls. "You've got a high school prom to supervise, remember?"

He's a curmudgeon, but he's our curmudgeon.

I kiss his cheek before waltzing out the door after Jack.

"Mom...*MOM*! Where's Dad?"

Jeff stands right outside my door, which is shut because no child should see how much makeup is troweled onto his mother's face before she is ready to make her grand entrance. Otherwise, it may frighten him away from the opposite sex for the rest of his life.

Because his shout startled me, I now sport a lipstick mustache. I'm still wiping it off as I open the door.

"Dad took Trisha up the hill to Janie's house," I explain. "Is there something I can help you with?"

Sheepishly, he hands me his bowtie—hot pink, to match his date's prom dress.

I wince. "Are you sure you don't want to wear one of your father's black ones? It would be so much more...debonair."

"I probably won't be called a wuss, either. And maybe I

won't come home with a black eye for defending myself, or be suspended for fighting on school property."

"I get the picture. So, why wear it?"

"If I don't act like colors are gender-neutral, I'm not woke. At least, that's what Felicity says."

As I place the tie around Jeff's neck, I mutter, "Well, I hope one of Felicity's parents is a dentist, just in case being 'woke' results in a tooth getting knocked out."

A twist, a fold, and a loop later, and my son is quite the woke gentleman. Satisfied, I pat the tie proudly. As Jeff admires my handiwork in the mirror, I ask, "So, before we pick up Felicity, are there any topics you'd prefer Dad and I avoid?"

"Anything to do with my bodily functions would be appreciated. And *please, please, please* don't pull up any of my baby photos from your iCloud." Suddenly, Jeff frowns. "Oh yeah—Felicity moved to Hilldale just this summer, so she doesn't know about...you know, what happened at my middle school prom."

It was the second time I was saddled with supervising a prom. Unfortunately, it was held in the same hotel as former President Chiffray's top-secret international summit on terrorism. A few party crashers showed up: a terrorist cell sponsored by the Quorum.

Jeff was taken hostage. The terrorists were going to behead him on television if Lee didn't take his place.

I shot the terrorists' mission leader instead.

She turned out to be an old friend of Jack's—and not in a good way.

At the time, I'd already given Acme my notice. After he was pulled to safety, Jeff talked me into staying on. I look forward to the day the world is rid of those who think nothing of taking innocent lives.

My way of putting a smile back on my son's face is to kiss him.

He mutters, "*Agh*! You smeared me with lipstick!"

But he's also smiling.

"So, Felicity, what's your favorite class?" Jack's question is definitely in Jeff's "safe" realm: that is, anything that won't elicit a sigh or a groan from him.

"I'm really good at algebra," she exclaims. "It's where Jeff and I met." She prods him. "Don't you remember? You asked for help with linear equations."

"Is that so?" I coo.

Two years ago Jeff was solving something much harder: quadratic equations. He must really like this girl to have dummied himself down for the chance to meet her!

Jeff blushes. I guess any talk about cute meets will now be relegated to the Verboten Topics list.

"By the way, Jeff, thank you for my beautiful corsage!" Felicity dimples up.

"Oh…you're welcome. Hey, I'm sorry I poked you with the pin when I…you know…when I put it on your, um… breast…I mean *chest*…" Jeff is bright red.

Jack chokes down a guffaw.

"Stay on the road, dear," I warn him.

Jeff scowls.

"I'm so happy you were able to get us front row tickets for Talon!" Felicity exclaims. "I'm a real fan!"

Jeff sighs, relieved. "Me too! My Aunt Phyllis got us hooked up. She and the lead singer go way back."

I turn around, surprised. "She does?"

Jeff nods. "She says she was one of his very first groupies."

WAY, WAY, WAY TOO MUCH INFORMATION.

"It's why he cut her such a great rate for the prom," Jeff adds.

"Good to know," I reply. Well, then, that should help tremendously with the PTA's red ink problem.

Hey, I may actually enjoy myself tonight. You know, just relax...

Jack pulls me out of this wishful fantasy by declaring, "We're here!"

He and Jeff quickly jump out of the car. In a flash, they are opening the doors for Felicity and me.

"Thank you, gentlemen," I say. I step up to give Jack a quick smooch—

But when he leans in, I know he wants more.

Sure, why not? He's earned it.

When our lips meet, all my worries melt away.

I hear Felicity whisper: "Your parents are so cool."

"Yeah," Jeff says. "I know."

WHILE JACK PARKS THE CAR, I WALK TOWARD THE GYM—

Only to hear Aunt Phyllis yell, "You better believe I'll whack you with this sword! *How dare you!*"

Oh, heck! The prom hasn't even started, and already my aunt and Penelope are at each other's throats!

I run as fast as I can to the ruckus, which consists of Aunt Phyllis, Penelope, and three hulking guys in tuxedos. The boys must be juniors because I don't recognize them as Mary's classmates (all of whom I've had run through the Hilldale Police Department's mug shot archives), and they are too large to be sophomores like Jeff.

Aunt Phyllis is wielding the sword at them.

They are standing over an older man. Though he is filthy and bloodied, I recognize him: he is Hilldale's one and only homeless citizen.

We Craigs call him Mr. Red Sweatshirt.

When Jeff was seven, he came up with the name. "It's all he ever wears, so that has to be it," Jeff explained at the time. "Too bad it's so dirty."

Because Hilldale is a gated community, sightings of Mr. Red Sweatshirt are rare. He's usually found in the alleys between and behind the township's supersized McMansions. That's where all trash and recycling bins are located, as per Hilldale's strictly enforced CC&Rs (covenants, conditions, and restrictions). Mr. Red Sweatshirt forages through the trash for cans and bottles, which he resells to the local recycling center.

I once caught him picking through our food scraps. Since then, I've put our leftovers in recyclable plastic containers and leave them on top of our bin, along with a few unopened bottles of water.

With our Thanksgiving leftovers, I also include a gift bag. Inside is a new red sweatshirt, black sweatpants, a twelve-pack of tube socks, sneakers, and a rainproof jacket.

Now that we're face to face, Mr. Red Sweatshirt turns his head, ashamed.

"What's going on?" I ask.

"This—this *vagabond* attempted to enter the auditorium!" Penelope huffs.

"But...I'm here with the Muggalos!" Tears well up in Mr. Red Sweatshirt's eyes. "I've got to see Talon!"

"Talon, Talon, Talon!" Penelope sneers. "I've heard that name all week, and I'm sick of it!"

If what Aunt Phyllis told me about Cheever's infatuation with the band's leader is right, no wonder it's the last name Penelope wants to hear.

Penelope whips around to face me. "We've got a sold out event! People have paid good money to see this weirdo band and yet you want to seat this...this *bum* sitting among our innocent children?"

"Our so-called innocent children won't be hurt by an act of charity," I counter.

"That *person* does not have a ticket," Penelope argues.

"He's got something better," Aunt Phyllis declares. "A backstage pass! I gave it to him myself."

"By that, you mean you made one from your home printer!" Penelope retorts.

"Doesn't matter," I growl. "Problem solved."

Penelope shakes with fury, but she's smart enough to zip her lip. Her heels clack angrily as she walks toward the gym.

I snap my fingers at Penelope's goon squad. "Go join the party—*now*." The look on my face warns them not to argue. They skedaddle.

Phyllis and I help Mr. Red Sweatshirt to his feet. All the while, Phyllis grouses, "This posh prison you call a neighborhood has only one person who needs a helping hand! You'd think there'd be enough heart and soul in these ten square miles to band together and help him back on his feet! Why doesn't someone let him do chores for a room over one of these three-car garages? Or, get him a job at one of the shops in your little 'town square?' So much for 'It takes a village!'"

"That was said about raising kids," I point out.

"Pshaw!" Aunt Phyllis snaps. "We're all God's children, aren't we? And reality check: this poor guy was someone's child once."

"No arguments there." I give her a kiss on the cheek. "Go ahead and escort your date inside. And make sure he gets a plate of all the great grub we've already overpaid for."

Phyllis nods gratefully. "You are your mother's child."

There goes my mascara.

I wait until my tears dry before I go inside.

13

Leo

Those born between July 23rd and August 22nd are under the zodiac sign of Leo.

These folks are charming, outgoing, and love to laugh. A Leo is the life of every party!

Of course, there is the other side of Leo's personality. Leo has an inflated sense of self. When he is wrong, he hates to admit it.

Should a friend be down on his luck, Leo will rub salt in the wound with an "I told you so."

If you are a Leo, go ahead and let others see your kinder, gentler side. Be the person they appreciate for your humor and your joie de vivre.

In other words, play to your strengths—just like your spirit animal.

A JUNIOR GIRL TAPS ME ON THE SHOULDER. "MRS. CRAIG, I think one of the kids must have spiked the punch!"

She then proceeds to throw up on my shoes.

Dammit! These were my favorite Kate Spades.

Like wallflowers, a group of clueless parent volunteers leans against the far side of the gym. I assume it's the same pose they struck when they were the age their children are now.

I whistle loud enough to catch the attention of the one wallflower mom who isn't stunned into silence by the sight of students having *GOT*-worthy sword fights (thank goodness the swords are soft plastic), tossing food around (those turkey drumsticks pack quite a punch), or busting out dance floor moves—booty dancing, perreos, butt slaps, daggering, hair whips, and drops—that could easily pass as pornographic acts.

(When one female student did a slow, slinky come-up, Jack had to slap away the hand of a chaperoning dad who attempted to put a Benjamin in her thigh-high boot! The things kids wear to proms these days...)

Now, having been pressed into service, the Wallflower Mom takes the drunk student outside to puke out her guts.

And not a moment too soon: Talon's fans—the Muggalos —have entered the building.

Like Moses parting the Red Sea, the students open a path to let them pass. As the Muggalos march through, they chant: *"TALON! TALON! TALON! TALON!"*

When they reach the front of the gym, two of them—a boy and a girl—jump up onto the stage. Like orchestra conductors, they raise their hands over their heads, egging on the crowd.

The boy is Cheever. At least, I think it's him. Frankly, it's hard to tell considering that his face, like these hundred other kids who've swarmed the prom, is slathered in red war paint. The Muggalo's heads are either shaved, or their hair stands tall in stiff Mohawks dyed in rainbow hues of lime green, bright yellow. In Cheever's case, his mohawk is baby blue.

He holds the electric torch that will allow his girlfriend to light the flame in the dragon's mouth. I'm not surprised he had the highest bid. Once again, Penelope's attempt to buy her son's loyalty from his father has worked in Cheever's favor.

Cheever hands his girlfriend the torch. Bald, her whole head is painted hot pink. Bright yellow circles are drawn on her cheeks. Large black cartoonish lashes are painted above her eyelids. She is dressed in a leather skirt. Her tank top cropped above her waist. When she opens her mouth, I see a spike piercing her tongue.

Cheever must find it a turn-on because suddenly his mouth is on hers. Their dance moves mimic bonobos in heat. When the song ends, The crowd goes crazy.

Penelope shouts in my ear, "My God, just look at those two animals on the stage! They're disgusting..."

But her voice trails off when she realizes one of those "two animals" is her precious little boy.

Suddenly, the stage's curtains pull back to reveal the band. Recognizing the first chords of their classic hit, "Bite Me Harder this Time," the crowd's roar causes the gym's roof to shake.

The lead singer, Talon, stalks the length of the stage. He's quite a vision in his skintight leather pants and a crop top that hugs his massive chest and shows off his well-defined abs. Talon's face is painted the Muggalo's official fire-engine red hue, and his blue hair is in the tall Mohawk that is the trademark of his band.

Each of the bass player's guitar licks is accompanied by a thrust of Talon's hips.

Penelope was right. The prom is a disaster.

As if reading my mind, Penelope jabs my shoulder and shrieks, "Your aunt has made our dance a den of iniquity! You'll pay for this, Donna Craig! But first, I have to get that —*that lascivious clown* off the stage!"

Cheever watches his mother stalk off. He frowns anxiously.

I shove my way through the crowd after her. I don't know what kind of damage control I can do at this point, but if Penelope sends the band packing, we'll have a riot on our hands.

AN EXTENDED DRUM SOLO IS SO NOT WHAT WE NEED RIGHT NOW.

Unfortunately, it's what we've got.

Talon uses it as an opportunity to slip backstage and share mugs of the prom's spiked grog with Aunt Phyllis and Mr. Red Sweatshirt, who can't quit high-fiving the lead singer, as if they're long-lost brothers.

Seeing this trio of tyrants is more than Penelope can take. It gives her the strength to toss off Talon's two bodyguards.

I watch as she gives him a piece of her mind. To his credit, he takes it like a man. I guess she's not the first mother who's cursed him out for turning her child into a paint-sopped Mohawked hellion.

But what may make Penelope unique is that she may be the first mom he's shut up with a lip lock.

When they resurface, he gasps, "Penny Pucker-Up! Wow! It really is you!"

Penelope's eyes open wide. Though in shock, she nods.

He turns jubilantly to my aunt and Mr. Red Sweatshirt. "First Phyllis, then Tommy, and now Penny? Jeez! It's like old home week!" Noting Penelope's puzzled frown, he exclaims, "Babe, *it's me*—Benny Gallo! Remember? Benny and the Erectors!"

"Benny?..." She faints in a stupor.

Thankfully, he catches her before she hits the floor. Cradling her face in his hands, he declares, "Girl, do you know how long I've waited to see you again? Hell, you're the only reason I booked Mendocino all those years!"

Mendocino? What the heck is he talking about?

Hearing that, Penelope is suddenly laughing and crying at the same time. The next thing I know, she's giving Talon mouth-to-mouth resuscitation.

Among other things.

Delighted, Aunt Phyllis throws up her hands. "My work here is done! Oops! Except for one thing. The grand finale!" She trots over to the backstage technical dashboard and pushes a button.

Heaven knows why but the crowd has begun a countdown: "Ten...Nine...Eight...Seven..."

Suddenly, the hard-fought but much anticipated fire-breathing dragon swoops down from the ceiling toward the stage.

Penelope is wrapped around Talon like a vertical John-and-Yoko, totally oblivious to what's flying over their heads.

The pose is so damned passionate that even I turn away. Not Mr. Red Sweatshirt. He stands there, fascinated.

Come on, guys! Get a room already…

Suddenly, I see Cheever headed my way. "Mrs. Craig, we've got to stop my mom before she ruins everything!"

Too late, kid…

Before he can see them, I shout loudly, "Nope, doesn't look as if your mom is in here, Cheever!"

Sadly, I don't think they hear me over the crowd, which is now shouting, "…Three…Two…*ONE!*"

Unfortunately, that's when the auction winner—Cheever's girlfriend—chooses to light the cord to the dragon's flame.

As always, Penelope's timing leaves a lot to be desired. Just as she's disentangling herself from Talon, the dragon is directly over her—

And an errant spark sets Penelope's hair on fire.

Talon does what any hero would do: dunks his grog mug over her head.

Not a great idea, considering its alcohol content.

In the hope that I come up with a better solution before she goes up in flames, I run to the backstage refreshment table, where I hope to find a pitcher of water. No such luck. There is, however, a cake designed to look like *Game of Throne*'s Winterfell Castle. It sits in snowdrifts made of powdered sugar.

It'll have to do.

I toss the cake off of its stand. Then, taking the stand in hand, I run back as fast as I can in my smelly Kate Spade kitten heels—

And toss the powdered sugar over Penelope's head.

As I'd hoped, the sugar puts out the flames.

In the meantime, Penelope has fainted.

Perhaps it's a blessing in disguise.

The EMTs are there in seconds. Hilldale's fire chief has gotten into the habit of calling the school district to inquire up front if Penelope is expected at its events. By now, he's quite aware that Penelope, proms, and pyrotechnics are a terrible combination.

I wonder if she's a fire sign...

TALON LOOKS HEARTBROKEN. "I'VE BEEN LOOKING FOR THAT woman all my life," he murmurs.

I can't believe my ears. "Who...*Penelope?*"

He nods slowly. "Best groupie ever! Those lips of hers could..." Suddenly, he realizes who he's talking too. "Well, let me put it this way. She was worth the road trips to that podunk town of hers."

"I thought she grew up in San Francisco!"

"Who...Penny? Nah! Mendocino!" He mimics taking a toke. "Mendo Goldilocks is what we used to call her! But then one day she just disappeared. That was, what...sixteen years ago?" He shrugs. "Eventually, they all grow up."

"Awesome," Cheever whispers. "My mom was a groupie?"

Talon chortles. "I don't tell tales out of school, little buddy." He wiggles his eyebrows. "But...hum...YEAH."

Oh, heck! Penelope is going to flip out when she realizes her deepest, darkest secret has been revealed.

I pray I'm not around when that happens.

"Why didn't she recognize you too?" I ask.

"Under all this goop, why would she?" To prove his point, Talon takes off his kerchief to wipe the crimson makeup from his eyes, revealing tiny spidery lines. "Besides, it was another era, and another band altogether. I only became 'Talon' eight years ago."

Onstage, thrusting in those tight leather jeans, I thought he was around my age. But now that we're up close and in full light, it dawns on me that he's in his forties, easy. I give him the once-over. "You're in pretty good shape. How old did you say you are?"

He chuckles. "I didn't."

"I guess the makeup hides a lot."

"So does the blue mohawk. Otherwise, my fans would notice all the gray." He snickers. "Trust me, no rock star can afford to act his age."

"I guess you've been doing some version of this gig for quite some time," I say.

"It was the best way to pay my way through college. Got a degree in financial management. Interned at Goldman Sachs. Then one day I just walked away from it all. This is what I wanted to do. Even now."

"You don't say." Suddenly I notice the tattoo on his neck: the Zodiac emblem for Leo.

He's also wearing a Stanford signet ring.

Interesting.

I point to the ring. "Stanford grad?"

He nods. He shows it to me.

He graduated nineteen years ago—the same year as Jonathan.

"You didn't happen to take an astrology class while you were there, did you?"

"Ha! Funny question. But yeah, as it so happens." He shrugs. "But it was weird shit—robes, masks, anonymity! Still, I learned a lot about people."

"Like what?"

"Well, like I discovered we all have our dark and dirty little secrets." He shrugs. "And that we create our own destinies." He tosses a thumb toward his chest. "Hell, I'm proof of that! The class made me realize that what I really wanted was to play guitar, make out with groupies, and never grow up."

"But isn't that the antithesis of astrology? You don't believe your fate is written in the stars?"

"I want nothing to do with that pseudo-science," Talon declares adamantly.

"Then why the tattoo?" Cheever asks.

"To remind me of who I'm *not*." Hearing Talon's growl, Cheever recoils.

"I think I met a couple of classmates of yours," I say casually. "Did you know a guy by the name of Jonathan Presley?"

"The name's familiar." Talon thinks for a moment. "Yeah! I'm pretty sure he was in a math class."

"He was also in your astrology class."

Talon's eyes open wide? "No shit! Well, what do you know!"

"Jonathan died recently," I watch intently for his reaction.

It's a frown and a shrug. "That's rough. Let me guess: heart attack. We're all getting around that age. When I was thirty-five, my doctor told me I should quit either smoking, booze, or sex. I dropped the cancer sticks. When I turned forty, the ultimatum was drink or sex. Let me put it this way: I'm no monk." He winks at Cheever.

"Jonathan's death was a hit and run," I reply.

Talon shakes his head sadly. "I want to die in my bed." He smiles slyly at me. "Not alone, of course."

Cheever's eyes open wide. "Surrounded by groupies?"

Talon laughs uproariously. "There are worse ways to go, little bro."

"Do you remember any of the women in the class?" I ask. "I heard there was one named Lilith."

Talon's grin fades. "That bitch? Yeah, I knew her."

I snicker. "I take it you didn't like her."

"You got that right! The slut did quite a head trip on poor Tommy."

"You mean…" I look around for Mr. Red Sweatshirt, but he's nowhere to be found.

Tommy.

He's Libra!

Talon chuckles. "Yeah, you know, the dude who was just here. I guess he split when the fire department showed up." He taps his forehead. "If Tommy hadn't fallen for Lilith, he'd have been something great. He was also in our math class. He was a genius!"

"What was his major?" I ask.

"Physics. He minored in Ethics. All he wanted was to make the world a better place."

"What do you think happened between him and Lilith?"

Talon frowns. "I don't think. I know. She wanted him to convert."

"To her religion?"

"Of a sort. Communism. Back then, it was called the KGB." Talon rolls his eyes. "When Tommy refused, she dropped him. He was so depressed that he jumped off a bridge. Broke his back. He's never been the same since." He stares off. "Penny of all people! I still can't believe it." He leans in so that I'm the only one who can hear him. "Which hospital do you think they took her to?"

"Hilldale Medical. It's about five miles from here."

Talon nods. "We're here for a few nights. I think I'll stop in tomorrow, see how she's doing."

"I'm sure she'd appreciate that."

Talon hands Cheever his makeup-stained kerchief. "See you around, kid."

He walks off toward his band's bus.

JACK, MARY, AND EVAN HANG AROUND TO HELP AUNT Phyllis and a group of student volunteers to do clean-up.

When Jeff asks Cheever what happened to his date, he admits she dumped him for another Muggalo despite Cheever having bought her the right to light the dragon's flame.

He blames it on his mother catching on fire. "She always pulls that stunt to get attention!" he opines to Jeff. "Why can't my mom just be normal, like yours?"

Jeff rolls his eyes at that line.

I can't say I blame him.

Cheever takes me up on my offer for a lift home. After he climbs into the front seat, he pulls down the passenger-side visor. "Cool, a mirror! Now I can watch Romeo's backseat action."

Jeff warns Cheever against this terrible idea with a punch to his shoulder.

As I drive, none of the kids say a word. A quick peek in the review mirror confirms my suspicions: Jeff and Felicity are necking.

Oh boy.

As for Cheever, he's still in awe of having been in the presence of his idol. Every now and then he'll stroke Talon's kerchief, as if it holds some secret power.

As we're hit with the headlights of a passing car, I glance over at him. Suddenly, he doesn't resemble Peter in the least...

Nah. My eyes are just playing tricks on me. Everyone in red makeup and sporting a blue mohawk looks the same, right?

Still, I do the math. "Penny" had Cheever fifteen years ago. If she were my age, when I had Jeff, she'd be—

I don't want to go there.

It's none of my business, anyway...

That's never stopped me before.

14

Libra

One of the wonderful traits about Libra—those born between September 23rd and Oct 22nd—is that they are tactful. They are also romantic (but of course! After all, their ruling planet is Venus), charming, diplomatic, and seek balance in every part of their lives.

If there were any flaws inherent in this sign, it would be that Libra can be superficial and somewhat detached from others, as well as reality.

Here's the bottom line: if you can live with these few niggling issues, you'll still have a partner who will strive to make you happy.

Let's just say this guy's a keeper.

As long as he holds onto his marbles.

"WHERE WERE YOU ALL NIGHT?" JACK LOOKS UP FROM HIS iPad, where he's reading the morning's news.

I'm up so late that Mary and Evan are making the family's breakfast. They make a great tag team. As she whips the scrambled eggs into a frenzy, he lays strips of bacon on the griddle in perfectly straight lines. When he's done, without a thought he reaches over to wipe his hand on her apron. Smiling up at him, she uses her free hand to smooth his cowlick into place.

The prom was so crowded that I only caught glimpses of them. Ah, well, maybe Ryan is right: all's well that ends well, even without an assist by me.

I guess it's time that I accept this new reality…

As if.

Trisha is still at Janie's. Aunt Phyllis is nowhere to be seen. That's okay. She's earned the right to sleep in. Jeff is texting furiously. My guess: it's with Felicity, and no math equations are being exchanged.

Hopefully, her hickey isn't as prominent as his.

Still bleary-eyed, I drop down on the kitchen banquette beside Jack. "I spent the bulk of last night walking all of Hilldale in search of Mr. Red Sweatshirt, a.k.a. Libra, a.k.a., Tommy Alston."

All actions cease. All eyes turn in my direction.

Mary's whisk drops into the bowl. "You learned his real name?"

I nod. "Thanks to Aunt Phyllis. She was kind enough to invite him backstage at the Muggalos concert."

"Why weren't we invited too?" Evan, Mary, and Jeff form a choir of hurt and condemnation.

I shiver. The thought of Penelope wrapped around Talon still haunts me. "Trust me, you did *not* want to be there."

Mary shrugs. "No biggie. We've all seen Mrs. Bing on fire before."

She's got a point. For Mary, this tradition began with her Father-Daughter dance in middle school.

Ah, good times.

Maybe out of habit I sniff the air. "Speaking of which, how's that bacon coming?"

Mary and Evan turn to stare at the stove. Grease dances gleefully on the charred remains of our bacon strips.

Instinctively, Evan grabs for the pan's handle—without a potholder. By the time he tosses it into the sink, he's scalded his hand. His groan rocks the room.

Mary turns on the cold water and holds his hand under the faucet. She yells, "Jeff! Get a sterile bandage from the downstairs bathroom!"

As Jeff takes off, Jack turns to me. "I take it you didn't find Tommy."

"No," I admit. "But Talon—that is, Benny Gallo—gave me some interesting insights into him."

"Such as?"

"Turns out that they knew each other in college. Can you guess where they went?"

His jaw drops. "Stanford?"

I nod. "And they were in Jonathan's astrology class. At the time, Talon majored in finance and Tommy was a Physics major. They also shared a math class with Jonathan, which is why Talon recognized Tommy in astrology."

"Did either of them have run-ins with Lilith?"

"Tommy. Sadly, she made him the shell he is today. Talon hated her for that. He knew she was bending Tommy's ear about sympathy for Russia."

"Maybe she used Tommy to make the change in Horo-scope's coding. If so, he may know how, when, and where Horoscope is launched," Jack reasons. "We need to find Tommy, pronto! Let's get moving!"

I groan. "That's easy for you to say! You've had your coffee, and you weren't wandering the mean streets of Hill-dale 'til the crack of dawn doing just that!"

Jack moves to the coffee pot, pours a cup, and walks it over to me. "Sit. Sip. You've got as long as it takes for me to scramble those eggs Mary has abandoned while not burning what's left of the bacon."

As he heads to the stove, he grabs an apron off the pantry hook. It is embroidered with the phrase:

HOT STUFF COMIN' THROUGH

Indeed.
Perhaps I should sleep in more often.

As Jack and I walk block by block through the alleys of Hilldale, I put in a call to Ryan. "We've identified two more sun signs."

"Between now and when you left the office?" He sounds dubious.

"Hard to believe, but yes. Leo is now a rock musician known as Talon. He has a cult following—many of which showed up at the prom last night."

"Don't tell me he's recruiting for the Russians too."

"That's a resounding 'no.' Lilith's attempt at recruiting him backfired—with him, anyway. But she did snare a good friend of his: the one and only Tommy Alston."

"Ah, Libra!" Ryan declares. "But, sadly, he's dead. At least, that's what Capricorn told you."

"Carlton Miller assumed he was dead—that even perhaps Lilith had killed him—because he couldn't find a trace of Tommy anywhere, online or off. As it turns out, Tommy is alive, if barely. For the past several years he's been homeless."

"Did Leo tell you where you might find him?"

"He didn't have to." I take a deep breath. "Periodically, Tommy shows up in Hilldale. He's our town's—well, to put it bluntly, he's the town's one and only homeless person."

"You make him sound like a pet."

"If only that were the case! The animals of Hilldale are treated better and get a lot more respect."

"So, go to the nearest homeless shelter and get him."

"I went there first. No one there has seen anyone who matches his description. Tommy is always foraging in Hilldale's garbage cans. Jack and I are walking the town now, to see if we can find him. But we could speed things up if Acme could initiate an aerial search."

"Sure. Can you get me a photo for facial recognition cues?"

"Arnie can pull it off Hilldale High's surveillance footage from last night. Tommy was backstage with Aunt Phyllis, Talon, and me."

"*And you didn't detain him there?*" Ryan is cross.

"There was an emergency. Someone…caught on fire."

"Sounds like a heck of a prom!"

"It's become a local ritual," I mutter.

"So, you were backstage with a rock star, and no one took a selfie?" Ryan snickers.

"Wait!…You're right! Aunt Phyllis may have taken one, if for old time's sake. She and Talon go way back. Apparently, she was one of his first groupies."

Ryan sighs. "Why am I not surprised? Okay, send it over as soon as you can, and we'll program the search."

I KNOCK ON AUNT PHYLLIS'S DOOR. NO ANSWER, BUT I CAN hear her snoring.

In fact, she's snoring in harmony.

How could that be?

I open the door:

She's got a man in bed with her.

Oh my God! Is it Talon?

First, he hits on Penelope—and then he sleeps with my aunt?

What if they're naked?

Dammit, Ryan is waiting for my call. I'll just have to avert my eyes…

I sneak up to the bed. The covers are over their heads. From the curves of their bodies, I can tell they aren't snuggling. Well, that's a relief.

Now, to decide which body belongs to Aunt Phyllis. *Eenie, Meenie…*

Oh, the heck with it! The left side of the bed is closest. I walk over and, very gently, I lift the corner of the comforter.

Thank goodness, I recognize Aunt Phyllis' favorite flannel nightshirt. I nudge her—

But it's not her. The man wearing it lets loose with a blood-curdling scream.

Oh my God—it's Tommy!

Phyllis leaps up from the other side of the bed. She too screams—an octave higher, but still ear-piercingly shrill.

"*Shhhh! Shhhh!*" I raise my hands so that they see I have no weapons.

Tommy calms down, but he's still whimpering.

As Aunt Phyllis comforts him, she glares at me and hisses, "What the heck are you doing in here?"

"The more interesting question is, what is he doing here?"

"When I got home, it was below forty degrees. What was I to do—just leave him beside your garbage can?" She wraps the blanket around the scared, shivering man.

"No, of course not. You did the right thing." I pat Tommy's arm. "I'm sorry. I didn't mean to frighten you."

He nods, and whispers, "I...I know you're a nice person." He points to his sweatshirt. It's folded over a chair. "And...I heard you talking to Benny. I know you know about–*about HER.*"

"You mean Lilith," I reply.

Tommy flinches at the very sound of her name. Finally, he whispers, "Yes."

"I'll let you two talk." Aunt Phyllis grabs her robe off the bedpost and rolls out of bed. Suddenly, she sniffs the air. "Do I smell bacon? Nah, can't be. It's burnt. I must still have the stench of Penelope's hair in my nostrils."

She shuffles out to the hall, closing the door behind her.

A MAN HAUNTED BY THE SHAME OF PAST DEEDS STRUGGLES TO hang onto his soul.

In a voice no louder than a whisper, Tommy Alston speaks slowly and precisely as he tells the tale of his fall from grace.

"They tell me I was once a genius." He says this with absolutely no guile. "If I was so smart, why did I think she cared about me?"

"People will do anything, say anything, to get what they want from others," I remind him.

His nod is slow, weighted with his sadness.

"How did you meet Lilith?" I ask.

"In that class—astrology. But it wasn't meant to be, you know? Because we weren't supposed to talk to each other." He looks down at his rough, blistered hands. "I was surprised when, one day, she walked up to me on campus. Even when she whispered, 'Libra, right?' I knew I should have pretended I didn't know what she meant. But I didn't. She was so beautiful."

"Did she explain how she figured out it was you?"

Tommy nods. "She said she'd noticed the cuff of my shirt. I'd raised my arm in class, and my robe slipped away from it."

"Did you believe her?"

"At the time, yes." He frowns. "And that's how it started with us. We'd meet up every couple of days, exchange notes about the class, and laugh at the fact that none of the others knew our little secret. I loved her laugh." He pauses, as if hearing it now.

"And then she seduced you."

"Yeah. I fell hard." His voice is so low he sounds as if he's talking underwater. "She was already engaged to be married and moving out of state. I was being courted by Northrup Grumman. It wasn't meant to be anything more than just fun and games."

"How long did your affair continue?"

"Years. Well over a decade. In the meantime, she moved away, and I tried to move on. But as far as I was concerned, no one could compete with her. And so whenever she came to town, she'd call. I'd come running. Always somewhere different. This hotel or that. Just like when we were in school." He coughs, as if clearing his throat will clear his mind too. "Then one day she asked me to look at some software code. What she handed me was classified. I realized that right off. She wouldn't tell me where she got it, just that I'd have to trust her that if it were left as is, something would go very, very bad."

"What could you tell about the coding?"

"I don't remember much…" He sighs. "A place…some location. The truth is, I didn't want to remember it at all. I wanted to die. It's…it's why I jumped."

"Off the bridge."

He nods. "I lived. But at least I forgot."

If only he hadn't.

"Did you ever hear from Lilith again?"

"No. But I did hear about her—from Jonathan. He'd also been duped by her. A few of the others had too! She'd been told who to…to seduce." He ducks his head, shamed.

"Told? By whom?"

"Arthur." The name comes out of Tommy's mouth as a growl.

"Which sign was Arthur?"

Tommy shakes his head. "He wasn't a sign. He was our instructor."

Bingo—Lilith's handler.

"Tommy, what was Arthur's last name?"

"Arthur...something." He stares up at the ceiling in the hope of finding it there.

"Please, Tommy, think hard! It would help me to know his last name."

"I forget a lot." Tommy closes his eyes. "Strange name. Like the poet."

"Poe?"

Tommy shakes his head.

"Byron?...Shelley?...Keats?...Whitman?"

"No, no, no, no!" With each name, Tommy's head shakes decidedly. Then, as if awakening from a trance he says, "It's...Yates...YATES! That's it!"

"Good, Tommy, good! Thank you!" I pat his hand. "One last question, Tommy: when was the last time you saw Lilith?"

Fright fills his eyes. "I hadn't seen her in a long while—until last week."

"Did she say anything to you?"

His hands shake. "I left as fast as I could. She was with someone—*who would have killed me.*"

"Tommy, when you aren't here in Hilldale, where do you go?"

"There are other Hilldales. Safe havens. Edible garbage." His grimace quivers on his lips. He may be cracking a joke.

Or he may want to reassure me that he knows how to take care of himself. "Better than the shelters and missions, right? Or, like everyone else, I just head for the beach."

I force out a chuckle. "That's nice. I've always wondered. Venice?"

"Nah. Too many bums. Manhattan Beach."

I try not to frown. Manhattan Beach is memorable for me, but for all the wrong reasons. Jack's first wife was killed there by Carl.

It's a small world after all.

"Why does that make you sad?" Tommy has picked up on my uneasiness.

With as much nonchalance as I can muster, I reply, "Nothing. I just know that the cops there aren't so friendly with, um, non-residents."

"They don't bother me. I stay with Cancer."

"Cancer—from your astrology class?"

He nods.

"What is his address? I'd like to talk to him."

Thunderclouds of anxiety cover his eyes. "I don't know. She gets upset when I mention...back then."

Cancer is a woman.

"Please, Tommy. It's critical. The lives of others depend on it."

He wraps his arms around his waist, as if willing himself to hold back from this secret. Finally, his arms flop down. "On the Strand, all the way north. It's the smallest house. Yellow, with bright blue trim." He grabs my arm. "Please... promise me you won't hurt her!"

"I swear."

Once again, trust clears the clouds in his eyes. "Without

her, I'd be dead." His head falls onto his chest. "I should have listened to her back then. Jonathan too."

"Cancer knew Jonathan?"

It's his turn to laugh. "He was her brother!"

My God.

As I cross to the door, his wistful soliloquy haunts me:

> *"Love, whose month is ever May,*
> *Spied a blossom passing fair,*
> *Playing in the wanton air:*
> *Through the velvet leaves the wind,*
> *All unseen can passage find;*
> *That the lover, sick to death,*
> *Wish'd himself the heaven's breath."*

JEFF LOOKS UP FROM HIS TEXTING TO REPORT DUTIFULLY: "DAD and Mary took Evan to the airport."

"Darn it. I wanted to say goodbye to Evan," I reply.

"At least you wouldn't be crying your eyes out, like Mary."

"I have to run an errand. When your dad gets home, tell him. I'm headed over to Manhattan Beach. I...I found Cancer."

Jeff's mouth drops open: "*You found the cure for cancer?*"

"Ha! If only!" At the very least, it may be the cure for our current problem.

Before I leave, I take a moment to search for Tommy's verse. Ah! He was quoting *Love's Labour's Lost* by Shakespeare.

The first line breaks my heart:

Love, whose month is ever May

MAY IS TAURUS.
    May is Lilith.
    Despite everything, he still loves her.

15

Cancer

You would be Cancer if you were born between June 21st and July 22nd.

Friends and family appreciate your sensitivity, desire to nurture, and your hospitality. However, take note! You may also be moody, pessimistic, and clingy.

Perhaps you've noticed that your friends no longer accept your invitations to hang at your place, even when you try to entice them with your vegan specialties or offer to treat them to mud facials. (How healthy! How nurturing! Such a great friend you are!)

Reality check: They'd change their minds if they weren't afraid you'd also chastise them for "being strangers" or "forgetting to return your calls."

In other words, a true friend doesn't have to cajole or bribe others to play with her. She just accepts their schedules (even if you aren't penciled in as often as you'd like), their decisions (even if they didn't take your advice), and their optimism (which you may not share).

Real friends accept each other's foibles. Otherwise, they're just "acquaintances."

THE STRAND—A GREENBELT BETWEEN MANHATTAN BEACH'S homes and its shoreline—runs north of the pier for a couple of miles.

I park on the block that parallels its full length: Ocean Avenue.

Cancer's house is on one of the many footpaths running perpendicular to the Strand. Thankfully, by initiating an aerial scan, Emma located my destination—a small, yellow cottage trimmed in blue—saving me an on-foot search that would have taken at least an hour.

Public records show that a woman named Mary Ann Harrison owns the cottage. Since her last name is not Presley, I assume it's a married name.

I give Emma her next task: finding Arthur Yates. "I'll pull up anything I can find in Palo Alto, circa the early 1980s," Emma promises.

Mary Ann Harrison's tiny front yard is neat as a pin. The windows are shuttered, so I can't look inside.

No one answers my repeated knock.

I walk around to the side of the house. It is blessed with a straight-on view of the Pacific Ocean.

In the tiny backyard, a woman is waxing a surfboard. Her slim frame is gloved in a wetsuit. Her white-blond hair, cut gamine short, clings damply to her skull.

Because I'm out of her peripheral vision, she doesn't see me as much as feel me. I know this because she stops rubbing the board, shifts her shoulder slightly to pick up something, then straightens up and declares without turning around: "Who are you and what do you want?"

It's easy to figure out what she now holds in her hand: a gun. By the time she turns around, sights me, and fires, I will have already put a hole in the back of her head. But since a footpath leading to a popular beach on a beautiful Sunday should not be the scene of a needless murder, I say instead, "I want to stop Taurus, and I think you can help me."

This gets her attention. She drops the gun in the sand before turning around and saying, "Would you care to join me inside for tea?"

WHILE MARY ANN STRAINS THE TEA INTO TWO MUGS, I SCAN the photos intermingled with the rows of books on her wall-to-ceiling bookshelf.

She has her brother's cornflower blue eyes. She also has his slight overbite and the spray of freckles across his nose. In the photos of them at all ages and standing arm in arm, they seem to also share a fierce love as only siblings can.

When she sets the tray on the coffee table, I join her on the sofa. I sip my tea. She holds her mug between her hands, taking in its warmth as she sizes me up.

Finally, she asks, "How did you find me?"

"Tommy Alston. I live in Hilldale. I've seen him for years, foraging in the alley behind my home. Sometimes I leave food. Sometimes it's clothing."

"The red sweatshirts," she acknowledges. "He appreciates them." As she reaches for a teaspoon, I notice her hand is shaking. "I'm surprised he told you about Taurus—or for that matter, about me."

"Just so you know, he never gave me your name. He described your home as a safe haven."

She acknowledges this with a slight nod. "I don't think he remembers my name anymore. His mind...it goes in and out of focus."

"He mentioned a fall from the bridge," I reply.

"You know, he and my brother were best friends." She wipes away a tear. "I haven't yet told him that Jonathan... that he's dead. If Tommy knew that..." She sighs.

"I haven't mentioned it to him either," I reassure her.

She nods gratefully.

"Mary Ann, what did Tommy tell you about Taurus?"

"I know she was the one who brought him to ruin if that's what you're asking."

"And yet, when he thinks of her he quotes Shakespeare," I point out.

"That's prophetic, somehow." Her voice is barely a whisper. "She broke him."

"Stanford has no record of the horoscope class in its archives. Why is that?"

Mary Ann shrugs. "I'm not surprised. We only learned of the course on the first day we went to work for the corporation sponsoring our senior projects. It was taught at the company's headquarters."

"What is that company?"

"Dartmouth Analytica. It makes census and social media software." She rolls her eyes. "I should say, 'made.' It's now out of business. It got caught up in those international voter influencing scandals a few years back."

"Yes, I remember it." Only because Dartmouth Analytica was one of the Quorum's shell companies. It was using social media to influence elections in democratic countries. Much of its funding came from the Russians. No surprise there.

To draw her back to the here and now, I reveal, "The organization I work for is charged with solving Jonathan's murder."

Mary Ann's eyes narrow. "It was a hit and run."

"You and I both know better. He was targeted and killed because he gave intel on Project Horoscope to the Russians."

Mary Ann's mug shakes ever so slightly in her hand.

"Around two years ago Lilith approached Jonathan about altering some code inside one of Blacktech's military projects: Operation Horoscope," I explain. "He refused. Later, she circled back around and let him know that someone else did it for them."

Slowly she nods. "Tommy."

"Did Tommy ever mention what he changed for her?"

"GPS coordinates."

Shit.

"Knowing what he did made him a shell," she continues. "Afterward, he gave away whatever money he made that didn't go toward booze, or up his nose. It's why he disappeared."

"Tommy wouldn't have known it, but his code sealed Jonathan's death sentence," I explain. "When Lilith taunted Jonathan with this information, he was smart enough to realize that the moment Horoscope is initiated, he'd be exterminated. It's why he put his confession on a thumb drive—the one he left with you, so many years ago, in case of such an 'accident.' And he had already addressed the envelope: to Robert Martin, the owner of BlackTech."

Silently, she stares at me.

"It was you who mailed it. Am I right? You sent it from Catalina Island."

The tick at the corner of her mouth proves it.

"You had no way of knowing that Robert died a couple of years ago. The letter went to his college-age son, Evan."

"I'm so sorry...for his loss. Jonathan always spoke highly of Robert." Pain closes her eyes. "My brother's confession must have been devastating for Evan."

"It was. It's why our firm is investigating Jonathan's death. Mary Ann, did Jonathan ever tell you about his work at BlackTech?"

"In the beginning. But even within the first year, he stopped talking about it. He wasn't supposed to discuss any government contracts. But I knew he was unhappy about them."

"We want to bring your brother's killers to justice. But, first I need to piece together how it started: how he was compromised along with a few others in the class."

"You mean Jonathan and Tommy weren't the only ones?"

"No. We've discovered a few more. Like Jonathan and Tommy, they were seduced and recruited through Lilith as well. Others were killed."

She sighs. "Ask away."

~

"Considering the anonymity policy, how was it that you and your brother ended up in the astrology class together?" I ask.

"Yeah, it was fortuitous, right?" By her snarl, I can tell her comment isn't a joke. "Jonathan and I were twins. But because I was born two minutes after midnight, this made me a Cancer."

"And because you didn't share a last name, your instructor—Arthur Yates—didn't realize you were related."

She nods. "Our parents divorced when we were twelve. I took my stepfather's last name. Jonathan refused to do so, even when my mother begged him." She shrugs. "Later, I wished I hadn't. Our stepdad was a lecher."

"What was your major?"

"Like Jonathan, I was a Computer Science major." She shrugs. "Two scholarship kids who held golden tickets to life's most successful professions—had we not been chosen to intern at Dartmouth Analytica."

"If Jonathan, Tommy, and you were close before the course, you must have hidden your relationships when you were assigned the class."

Mary Ann snorts. "Of course we did! If we were to graduate, we had to keep it on the QT! It was our final semester —much too late to get another accredited work project."

"Anytime during that semester, were you aware of Lilith's relationship with Jonathan?"

"Not at all! Jonathan kept it a secret, as did Tommy." She shakes her head angrily. "Ha! If only one had let it slip to the other! Maybe they would have both walked away from her."

"By happenstance, I discovered Tommy's involvement through one of the few classmates who didn't fall under

Lilith's spell. Here's the thing, Mary Ann: to stop the catastrophe set in motion by Jonathan's duplicity, I have to track down a few more of your classmates. We don't have time to lose. Were you able to identify anyone else in the class?"

Mary Ann nods. "Vera Gantry. Aquarius. She was a language major."

"How did you do this?"

Mary Ann laughs. "Men don't realize how often we ladies head to a lavatory after class. There were only three women in Astrology: Lilith, Vera, and me. My CS degree had an emphasis on AI. My senior project dealt with robot humanization. Despite the voice masks, after a month in class, I recognized the cadences in the other women's voices. One day I made it a point to be the first person out the door. Then I waited in the closest lavatory and lingered by the basin. Anyone who came in after me was asked something simple—usually, a direction to another building—so that I could analyze the lilts and pauses in her voice. I struck gold with Vera. Some phrase she used sounded familiar, so I looked the woman in the eye and said, simply, "'Hello, Aquarius.'"

"How did she respond?"

Mary Ann laughs. "As you can imagine, at first, she was petrified! But I assured her that by breaking the anonymity rule we'd really be helping the instructor with his theorem—if only by disproving it. That's when I pointed out I'd already done so."

"So, you told her you were Gemini's—that is, Jonathan's twin."

Mary Ann nods sadly. "I wish I hadn't."

"Why do you say that?"

Mary Ann shrugs. "I wouldn't have been his target."

"You—a target? To Jonathan?"

"No. Scorpio." Mary Ann's lips curl into a smirk. "A couple of our classmates were from other schools. He was one of them. I learned this later—when he approached me a few hours after class one day." She closes her eyes, as if watching the incident play out in her mind's eye. "He claimed to go to UCLA. He flirted. I was flattered. One thing led to another…" Opening her eyes, she shrugs. "I was young and dumb. He was handsome and horny. The rest, as they say, was inevitable."

"What do you mean?"

"The sex was good. No—to be honest, it was great. And besides, he mixed a mean martini." Her sky-blue eyes cloud over. "I became his booty call. You know, when no one else is around. The one who's always available. And then, one night, I was too available."

"In what way?"

"He invited me to a party at a friend's house. I felt honored. I thought my dream had come true and that he was finally taking the relationship seriously. But I misinterpreted his intentions." As Mary Ann bows her head, her bangs skirt her eyes. When she can speak again, her voice comes out in a whisper: "He wanted to share me with his asshole friends."

My heart sinks in my chest.

"I didn't even want to drink that night. When I refused, he offered me a soda. The drug must have been in there because I didn't remember a thing."

"A roofie?"

Mary Ann nods. "When I woke up, I was in my dorm room. Sore all over. Bloodied…" She shrugs. "I stayed in bed for two days. When I finally got up to go to class, I avoided him. But the following Saturday he was waiting for me outside my apartment. He said he had to talk to me. He sounded contrite. I agreed I'd meet him after my library shift, but I insisted that we do so at a public place. He suggested that we meet at a coffee shop within walking distance. Once we were there, he wasted no time in calling me a whore—in shaming me—for, as he put it, 'getting out of control.' He told me that the amount of grain alcohol I drank was embarrassing. And that the way I came on to his so-called 'friends' embarrassed him. Him! Can you imagine! Then he showed me pictures." She shudders at the thought. "Me with...with men I'd never met before! Me, doing...*things!*...Horrible things!"

As she sobs, I lay my hand on her shoulder.

She sighs, but she doesn't push me away. "He then pulled out an envelope. There were pictures inside of...all of it. He said he'd done me a favor buying the photos and the negatives, which he claimed he destroyed. He handed me the photos." Mary Ann rolls her eyes. "Can you believe I actually thanked him?"

"You weren't thinking."

"You're right. I wasn't. Otherwise, I would have known he never loved me." The tears clinging to her lower lashes finally fall and roll down her face. "But hey, it was a different time. We didn't talk about those kinds of things back then."

"Who is Scorpio?" I ask.

"Other than the biggest mistake of my life?" Her laugh is filled with cruel memories. "Nope, sorry! If I tell you, I'll be the next victim on his list—and so will you."

To encourage her to speak, I'm just about to tell Mary

Ann that Lilith is no longer a problem when she adds, "You know, Tommy and Vera were an item even before the class."

"I take it his disappearance frightened her too."

"She had an additional reason to be scared. Scorpio made a move on her too." Mary Ann shudders at the memory. "When I heard about it, I told her my own sad tale. I don't think she ever told Tommy. He would have killed Scorpio!" She pauses to consider that. "Maybe it would have been for the best. Instead, all of us—Jonathan, Tommy, Vera, and I—allowed Scorpio and Lilith to ruin us."

"Where is Vera now?"

"She teaches languages at USC. Russian."

A chill runs through my veins.

As casually as I can, I ask, "Do you have a picture of Vera?"

She nods. "Follow me."

We walk into one of the bungalow's bedrooms. It's set up as an office. Mary Ann points to a billboard—really, a collage of photos. One picture, tucked far into the upper right-hand corner, shows two women—girls really: in bikinis lying on the beach.

Beside the photo is another more recent one. It was taken recently because it is Vera as she looked when I saw her with Jack.

Aquarius—Vera Gantry—is the woman Jack killed.

How can that be? Lilith was Taurus…

Unless Jack killed the wrong woman.

"Have you heard from her lately?" My voice is shaking. I pray Mary Ann doesn't hear that quiver.

She shakes her head. "No, but she has a habit of going dark. I guess she's like me: always looking over her shoulder." Mary Ann shrugs. "You know, Vera took in Tommy after his accident. Otherwise, he'd have been homeless. The medical bills alone wiped him out! The last time I was at her place, she mentioned she was holding onto some of the remnants of his old life: his school books, notebooks, his old computer—just in case, by some miracle, his brain fog cleared. It was wishful thinking on her part. We both knew it," she grimaced. "I'll give you her telephone number and her address."

"I'd appreciate that. Thank you." I don't want to be the one to break the bad news to Mary Ann.

Not yet, anyway.

She writes it down and hands it to me. "Donna, will you let me know how everything turns out?"

I stop myself from replying, *You'll know one way or another.*

Instead, I merely say, "Of course."

Vera's apartment, in Culver City, is a half hour north.

I can't altogether avoid the surveillance cameras surrounding her apartment complex, but I can park far enough away and enter through an alley to avoid being seen breaking and entering through her back door.

From her desk calendar, I see her next classes were to commence again on Monday. When the body is finally called in, the coroner will rule it a heart attack.

Jack killed her on Thursday—three days ago. Plenty of time for the stench of decay to set in. I do my best not to gag as I open closets and drawers, looking for anything with

Tommy's name or initials on it. Finally, tucked on the highest shelf of a linen closet, I find a canvas bag containing an ancient laptop computer. It also holds some lined notebooks. The initials *T.A.* are marked on the bottom right-hand corner of each one.

I take Vera's computer too.

I go out the way I came in. If I'm lucky, the only thing I'll leave behind is the prayer I say over her corpse.

Jack is in his favorite spot: the hammock in our backyard.

I once asked him what he thinks about as he lays there. His answer: "Absolutely nothing."

I envy him. We all need a haven from the world now and then. Swaying gently between two shady oaks is as good a place as any.

"How was Manhattan Beach?" he asks as I fall in beside him.

"Enlightening."

And then I proceed to tell him the good news first:

That Cancer confirmed she sent Jonathan's thumb drive to Evan.

That she revealed another Russian asset in the class: Scorpio.

I save the worst for last: that Jack killed an innocent woman.

Hearing this, he sits straight up in the hammock. "But... she was already verified as a foreign agent!"

"By POTUS," I confirm. "But did he tell you how he came across that intel?"

Jack's head shakes from his anger and confusion. "He claimed it was a valid source."

"But he wanted you to keep it from Branham."

Jack nods. The way he frowns, I know that, like me, he questioned Edmonton's motive at the time. Still, he did as our Commander in Chief requested.

"He allowed me to clear it with Ryan," Jack points out. "We should call him now."

He rolls out of the hammock. As I follow behind him, I notice his head is bowed, but his strides are deliberate.

He thinks he was played for a fool.

I hope he's wrong—for Edmonton's sake.

16

Void of Course

[Donna's horoscope today]

A "void of course" takes place when the Moon rules your planet. Warning: This is never a good time to begin a new project! Instead, use this period to review, reconsider, and reorganize.

Introspection usually means looking inward for answers. What others tell you may be contrived to lead you down a rocky path with twists and turns that can lead to a fatal misstep.

Despite the complications laid at your pedicured toes, you can, and will, agilely step over them without twisting your pretty little ankle—if you heed the advice coming from your head as opposed to your heart.

"NOT GOOD." RYAN'S REACTION TO JACK'S BAD NEWS IS understated, to say the least.

"I've got to report this to POTUS," Jack insists.

"Agreed," Ryan says. "Perhaps you should do it from here, officially."

"I'd appreciate that," Jack replies.

"So, we're back to square one with Lilith," I mutter.

"Seems that way," Ryan admits. "Donna, what can you tell me about your stop in Manhattan Beach?"

"Cancer—that is, Mary Ann Harrison—revealed that Scorpio may also be a Russian operative."

"Does she know his real identity?"

"She did, but she refused to tell me. She feels he's just as dangerous as Lilith." Who is now back in play, damn it. "And whereas Tommy can't seem to recall the exact code change he made to Jonathan's original software, he remembered it had to do with a GPS coordinate."

"Well, that's a shame." Ryan's irritation deepens his voice to a growl.

"There is one mitigating circumstance, sir. Mary Ann mentioned that Vera Gantry and Tommy were lovers before taking the class. Vera had also been approached by Scorpio, but unlike Mary Ann, she turned down his advances. She never told Tommy about it because she didn't want to upset him. Vera must have forgiven him for his affair with Lilith because after his suicide attempt, like Mary Ann, she allowed him to stay with her periodically. She even stored some of his things from before his suicide attempt. I retrieved them today—his computer and some notebooks."

"That was probably him banging on her door that night when she asked me to leave through the back door." From Jack's tone, I can tell that this realization saddens him.

"Have Jack bring the items in with him. We'll have the rest of the team look through it."

"If they need my help—"

"Thanks for the offer, but you'll be busy."

"Doing what?"

"Emma found Arthur Yates," Ryan explains.

"The astrology instructor-slash-Russian-handler?"

"One and the same."

"Where will I find him?"

"The Loma Linda Comfort Care facility in Santa Monica."

"A nursing home?" Jack is just as surprised as me. "Why didn't the Russians bring him home?"

"Good question," Ryan responds. "I suppose it's a combination of factors. Apparently, he had a stroke in the 1990s. At the time the Soviet Union was crumbling. The KGB had its hands full at home as well as abroad. Many Russian assets had already defected, and Russian citizens were leaving the country in droves. According to Arthur's health files, he never really recovered. In the decades since, he slipped into dementia. Maybe they felt it wasn't worth the risk."

"But you think he's worth a visit?" I ask.

"At this point, every lead is crucial." Ryan sighs. "Craigs, you've got your marching orders."

After we hang up, Jack takes my hand. "I'm sorry you had to go back to Vera's place."

At all costs, our role as assassins means to do the job and get out with little if any notice. Still, I know Jack well enough to imagine he's wracked with guilt about Vera. Otherwise, I would not now say, "You know, Jack, we could break protocol."

"You mean call it into Emergency Services?" He thinks about that for a moment. "You're right. It's the very least we can do. First, I'll ask Arnie to scrub the apartment complex's surveillance of us—but yes, her loved ones need to know."

That would include Mary Ann.

What a shame. First, Jonathan, now Vera.

I'll break the news to her myself: Vera was found dead of a heart attack.

"You're here for Mr. Yates?" Jennifer Crenshaw, the director of Loma Linda Comfort Care, gazes at me from above her glasses.

"You seem surprised." I keep a benign smile on my lips.

"Only because…well, he rarely has visitors. In fact, I've been here nine years, and I only remember one…maybe two."

I shift the dozen roses I've bought along with a copy of a spy novel—*Red Sparrow* by Jason Matthews— to shake her hand. When the book drops anyway, she leans down with a grunt to retrieve it for me.

"Thank you!" I exclaim as she hands it back. "Uncle Arthur loves spy novels. I don't read them myself, but the clerk at the bookstore said this was a good one. I just hope he hasn't read it yet."

Mrs. Crenshaw shakes her head sadly. "I'm sure he hasn't, dear. You see, Mr. Yates' dementia is quite advanced."

"I figured as much. Still," I let a few tears flow. "They say I sound and look like my mother. I thought that seeing me might spark something in him."

The woman looks at her watch. "I'm sure he's napping. Even if he's not, visiting hours are almost over—"

"Look, Mrs. Crenshaw, Arthur was my mother's only brother! She's passed now, and since I'm out here on business, I felt I should stop in and pay my respects. I may never get another chance!" I wipe my damp face with the back of my hand—and immediately drop the book again.

Again, Mrs. Crenshaw reaches down for it. As she hands it to me, she shrugs. "Well, I guess it wouldn't hurt. It is a special occasion after all. Follow me."

The facility is a single-story U-shaped building. We walk down the long hall, almost to the very last room. A thin floor-to-ceiling window beside the door allows us to look into his room. Arthur, slack-jawed, sits alone, in a wheelchair. A television, mounted to the wall, is tuned to a game show.

Mrs. Crenshaw whispers: "Don't be disappointed if he doesn't respond. This hasn't been one of his better weeks."

I nod. Slowly, I walk over to him. Bending beside him, I murmur, "Hello, Arthur. It's me—Lilith."

His eyes widen. They roam over me hungrily.

Thank goodness, Mrs. Crenshaw has already stepped out and shut the door behind her as he places his hand on my breast.

So Lilith looked like me, once a long time ago.

As repulsed as I am, I squelch the urge to slap away his shriveled old claw. "We don't have time for that," I keep my tone promising. "I'm here about Horoscope."

His eyes gleam with recognition of the name. "My God! Is it time?"

"This week. Horoscope launches this week," I answer.

"All these years…" He shuts his eyes, lost in the past.

"Arthur, I'm worried."

"What about, my sweet?"

"I was just wondering: Was there ever a way in which I let you down?'

Although shaking, he reaches up to pinch my cheek. "Never, my dear! Just look how far you've come!" He chuckles. "Not as far as Scorpio, but still…"

Noting my grimace, he adds, "On the other hand, you are fearless!" Arthur leans in. "However, Scorpio is ruthless. And sadly, my dear, when it comes to power, the rule has always been survival of the fittest."

"I'll remember that," I retort. I think about the only other unaccounted students: "To tell you the truth, Arthur, Scorpio is worried about Sagittarius and Virgo."

"Why? They have proven themselves to be loyal! One to the cause, the other to the man," Arthur huffs. "Don't play the silly, worrisome little woman, Lilith. It doesn't become you."

At least now I know Sagittarius and Virgo are in play—or were. If Arthur's mind has slipped so far as to mistake me, a perfect stranger, for Lilith, he may not really know their status—or, for that matter, Scorpio's.

Their actual names and whereabouts aren't nearly as crucial as Horoscope's launch date and location. Time to turn on the charm. I lean in: "Oh, by the way, Arthur, what target did the Kremlin finally decide on? New York? DC?" I pause before adding, "Los Angeles?"

He gives me a strange look. "Don't be such a fool! Why would the US aim its most diabolical weapon on one of its own cities? You know as well as me that it was London all along—Westminster, to be exact." His eyes gleam. "The moment it's discovered that the US used Horoscope on its most vital ally, all the other Democratic nations will also turn against it! And who will they ally with next? Russia, of course!"

We are launching Horoscope?

But how? And from where?

Arthur takes my hand. He runs the tip of his index finger up the center of my wrist. "You must know how pleased I am with you," He whispers. "And of course, Scorpio will be here soon too. He'll want me at his side when Horoscope is initiated." He looks around, as if saying so will make it true.

It takes all my power not to shiver at his touch. "Where is Scorpio now?" I purr.

"Don't play games!" He says impatiently.

"I haven't seen him in a while."

He looks up at me sharply. "You know exactly where he is! In the…" his eyes narrow as he scrutinizes my face. He looks down at my neck. "You're not wearing it…"

At that moment, he realizes Lilith is not here after all.

Before I can react, he grabs his fork off the luncheon tray on his side table and stabs it in my thigh.

Son of a bitch!

I leap back into a bookcase, hitting so hard that its books topple off the shelves. The ones high above me fall onto my head and chest. Stunned, I fall to the floor.

With all his might, Arthur stumbles out of his wheelchair toward the nightstand. He opens a drawer and fumbles around until he finds what he's looking for—a tiny vial. With shaking hands, he pours something into his hand:

It's an L-Pill—cyanide, the Russian operative's final solution.

I've got to keep him from taking it!

I stumble to my feet and run to his side—

But it's too late.

It doesn't go down easy. He gags. He foams at the mouth. Soon he is shaking. His heart pounds too fast for the blood rushing through it.

Death comes with a jolt and a sigh.

Ah, hell.

It's not easy undressing a dead man. After I lay him out in his bed, I cover him with the blanket. There is a vase in the bottom cabinet of his bathroom sink. I put the roses in there, and then lay the book, open, on the nightstand.

There are a few items in the drawer: a pencil, a notepad, and an address book that is anything but what it seems: no names, just a series of innocuous words in two columns on each page.

One more thing for Emma to decipher.

By the time I get home, Jack is already there.

He's packing.

"You're going to DC?" I ask.

"No. Just up the road: north of Santa Barbara. POTUS refused to discuss my mission on the phone. Instead, he suggested that I report to him there. It's some posh political fundraiser tied to an art installation. I guess he wants to mix business with the pleasure of firing me in person."

"He can't do that!" I insist. "You were just following his orders!"

"He can do whatever he wants."

"And Ryan is going to let him?"

"If he wants to keep Acme operational, he has no choice."

I watch as Jack buttons up his tuxedo shirt. If he's going to get sacked, at least he'll look like a million dollars.

And if I'm going to do the voodoo that I do so well, I'll have to do the same. I know just the dress: a long-sleeved backless diamond studded indigo sheath that hugs every curve.

I fold my arms at my waist. "I'm going too."

Jack eyes me suspiciously. "Let me guess: you think you can charm him the way you did our previous Commander in Chief."

"It's worth a try, right? And besides, what have we got to lose at this stage?"

"Other than my career and your dignity? Absolutely nothing," he retorts blithely.

I wrap him in my arms. "You won't win this argument, Mr. Craig. Besides, Acme's plane is waiting."

His kiss is sweet and all too short.

Something may go down in flames tonight, but it won't be Jack's career.

17

Ascendant

Ascendant refers to the angle at which the next zodiac sign approaches from the East.

The term is also used about one's birth! Astrologers note the specific time and location of your "rising sign" as it ascends from the East because it guides your actions: how you present yourself to the world, and how you cope with adversity.

We enter the world with such high hopes! Do we ever live up to the expectations of our destiny?

Your mother would answer with a resounding, "YES!"

Bless her! She's always on your side, even when the sun, the moon, and the rest of the universe aren't—beginning with those snotty little girls in your kindergarten class.

"You're awfully quiet, Mrs. Craig." If Jack's mild tone is supposed to counterbalance the worry in his eyes, the attempt has failed miserably.

The flight isn't a long one: a good deal less than an hour. Still, we've been quiet since settling into our plane's seats. I've been staring outside the closest window, following the coastline. It's always a beautiful sight at sunset.

I force a smile on my lips. "I'm just enjoying the view."

He knows I'm lying. We've tried to hide our anxiety from each other. We're failing miserably.

Suddenly, I notice something odd. "We're passing over the Santa Barbara Airport!" I point below us, where another private jet is now landing.

"Actually, we're touching down at Vandenberg," Jack replies.

Makes sense, since it's where POTUS will have landed.

Maybe he's planning to sack Jack right on the tarmac. If so, Jack was right. I didn't need to get all gussied up.

Not that I say this to Jack.

"POTUS's host lives a half-hour away," Jack explains. "The event is being held at the weekend hacienda of some venture capitalist: a guy named Charles Riley. He owns his own vineyard outside of Lompoc."

As we get closer to Vandenberg, I notice that ours isn't the only private plane circling for a landing. There are at least three others. "This must be some shindig. And they also have clearance to land at a military base?"

"Sure, why not? It's a political fundraiser. The stated excuse is that it's some art installation. I expect a few other illustrious politicians will be there too, swilling at the donor trough." There is a tightness in Jack's tone.

I'm beginning to think he has every right to be concerned. Edmonton is such an arrogant prick.

So that Jack doesn't see the concern on my face, I stare

down at the landing field. Our plane must now be cleared for landing because there's a steady drop in altitude.

Something on the base's largest launch pad catches my eye. "What's that?" I point it out to Jack.

"My guess: the next payload to JSOC–the Joint Space Operations Center. You know, the 9th Combat Operations Squadron is based here." He takes a closer look. "Nope, on second thought, it's not large enough. Maybe it's a MilStar launch: satellite communications. The 148 SOPS—Space Operations Squadron—is located here too."

We are now close enough to read the writing on the missile's bulbous head:

ASCENDANT
The World's Largest
Communications Satellite Constellation

"Charles Riley holds the controlling interest in Ascendant," Jack explains.

"The commercial space load company?"

"One and the same. There must be a commercial launch happening soon."

Written on the center of the one-hundred-plus-foot-long missile's vertical body are the words:

Universal Peace

"Wishful thinking," Jack mutters. "Or a public relations stunt."

"If I were to guess, it's the latter." I lay my head on his shoulder. "Still, one can dream, right?"

As our plane approaches low and slow, I notice the plane landing ahead of us. It's painted with an interesting logo—

A blue Mohawk logo with a frantic scroll of letters that spell out

TALON

Well, what do you know? This should be quite some party.

For everyone but Jack and me.

SECURITY ON THE BASE IS HEAVY. TALON IS STILL BEING detained by the time we're on the tarmac.

I hope he was smart enough to leave any drugs or dope at home.

Seeing me, he mimics a double-take. The next thing I know, I'm enveloped in a bear hug. "Well, if it ain't the gorgeous gal with the great gams!" He holds out his hand to Jack. "You're one lucky dude."

"Thanks. I think so." Jack shakes his hand. "The name's Jack Craig."

After we settle into one of the limousines ferrying guests to the party, I ask Talon, "How did you get on the VIP list?"

"I know the artist, Jacob Grommet, personally! I already own some of his works."

"Nice." For someone else. My preference in art is less bland, more provocative.

"Not really," Talon admits. "Myself, I like it when they paint body parts—particularly those of the female persuasion." He gives me the once-over, as if he's got X-ray vision.

He only wishes.

"The best thing I can say is that Jacob's paintings are humongous"—Talon separates his arms as wide as he can—"and that's what counts. I've got way too much wall space! Need to fill it up fast." He thinks a beat: "Frankly, I've got too many houses. Time to unload a few."

I won't mention that Penelope's ex is a realtor. In fact, I think it best not to mention her at all. I'm depressed enough without having to hear him bemoan his lost love.

In any event, he's still yammering away: "I'm proud to say I was the first benefactor to jump on board with this project: launching a GIGANTIC peace sign in the sky so that the whole world can join in one great oneness of love! How cool is that?"

"You're quite the wordsmith," I purr.

Talon blushes—something I would not have been able to see if he were still slathered in his iconic red paint.

"The launch is taking place tonight?" Jack asks.

Talan laughs raucously. "It's why we're all here, bro! Charles' spread is a perfect viewing site. Makes sense, since he's invested enough in Ascendant to have a front row center seat for its success. His crib is only two miles from the launch pad. Yo, check it out."

He nods toward the mansion beyond the gate now in front of us.

The large, modern, terraced glass-and-steel structure hugs its hillside like a second skin. We can hear the muted chatter coming from the guests mingling at the bars and buffets set up on the large terraces of all five levels. Tiny lights twinkle under recessed eaves, assuring that nothing will divert the guests' attention during Ascendant's launch.

Eventually, our limousine is waved through.

"So glad you could join us, Mrs. Craig." As with his other guests, Charles Riley greets me at the front door with a warm handshake and a hearty hello. He's got just enough gray in his sideburns and a pouch around his waist to give away the fact that he's a few years over forty.

Charles chuckles as he shakes Jack's hand. "Any friend of the President's is also a friend of mine. That goes double for his beautiful better half."

"I know I wasn't on the guest list, so thank you for accommodating me," I say, blushing.

"Speaking of President Edmonton, I promised I'd find him promptly upon my arrival," Jack replies.

"His motorcade is on its way. He asked me to have you wait in my study." He waves over a member of POTUS's advance team. "Please take Mr. Craig to my study on the top floor."

Jack nods casually before walking off with the Secret Service agent toward the grand foyer's elevator. He hides his gallows mood well.

Charles turns back to me. "Besides the President, my other guest of honor is Jacob Grommet." He beckons to the artist, who's been corralled by Talon. They walk over together.

Charles and Jacob are of similar age, but the resemblance ends there. The artist is short and wiry. His beard is unruly, as is his hair, which flairs out like a wire-coiled halo. He's so jumpy that his handshake is quick, limp, and damp.

I wonder if he's hopped up on something.

I look from him to Talon. "So, you and Jacob are old friends?"

"Yep!" Talon exclaims proudly. "I guess I was one of your first patrons, right, Jake?"

Grommet frowns. "*Jacob.*"

"Sorry." Talon shrugs. "Old habits die hard. Hey, I'm über-proud to be a small part of this endeavor. Tickled pink!"

Jacob grimaces. "Don't be so modest." His reply isn't appreciative but terse.

"It's true, bud! Hell, getting your satellite as part of the Ascendant's payload cost a pretty penny, right? And the biggest pile of chicken feed came from...what's it called again? Oh yeah—the Horoscope Foundation."

Horoscope.

"I've never heard of it," I reply coolly.

Talon shrugs. "Yeah, I hadn't either. But when it comes to art, there are angels everywhere, right? And tonight, after *Universal Peace* is launched, the angels can hover around the coolest light show ever!"

Jacob stares down at his watch. "Our esteemed President is cutting it close," he grumbles.

"Not to worry. Ascendant's launch won't happen until he gets here," Charles reminds him.

Grommet frowns. "I've got some last minute items to check on before the launch. If you'll all excuse me."

As he walks off, Charles turns to me. "Don't mind Jacob. Unfortunately, his 'brooding artist' act is real and twenty-four-seven." He shrugs. " What would you like first, a glass of champagne or a tour of the house?"

"I opt for the tour. Let's save the champagne for toasting Ascendant's launch."

"Sounds great to me." He leads the way.

"You've got quite a collection here." I'm admiring Charles' gun vault, which is a veritable munitions museum.

Our tour begins at the lowest level. After reviewing Charles' extensive wine cellar and poolside cabana, we go up to the second floor (a massive staff kitchen), then to the third level (four guest suites), before making our way to the fourth: a living room and dining room that could easily seat twenty-four guests. The floor's movable walls convert this cavern into cozy alcoves when the house isn't filled with two hundred of Charles' nearest and dearest acquaintances.

Somewhere along the tour, we picked up a couple of champagne flutes, but thus far we've held to our promise to toast as Ascendant is launched.

It's for the best. On the worst occasions, I'm a sloppy drunk. Should my husband get fired, I doubt I'll be able to hold my liquor—or in this case, my bubbly.

The gun vault is located on the top floor, next to the master bedroom suite and down the hall from Charles' study. It also doubles as a panic room which, Charles tells me, can only be accessed with his thumbprint.

The term "vault" is relative only in the case of access. When its steel-plated curtain is recessed, like the rest of the rooms in this house, it has an incomparable view of Vandenberg and the ocean beyond.

Charles' vault holds one heck of a private arsenal. One wall is filled with antiques: everything from 17th-century muskets to Korean War-era arms. A bolt-action Mauser is mounted next to a 1904 Springfield Rifle, which is next to a Gatling gun. A prized possession: a Thompson sub-machine gun once owned by Al Capone.

Another wall showcases today's most sophisticated military weaponry. An M4, a TAC-50, and a Tango 51 are displayed on floor stands.

"Are you expecting World War III?" I ask.

Charles grins. "Better safe than sorry."

I guess now is not the time to point out that he's not an octopus.

"Are you an enthusiast?" he asks.

"I wouldn't say that. I've never viewed guns as toys. But yes, I consider them necessary evils." I'm standing in front of the TAC-50. "May I?"

"Be my guest."

I position it against my shoulder before putting my right hand on the pistol grip with my finger hovering outside the trigger guard. To support the heavy weight of the rifle, I hold it under the front stock with my left hand.

As I sight down its fancy Swarovski scope, I casually ask, "How exactly will *Universal Peace* be seen from space with the naked eye?"

"It's one of the twenty-two satellites in Ascendant's payload. The others are the last of a constellation of telecommunications satellites—one hundred and one of them, to be exact. Each satellite weighs 850 pounds. However, they are fairly compact: only about forty-three inches long, with a depth and width of twenty-seven inches square. It also has two wings made up of solar panels that are twenty-six feet long and six and a half feet wide."

"Impressive," I murmur.

"You bet it is!" He beams proudly. "Unlike the others, though, Jacob's satellite is equipped with a laser beam. The message it emits will be short and sweet: just for a few seconds, in fact. But the whole world will see it."

"You're very generous to allow an artist such a grand platform," I say.

"It's got great public relations value for Ascendant, no doubt about it. Still, it wouldn't have happened if Jacob hadn't come through with a benefactor to foot the bill for the ride."

"What do you know about The Horoscope Foundation?"

Charles shrugs. "Nothing, really. But Horoscope Foundation's director is supposed to be here tonight. His name is Arthur Yates."

I'm glad my face is obscured behind the rifle scope. Otherwise, Charles might notice my shock.

"He should be arriving soon," Charles adds. "I'll be sure to introduce you."

I'm certainly not going to be the one to break the bad news to him: Arthur will be a no-show.

"But without Ascendant, none of this is possible! You truly are a great friend to Jacob," I point out. "And considering the amount of champagne flowing tonight, why not toast the man whose investment in Ascendant made Jacob's dream possible—you?"

Charles chuckles. "Sure, why not?" He reaches for the

champagne glasses and hands me the one in his left hand. As we sip, he proclaims, "Here's to *Universal Peace.*"

My eyes scan the room. Suddenly, I squeal with delight. "Is that plaque for real? You have the machine gun that once belonged to Al Capone?"

"The one and only," he says proudly.

"Would you mind if I held it? " I flutter my eyelids in anticipation.

My excitement is contagious. To fetch it, he puts down his glass. By the time he's walked over and unlocked the gun's glass case, I've switched our flutes.

He strides back over, tommy gun in hand. Taking it, I hold it at a jaunty angle like a moll. "Do you mind if we take our picture with it?"

He laughs. When he's by my side, I hand him my phone, holding it out so that the angle is horizontal. "Your arms are longer, so you snap it," I explain.

To do so, he'll have to tap the digital circle next to his right thumb.

"Say, 'Peace'!" he declares.

I vow, "Peace!"

With a thumb press, he's memorialized this momentous occasion.

At least I hope it'll be memorable: as the night the death star's launch was stopped.

The door is open, but someone knocks anyway, to get Charles's attention. Jacob is standing in the threshold. "President Edmonton is here now, in your office," he says tersely. "The guests are moving to the roof. He'll join us there in fifteen minutes." Jacob tents his fingers to signal his appreciation. The sleeves of his loose-fitting shirt rise, revealing a tattoo:

It's the sun sign, Virgo.

Like Talon, Jacob was in Jonathan's astrology class too.

"Yeah, okay, thanks." Charles sounds annoyed. He turns to me. "I guess we head up to the roof."

I nod.

As we walk out of the vault, the door slides silently behind us, locking into place.

We are almost at the elevator when I say, "I have to powder my nose. I'll be up in a moment."

"You'll find a bathroom that way." Distractedly, Charles points down the hallway to the left.

As I walk away, I wave my champagne flute to show my thanks.

Really it's his flute.

Further down, on the right, two of POTUS's Secret Service detail are standing guard in front of a closed double door.

It must be Charles' office, where POTUS is meeting with Jack.

How can I stop the launch?

This is a living nightmare.

"HOROSCOPE LAUNCHES TONIGHT!" THIS IS HOW I TELL RYAN, Emma, and Arnie that I'm having less than a great time at POTUS's invitation.

"How? Where?" Ryan asks.

"From Vandenberg! In, like, ten minutes! It's part of a

commercial satellite payload going up on an Ascendant rocket! We've got to stop it!" My mind seems to be running at warp speed. "I think I know how."

"As long as it doesn't involve hacking Vandenberg's control center," Ryan warns. "That would be considered treason—even for a black ops contractor such as Acme."

"It won't—but still, it's a long shot," I warn them. "And I'll need some technical help."

"We're listening," Arnie assures me.

I explain: "Okay, so: a while back there was a pretty bad mishap on a commercial missile launch—"

"I remember!" Emma interjects. "It was a SpaceX launch. It was carrying eleven satellites that were going to provide better telecommunications coverage over Africa."

"Yes, exactly! Only it blew up on the launch pad. Somehow, three helium containers within the second-stage oxygen tank blew. The investigation team's first theory was an act of sabotage—that a sniper shot up the tanks from a neighboring building."

"I remember that," Arnie replies. "Instead, it turned out the launch team used oxygen that was forty degrees cooler than what was typically used, which made it heavier than it should have been. Everything—200 million dollars' worth of a missile and the eleven satellites—went up like a Roman candle!"

"Donna, there's something else you should know," Emma adds. "The notebooks you retrieved from Vera Gantry's house did, in fact, belong to Tommy. One contains the code change Lilith requested. Horoscope's laser will be aimed at London!"

One shot could do it: save London—and our alliance with the UK.

"I could do it from here." The words are out before I know it.

"How?" Ryan asks. "You'd need a sniper rifle!"

"I know—and I've got one."

"The things you women can stuff in those tiny purses always amazes me," Arnie murmurs in awe.

"What I mean to say is, I have access to a TAC-50. Or I will just as soon as Arnie helps me hack into the surveillance system here." I wince. "And the gun vault."

"Donna, a hit like that—it's quite literally a long shot!" Ryan acknowledges. "The farthest recorded sniper shot was just a little over two miles!"

"I would guess we're that close," I reply. "Arnie, can you pull the GPS from my cell?"

"Give me a sec...Okay, I'm locked in on you now."

"Now, put in the coordinates to Ascendant's launch pad."

"Doing it now..." A moment later, he sighs. "It's just barely two miles."

"Ascendant launches in eleven minutes! Ryan, it's the only chance we have."

I try not to count the seconds. Finally, Ryan says: "Do it!"

18

Virgo

If you were born between August 22nd and September 23rd, your sun sign is Virgo.

On the upside, you are analytical as well as intelligent; practical as well as reliable.

On the downside, you can be a tad fussy. In friendships, you can be harsh or judgmental.

Simply put, others find you to be a great co-worker. But don't expect to be asked out for drinks after work. Since it's already in your nature to tell it like it is, your criticism won't be appreciated any better if you're two sheets to the wind.

FIRST THINGS FIRST.

"Arnie, put Riley's surveillance system on a loop that shows the hall outside this bathroom as empty."

"On it," he says.

"Ryan, I'll need to know how long a fifty-caliber bullet

will take to reach the target at two miles with all the shot calculations. I also need Emma to call the shot set-up quickly, so get on those calculations: distance, air density, wind speed and direction, bullet velocity, and the earth's curvature—you know the drill."

"Got it," Ryan replies.

"Heads up: Riley mentioned that Ascendant is one hundred and twenty feet long. Emma, you'll have to check that statistic," I add. "You'll also have to add in the height of its platform. By the way, I'm on a hill that looks down onto the launch pad. You can use my GPS coordinates to figure out how much higher I am than Ascendant so that we can account for the drop in altitude over the distance. We won't have time for a second shot. This is going to be full cold bore."

"On it!" Emma shouts.

Like me, Emma knows the round will drop, but it is markedly easier to fire in a descending direction than ascending. The toughest calculations are windage because it can change direction multiple times over that kind of distance.

"Now, Arnie, I'll need your help to get back into the gun vault. To do so, Charles Riley's thumbprint has to be scanned. I have his wine glass. Hopefully, the print will appear on it."

"That might work," Arnie replies, "if we can pull a full print."

"I also had him tap my cell phone's power button."

"Also doable, except for the fact that your prints are on there too," he says. "Let's start with the wine glass. We'll need to dust it with a powder, preferably one with color. The darker, the better."

"Will an eyeshadow do?"

"It's worth a try."

I hold the glass up to the light. "I see a print. It's large enough to be a thumb, but I can't tell if it's all there."

"Great! Now, what you'll need to do is crush the eyeshadow into a powder. Then sprinkle it over the finger-print. The powder should cling to the skin's oils on the print."

"Okay, doing it now," I mutter. Well, there goes sixty dollars' worth of midnight blue in my Yves St. Laurent Couture Palette.

First, I take off my shoes and place them side by side, heels out, on the lavatory's marble counter, leaving room between them just wide enough to cradle the flute. I place the flute on its side but leave the thumbprint exposed.

Next, using the pointed tip of my eyeliner, I crush the pan of eyeshadow until it's a loose powder. Next, very gently, I dip the shadow brush into the colored dust. I then rub the brush's bristles between my right hand's thumb and index finger so that I sprinkle the right location on the glass.

"How dark do you need the print?"

"As dark as you can make it without covering up the grooves completely," Arnie explains.

"Got it," I mutter.

I'm almost done when I hear footsteps. Someone is coming my way.

Quickly, I leap to the door and turn the lock.

Not a moment too soon. Someone is working over the

handle. "Hello? Is someone in there?" It's a woman's voice. "Hello?" Exasperation punctuates the question.

I stay silent.

The footsteps walking away are barely drowned out by the expletives coming out of the woman's mouth.

I breathe a sigh of relief—

Until I see that, by accident, I moved one of the shoes. Slowly, the flute rolls toward the edge of the counter—

And falls off.

I grab for it—

And catch it.

I close my eyes, relieved.

Then I remember the thumbprint. Did I smear it?

Slowly I open an eye…

The thumbprint is pristine.

Ryan thunders through the phone, "Watch the clock, folks!"

"Quick, Donna, Take a photo of the print and send it to me," Arnie exclaims.

I do as instructed.

"Perfect!" Arnie crows. "I see all the little whorlie-gigs: loops, whorls, arches…Oooh, the dude has a radial loop! Do you know how rare that is?"

"Arnie—*focus*!" Ryan growls. "From the chatter we're picking up at Vandenberg, Ascendant launches in ninety-eight seconds."

"Sure, Boss! Okay, Donna, so go ahead and open the jpeg on your phone's screen. When you get to the scanner, lay it directly on it—*and pray*."

"Thanks for your words of encouragement," I retort. "Emma, is the hall empty?"

"Affirmative," she reassures me. "POTUS and his security detail are with everyone else: on the roof."

In a flash, I'm out the door.

THE SCANNER'S SCREEN IS ON THE RIGHT SIDE OF THE DOOR, flat against the wall. A tiny green light above it blinks benignly.

I say a prayer.

Then I lay the phone face down on the screen.

Silently, the metal door swings open.

I close it behind me.

"Seventy-two seconds," Ryan mutters.

THE TAC-50 IS JUST AS I LEFT IT: FACING OUT THE WINDOW.

Two miles west, the launch pad is lit up like your craziest neighbor's house at Christmas: too bright, too loud, and too gaudy for words, leaving all who see it mesmerized.

There are a few drawers on the bottom half of the vault's display wall. As I'd hoped, they hold ammo and gear. After I put on ear muffs, gloves, and safety glasses, I grab the box mag and a suppressor.

One shot. One kill. That's the sniper's motto.

A second round would be iffy anyway. Although it will take three to five seconds for the missile to fully clear the launch pad, by the time I settle the weapon, cycle the bolt and chamber another round, sight, and shoot, the rocket will be miles away.

The window's shield is solid steel. Even if it recesses into the wall, can the single pane of glass be opened? Frantically, I look around for some sort of buttons…

I find some on the window's far right side.

Pushing one, the metal plate falls seamlessly into the wall below it. I push another and the bullet-proof glass slides to one side.

"Sixty-seven seconds," Ryan cautions.

The window's ledge is deep—three feet thick—and chest high: Good, because I'll need all this space and more for the fifty-seven inch-long rifle.

The MacMillan TAC-50 is already fitted with a bipod and a night scope. I unscrew it from its tripod stand and carry the twenty-six-pound weapon to the window, where I position it. I then position myself behind the rifle. I crouch slightly, to sight Ascendant. My left hand cradles the rifle on the front stock that hugs the barrel. My right hand hovers over the trigger: slowly, gently taking up the slack.

"I've got some stats for you, Donna," Emma exclaims.

"Perfect timing. Go for it."

Emma takes a deep breath: "We're in luck. There's very little wind tonight. Also, the Ascendant's height is confirmed at one hundred and twenty feet. Its platform puts it an additional fifty feet off the ground. From your height and distance—in this case, 3,540 meters—you can figure the bullet will take 8.5 seconds to reach the target."

"We're now at forty seconds." Ryan's warning is terse and guttural. "At that velocity, you'll need to fire nineteen seconds before lift-off."

"Count it down for me, from twenty-eight," I reply.

"Will do," he vows.

With the window open, I can hear the crowd above my head. Their excited murmur punctuates someone's speech—

I recognize Jacob's voice: "Technology has been man's salvation. It has become the fabric of our very lives. But it has also created atrocity. War depends on technology too. Tonight, when Ascendant launches carrying the *Universal Peace* satellite, humankind will be encouraged to communicate in new and different ways. Through art, we will share not only the awe of the cosmos. We'll be inspired to create similar peace here on Planet Earth! That should be everyone's goal, should it not?"

The crowd shows its agreement with enthusiastic applause.

"Donna: we're at twenty-eight seconds," Ryan says sternly.

I take a deep breath.

Seven…six…five…four…three…two…

"We're at nineteen!" Ryan declares.

As I exhale in time with my heart rate, I squeeze that final fraction on the trigger.

The heavy round leaves the rifle with a muted clap of thunder.

The TAC-50's recoil packs quite a punch against my shoulder, but I hold firm through the pain. When I climb out of this glittery glove of a dress, I expect to find a bruise on my shoulder.

The crowd is now counting down: "Ten…Nine…"

Not me. I am praying—

Until they scream: "One!"

The rocket lights up—

It lifts off—

No...

It blows up.

A fireball engulfs the rocket and its scaffold, leaving just a charred shell. As the missile's bulbous head topples off, the crowd gasps as yet another explosion follows. They are cowed into stunned silence by the fireball blazing before their eyes.

With so little wind, the black smoke from the fire envelops Ascendant's now skeletal frame. More flashes follow, as does a cacophony of additional explosions.

It sounds like a war.

Instead, Armageddon has been prevented.

Tiny whiffs of black smoke drift our way. Soon the crowd will be headed inside.

Quickly, I peel off my gear and put it back. Then I move the rifle back onto its stand, close the window and its metal shield, and get the hell out of there.

Jack must be upstairs with POTUS and our host. They are likely to be wondering where I've been all this time.

I go back to the bathroom. This time when I walk out, Arnie leaves it on the surveillance footage.

"AH, MRS. CRAIG—THERE YOU ARE!" HALF-HEARTEDLY, Charles beckons me over. He's no longer smiling. "I suppose you saw the fiasco."

"Yes—from a lower terrace." I pat his hand. "Charles, I'm so sorry."

His guests of honor are also sullen. Jacob's dark scowl is accompanied by a full-body tremor. Edmonton's face is bland, but his disappointment shows itself in his hooded eyes.

I don't suspect he's too upset. Despite the failed launch, his PAC's coffers are fuller, thanks to the many lobbyists and donors who used this event as an excuse to rub shoulders with him.

Edmonton greets me with an appraising gaze. "I'm glad to hear you didn't miss the launch altogether. When Charles mentioned he'd given you the grand tour and how enthralled you were with Capone's machine gun, I assumed you went back for a second look."

I chuckle. "If men wore Spanx, they'd never question why it takes women such a long time to leave a bathroom. Besides, his panic room is a fortress!" I glance around. "I do hope Jack was able to catch the launch too."

I don't want to come out and ask Edmonton if he sent Jack packing before the main event began.

Edmonton nods to the far side of the terrace. "He's standing over there with Congresswoman Grisham and a few other of her esteemed colleagues."

"Smart move. Ryan will be happy to hear he's so attentive to those who butter Acme's bread," I reply.

"Only I can do that, so tell Ryan not waste Jack's time— or yours." From his tone, he's not joking.

"Acme will always be at your beck and call," I purr.

"I'll hold you to that, Mrs. Craig."

I don't doubt that in the least.

~

CONSIDERING ALL THE SOMBER FACES, I'M SURPRISED TO SEE Jack and Elle Grisham sharing a laugh.

Or maybe more than that, by the way, she places her hand on his chest as she leans into him.

"Don't let our host see you giggling," I warn them. "He's not in the mood for any jokes."

Elle sighs grandly. "I can't say I blame him. At this point, his investment in Ascendant merits a breakdown." She shrugs. "But, he'll recover in no time. He has a fleet of rockets. Just as soon as Ascendant finds out the cause of this failure, another missile will be ready to go, filled with twenty more satellites. With the current demand, Ascendant could fly a payload a week."

So it was all for naught. Eventually, Horoscope will launch.

Something behind me catches Elle's attention. "Poor Charlie looks so forlorn! I know just the thing to cheer him up—a reminder that there's another government contract coming his way. If you'll excuse me..."

As she goes off in one direction, Jack steers me in another: to the elevator.

Neither of us speaks in the limousine back to the base.

I WAIT UNTIL WE'RE AIRBORNE BEFORE ASKING: "HOW DID IT GO with POTUS?"

Jack shrugs. "Fine and dandy."

"You mean, POTUS wasn't upset when you told him about Vera?"

"On the contrary, I informed him his target was exterminated."

I frown. "But she wasn't the target! She's not Lilith!"

"Edmonton wanted Vera dead, whether she was Lilith or not. And if I'd told him I knew her true identity, he would deny all plausibility, leaving me to be his scapegoat."

I arch a brow. "No surprise there."

"Besides, I found the real Lilith. She was at Riley's party, in fact."

"Get out of here! Who?"

"The esteemed Congresswoman Elle Grisham."

Suddenly, I remember something Tommy said:

I hadn't seen her in a long while—until last week...

I left as fast as I could. She was with someone—who would have killed me...

"You're right, Jack! Elle *is* Taurus. Tommy mentioned that he saw Lilith not too long ago. My guess: when she was on the greens at Lion's Lair."

"Tommy sure gets around. But hey, I don't blame him for climbing that hill. I'll bet Lee has the tastiest garbage in town." Jack shrugs at his bad joke.

"So, how did you figure it out?" I ask.

"She's wearing a necklace with a small Taurus charm."

Well, what do you know about that! "So that's what Arthur meant," I mumble.

"Why? What did he say?"

"He looked at my neck and said, 'You're not wearing it.' He must have been referring to the necklace!" *Stupid, stupid me.* "Arthur's other traitors had similar charms: Jonathan, Carlton Miller, Jacob Grommet—"

Jack's eyes open wide. "Grommet, the artist?"

"*Universal Peace* was Horoscope."

Jack laughs. "Then it's a good thing the damn thing blew up on take-off! Talk about luck."

"Luck had nothing to do with it," I proclaim.

It takes a few seconds until Jack grasps my meaning. Suddenly, he's laughing even louder. Why, Mrs. Craig! I can't wait to hear all about it."

"First, we have to decide what we're going to do about Lilith."

"'*We*' aren't doing anything," Jack warns me. "However, *I* will complete the mission POTUS assigned me."

I stare at him. "Jack—you can't! She's not just any terrorist. She's a U.S. Congressperson! What if you get shot by some security detail before you can explain her true identity?"

"She doesn't hold a position that merits any assigned security. Besides, by tomorrow, Acme will have the dossier on her. But before I give it to Edmonton, Acme will backchannel it to Branham." Jack shrugs. "A few minutes ago I had Arnie break into her top aide's calendar. She's in Los Angeles all day tomorrow."

I roll my eyes. "Another political fundraiser?"

"No. She's taking a personal day to attend a funeral. She's sending her aides back to Washington."

A chill runs through me. "It must be for Arthur. Have Emma find out where it's being held."

"Good call." Jack takes my hand. "Well, Mrs. Craig, I believe this nightmare is almost over."

I pray he's right.

19

Taurus

The sun sign known as Taurus covers those born between April 21st and May 21st.

Like its spirit animal—the bull—loyalty is the dominant trait of Taurus.

Other people skills are also clearly evident. You'll note that Taurus is sincere, patient, and will see any and all projects to completion.

But this sun sign has a few negative traits. If you are a Taurus, I'm sure you've noticed that you're a bit...well, narcissistic...

EXCUSE ME! Do you mind putting down that mirror when I talk to you?

The most troubling trait of all is indicative of this fact: the world's most heinous despots and dictators —Hitler, Pol Pot, Hirohito, Saddam Hussein, Jim Jones, Louis Farrakhan—were born under this sign.

Not to worry, Taurus! There is an easy way to mitigate any comparisons with these tyrants:

Leave no bodies.

Remember: dead men tell no tales.

JACK LEFT THE HOUSE BEFORE I WOKE UP. MAYBE HE'S HOPING to be first in line to catch Ryan. That way, he can make his case for going rogue.

At this point, I'd toss a coin as to whether Ryan will sanction a hit on Elle Grisham. It won't depend solely on whether Emma finds discrepancies in Elle's background. The decision to either exterminate or arrest a foreign operative—specifically one who has risen so high in our government—belongs to the CIA director. And his decision may need to be seconded by DI Branham.

As Jack predicted, by the time I walk into Acme Headquarters, Emma and her ComInt team—with assists from Dominic and Abu—have pieced together the life and times of Elle Grisham, a.k.a., Taurus.

In awe, I ask, "How did you do it?"

"We attempted a reverse timeline," Emma explains. "Although the media and public records have meticulously documented Congresswoman Grisham's voting record and her actions as a politician, the rest of her life is as emaciated as a model during Fashion Week."

"Before she was Elle Grisham, she was Ellen Lilith Black —at least, that's what she's claimed," Abu adds. "The name was stolen from the birth certificate of an Iowa-born infant who died from SIDS within a month of her birth."

"Lilith Black's school transcripts were bogus too,"

Dominic cuts in. "They mirrored those of a female student who graduated first in her class in a small agricultural town in the uppermost western corner of the state. When a Stanford admissions department clerk called to verify it, the response, given via fax and around midnight Central Time, was signed by the school's secretary: a spinster with a penchant for gambling. When she died a few days later in a freak accident, her heirs—two nephews—were surprised to discover fifty thousand dollars in a purse hidden in a shoebox in her closet."

"Except for her freshman year at Stanford, Lilith Black lived off campus, kept to herself, and aced all her classes," Abu continues. "After graduating with a degree in Political Science, she moved back to Iowa—if she was ever there, to begin with."

"There, she took the name 'Elle Black.' She signed on as a campaign volunteer with an incumbent congressman from a very rural district: James Tucker," Emma continues. "When he won, he invited her to join his DC staff."

"Was he the congressman Jonathan met through her?" I ask.

"If our timeline is correct, it had to have been. Tucker was on the Budget and Intelligence committees," Dominic replies. "Within a year, she married a Gulf War veteran— Luke Grisham, who suffered from PTSD. Less than a year later, he killed himself with his Army-issued pistol."

"Tucker was voted out of office six years later because of some scandal," Emma reveals. "Elle ran for his seat, using Veterans' rights as her campaign's rallying cry. The rest is documented history."

"My guess: she made sure that Tucker's scandal was

revealed," I mutter. "We should pass this information onto Jack as soon as possible."

"He already has it," Emma informs me. "I briefed him before he took off."

"Jack already left? So, Ryan gave him clearance?"

Emma stares blankly. "Ryan never met with Jack. He's out of the office until late this afternoon."

As I run to the door, Emma shouts, "Clearance? For what?"

THIS TIME, WHEN I CALL LOMA LINDA CARE AS ARTHUR'S niece, I'm sobbing because I've just seen the obituary notice of his death.

"Thank goodness you called!" Jennifer Crenshaw exclaims. "I knew how much Arthur meant to you, but I had forgotten to ask you for your contact information!"

"I read that he died yesterday—just after I saw him!"

"You were right to insist on seeing him that afternoon," Jennifer sniffles. "I feel guilty for having attempted to turn you away."

"Not to worry, Mrs. Crenshaw. And it was kind of you to make the funeral arrangements."

"Oh...but it wasn't me! It was your cousin. You know, his *other* niece. What was her name again? Oh, yes—*Lilith*. He talked about her constantly. It's probably why I never knew you even existed."

"She always was his favorite," I mutter. "Sadly, I've lost Lilith's telephone number. I'd love to attend the service. Did she mention where it was to take place?"

"I overheard her talking to the mortuary where he was sent. It's called Beyond Heavenly. She decided on cremation. It's to take place there. You'll find it on Venice Boulevard, close to Culver City. She's headed over there now."

I'm sure that's where Jack is headed too.

And now, so am I.

OLD HABITS DIE HARD.

In Jack's case, it means avenging a wrongful death.

It also means exterminating a traitor.

I break the sound barrier to get to the Beyond Heavenly Funeral Home and arrive just as Elle is getting into her limousine, urn in hand.

Jack is parked on the street. He's made the wise decision to hold off on the kill until he can get her alone.

He pulls out after her car, and I'm on his tail.

THE LIMOUSINE DROPS ELLE AT A SMALL BOUTIQUE HOTEL IN Beverly Hills—one that caters to out of town actors, directors, or billionaires. Its website boasts "only twelve sumptuous suites, three on each floor."

That should make things easy.

Jack pulls into one side street. I drive onto another.

He will tail Elle to her suite.

Jack rarely goes rogue. Having done so myself (admittedly, on far too many occasions) I've come to appreciate a team effort. It's truly a joy to have another watch your back

—your front, your sides; really, watching your every move—and constantly whispering sweet, very important somethings in your ear; feeding you details that allow you to do the job quickly with as little outside interference as possible.

Today, I'm Jack's guardian angel.

The lobby is grand for such a small hotel. Designer muffins and fruit are laid out for guests. There is only one receptionist and she's busy signing in a guest. Two others are also waiting for their rooms.

I'm sure there's a video monitor behind the desk. As busy as it is now, she won't have time to watch it as it switches feeds between the hotel's four floors and public spaces, which includes a pool off the lobby.

I walk in just as the door of the hotel's only reception elevator closes on Jack. I watch its light to see where it takes him:

All the way to the top floor.

I slip down a side hall, having guessed correctly that it will take me to a service elevator.

I take it to Elle's floor.

All the suites are on the same side of the hall. The doors to two of the suites are closed. A third is open. A maid's cart is in the hall.

Cautiously, I glance inside the open suite. The maid is in the bathroom. I hear her humming a Beyoncé tune. She has her back to me as she scrubs out the enormous tub.

I walk into the room and onto the balcony.

~

THE SUITES' BALCONIES AREN'T CONNECTED. NO PUN INTENDED, I must take a leap of faith. I climb over the railing, say a prayer, then stretch beyond the gap between it and the next balcony. Once I've grabbed hold of the railing, I pull myself onto it, tossing one leg over and then the other.

If it turns out that Elle isn't in this room, I'll have to repeat these contortions on the third and fourth balconies.

I'm in luck. The floor-to-ceiling sheers have been opened, filling the room with light. I peek through the balcony's French door in time to see Elle enter her bathroom.

I try the door: it's unlocked. I open it a mere crack. This allows me to hear the running water as she turns on the shower. Because the bathroom is angled against the far side of the suite, I can watch through the bathroom vanity's mirror as she drops her robe and enters the shower.

I duck low when I notice the front door open slightly.

Slowly, Jack enters the room. He scans it. He realizes Elle is in the shower.

Jack is wearing latex gloves. He pulls a syringe from his pocket, uncaps it, and then positions it in his right hand before moving to the bathroom.

Elle is shampooing her hair. The fact that she is holding both arms up over her head makes it easier for Jack to grab her from behind, hold her tight, and plunge the syringe of aconite into her armpit before she can react.

By the time she realizes what just happened, her muscles are already freezing up.

I watch as Jack waits for her last gasp.

He lets her drop onto the shower stall's tile floor.

Jack gets out of the shower stall. He's sopping wet. His

eyes narrow when he finally catches sight of me, seated on the bed.

I just have to ask: "Was it as good for you as it was for me?"

❧

"Mrs. Craig, what am I going to do with you?" he mutters.

Granted, Jack has a right to be annoyed. Still, I roll my eyes as I pout, "Oh yeah right—shame on me for crashing your unsanctioned kill!"

"You're now a witness," he reminds me.

"A wife can't testify against her husband," I counter.

That declaration earns me a long, deep kiss from my very wet husband. When we part, Jack murmurs, "I knew I married you for a good reason. Last one home feeds the dogs."

"Then, that will be me. I'm heading to Manhattan Beach. I have to break the news to Mary Ann about Vera."

"Mind if I join you? She may like to learn the fate of some of the others, too—especially Lilith and Arthur."

"I'm sure she'd be happy to meet you."

Jack stands still as I hold the blow-dryer to his shirt and pants until they are dry again.

He then follows me onto the balcony and over to the next one.

The maid has done an excellent job with the room. Two plush robes hang in the closet. We put them on before sauntering out the door to the elevator. Our embrace allows us to avoid the halls' security camera.

The lobby is just as busy as I left it. We walk down the hall toward the entrance of the pool. When we turn a corner blind to the surveillance cameras, we shed our robes, depositing them in a bin before walking out the fire exits. Separately, we walk in the opposite direction of our cars before circling back around to them.

Will someone notice the security footage of some strange man walking into one fourth-floor suite and then out another? Will they also realize that it was the suite in which the Congresswoman from Iowa was discovered dead of a heart attack?

Hopefully, not before we convince Arnie to scrub it of our presence. Maybe a potpie will assuage any doubt that it's the right thing to do.

And yeah, okay, I'll throw in a few pancakes.

MARY ANN IS NOT ALONE.

Despite this, she beckons us into her home, shaking Jack's hand warmly when I introduce them.

Tommy sits outside on one of the backyard chaises. His eyes are closed, and his face is tilted toward the sun.

I get right to the point: "Vera is dead."

Tears scrim Mary Ann's eyes. "I know. Tommy went there last night. When she didn't answer her door, he made enough of a ruckus that the neighbors called the police. For once they listened to him when he insisted they open the door." Her shoulders slump. "Her body…it had been several days since her heart attack."

I put my arms around her. She melts into them.

Finally, she breaks away. As she breathes deeply, I say, "I have some good news too."

She guffaws. "Boy, could I use some!"

I nod at Jack. His kill, his news—not that Mary Ann needs to hear the particulars.

"Lilith is dead," he says. "So is the class's instructor, Arthur Yates."

It takes a moment for this news to sink in. The realization comes with a ghost of a smile. "There is a God after all!"

"Mary Ann, please—can you now tell us who Scorpio is?"

She shakes her head adamantly. "Not while he's still alive! If he ever found out..." Her voice trails off. "Except for Tommy, everyone I've ever cared about is now gone. Donna, this isn't just about my survival! If Scorpio came after me, even if Tommy weren't on his radar, eventually Scorpio would discover he's still alive too." Her eyes open wide. "I almost forgot—I have something for you! When Tommy showed up, he had this on him."

She walks over to a bookcase. From its lower shelf, she pulls out a notebook. "I think the equation on the last page may be of interest to you. Tommy remembered he changed the code in the software that initiates the laser's kill shot." She hands it to me. "By the way, I hope you don't mind. I made a suggestion on how the code could be further altered."

"Will it completely immobilize the laser?" I ask.

"Oh, no." She grins impishly. "It'll still light up the sky—but only with the words, *Universal Peace.*"

We're still laughing as she walks us out the door.

"HAVE YOU SEEN THE NEWS THIS MORNING?" RYAN'S CALL, TO both my phone and Jack's, comes in much too early the next morning.

And, since he's not one to mince words, we know we don't have to wait for the punchline: "Jacob Grommet committed suicide."

It's not the one we expected. But hey, it'll do.

"Not surprising," I counter. "He knew too much, and he was too volatile to keep in play."

"No arguments there," Ryan concedes. "Oh! And, another item of interest: Congresswoman Grisham succumbed of a heart attack. It happened yesterday, here in LA."

"Oh…" I do my best to sound alarmed as the other shoe drops. "But, she wasn't that old, was she?"

"Forty-something," Ryan replies. "By the way, did you know she was a Stanford grad?"

"I…had no idea." I'm still praying my reaction is worthy of an Oscar nod. "Jack? How about you?"

"A lot of movers and shakers have come out of that school," he adds blithely. "I'm sure her colleagues will miss her dearly."

If any are left.

"May she rest in peace," Ryan mutters. "By the way, Branham wants a briefing as soon as possible on all operations."

"I'll write up the reports on Horoscope and Flame today," I promise.

"No need. He wants to do it face to face. We leave for DC in two hours."

I stifle a groan.

"Jack, I assume your mission is over as well." Ryan knows better than to ask anything else.

"Affirmative," Jack replies.

"You're welcome to come along for the ride." This is Ryan's way of saying that Branham wants to hear about Lilith in person.

"Sure, what the heck. DC is always a joy in January."

Jack's sarcasm is not lost on Ryan. He chuckles as he clicks off.

20

Scorpio

Scorpio is the sun sign for anyone born between October 22nd and November 23rd.

Scorpio is a passionate person. You'll also note that he has a charismatic personality!

Of course, both of these traits have their dark sides. Vengeance comes easy—sometimes to the point of self-destruction. Remember the fable of the scorpion and the frog? Yeah, like that.

Let me put it this way: fascinating folk, for sure. But get too close, you may get stung.

"Next stop, Liberty Crossing," Ryan declares.

He's referring to Branham's office, which is located in LX2 of the Liberty Crossing Intelligence Campus, in McLean, Virginia.

On the seven-hour flight to DC, conversation was kept to

a minimum. But now that we're a mere mile from our designated exit off VA 267E, Ryan is eyeing us warily. I don't think he likes being left out of the loop, or waiting to hear what we disclose to his superiors without it first having been vetted by him.

At the same time, he knows our silence gives him plausible deniability.

Like him, we want to protect Acme at all costs.

My phone buzzes softly. I look down to read the message just received. It's from Emma:

POTUS requests YOU meet him in the Oval.

I shake my head. "We have to take a detour first. POTUS wishes to see me."

Jack and Ryan turn to stare at me.

Neither of their phones was sent the same request. The message here: Edmonton wishes to see me alone.

"GREAT TO SEE YOU AGAIN, MRS. CRAIG." MARIO MARTINEZ meets me in front of 1600 Pennsylvania Avenue's iconic rotunda, which faces the White House's South Lawn.

By the time I shake his hand, Jack and Ryan's car has already been directed to one of the parking spaces further down the drive.

Somehow, I'm able to lift a smile that isn't quivering on my lips. "I was surprised by the President's invitation."

"He got word you were in town, so the timing of his request worked out," Mario replies.

He knew I was in town? How?

And what will he be 'requesting'?

The rest of the journey to the Oval Office is made in silence. Mario and I pass through several security checkpoints. Armies of aides scurry about; many new faces. In fact, I don't recognize any from my many visits when Lee was president.

Edmonton has cleaned house.

He has good reason to surround himself with only those who are loyal to him. Too many of us have reasons to doubt his allegiance to anyone but himself.

"AH, MRS. CRAIG! ALWAYS A PLEASURE!" EDMONTON STANDS to greet me. In fact, he goes as far as walking to one of the two facing sofas in front of his mammoth desk. As he sits down, he pats it. "Please, have a seat."

Do I have a choice as to where? I guess not.

If I had, heck, I wouldn't even be in this room.

While he waits until I get settled, his eyes never leave me. His thin grin never fades. It may only be a few minutes but it seems like an hour before he finally speaks:

"You were there when Arthur Yates took his poison pill."

How would he know this?

Edmonton shrugs my stunned silence. "Not to worry. Your people did as instructed and scrubbed the facility's security footage. How were you to know there was also an unrelated surveillance camera inside Arthur's suite?"

"So, the CIA already knew of his actions?" I ask.

Edmonton's laughter rings through the oval office.

"Now, wouldn't that have been an interesting twist to this sordid little tale!"

Suddenly, it dawns on me: Russia would have never let Arthur go. Not as long as his assets were still in play.

Not while he was alive.

Not as long as he was still a loose end in Russia's web of embedded spies.

But there's still one traitor left:

Scorpio.

I lay my hand on his chest, between the first and second button of his white oxford shirt.

He's not surprised, let alone offended. In fact, he smiles.

I slip two fingers around the second button. When it's undone, I pull out a chain.

It holds a charm: the sun sign, Scorpio.

Bradley Edmonton.

I rise, but Edmonton grabs me by my arm and jerks me down again, closer this time. "Only those operatives with vast knowledge of our past successes and current missions were given L-Pills. As for the horoscope talismans—well, they were Arthur's personal touch."

So, now I know.

I shrug at the irony of it all. "In your position, Scorpio, you'd have certainly earned yours too."

Edmonton cackles. "Mrs. Craig, you are too smart for your own good!" He stops, angrily hissing, "But not smart enough to have realized this before now." He grabs my hair and yanks me so close that we're face to face. "Otherwise, you wouldn't be sitting here now. You and your husband—your family—would have all disappeared."

"We would have never run," I retort.

Okay, maybe. But telling him so gives us cover if and when the time comes.

"Foolish bitch! I mean you would have been *exterminated*." He leans back, but he holds firm to my wrist. "Instead, I have greater plans for you—and you'll agree to them. Or else, Jack will be tried for treason."

I pull away from him. "On what grounds?"

"The murder of U.S. Congresswoman Elle Grisham." He lets that sink in.

"She died of natural causes," I point out.

He wags a finger at me. "We both know that's not true."

Edmonton had her room bugged too.

Fuck.

Edmonton peers into my eyes and then crows, "Thank you for the confirmation! Up until now, it was just a guess on my part. You see? Already our little partnership is paying off."

"Partnership?" I frown. "What do you mean by that?"

His eyes run over me. "Congratulations, Donna. You're now the newest member of the White House staff."

"Oh yeah?" The thought is so ludicrous that I can't help but smirk. "In what capacity am I to serve?"

Edmonton jerks me close. As he runs his finger over my cheek, he whispers, "Any. All. As you so preciously put it, you'll be totally at my beck and call."

His mouth finds mine. In no time his tongue separates my lips, probing deep into my throat.

I try my best not to gag. A harder reflex to squelch is the urge to bite his tongue in half.

Finally, he pulls away. He shrugs. "You'll learn to like it. All of it."

I've been duly warned.

Noting my silence, he adds, "If you must have an official capacity, we'll call you 'Senior Security Advisor to the President.' That should keep tongues from wagging."

All but yours, unless it finds its way into my mouth again.

He leans in as if he's got a secret to tell: "Frankly, Jack did me a favor. You see, Lilith was somewhat greedy. She insisted that I make her my vice president before the upcoming election." He shudders at the thought. "Could you imagine having that viperous slut down the hall from me? How long do you think it would have taken before she set me up for...well, I don't know—perhaps treason?" His eyes dance at the thought. "Or maybe she'd have had me killed."

I could see the attraction to that theory.

His fingers move down over my body. I resist any urge to move, to give him the pleasure of seeing me scared or angry.

Certainly not turned on.

Disappointed, he mutters, "You're dismissed, Mrs. Craig."

I do my best to walk out with my head held high.

"WHAT DID POTUS WANT?" THE QUESTION COMES FROM Ryan, not Jack. My husband has already read the answer on my face: *I've been asked to pay the price for his unsanctioned deed.*

Because a half-truth is not a lie, it is much easier to tell: "He has his suspicions about Lilith's death," I admit. "Let's see Branham."

Ryan nods. "He's waiting for us now."

As Jack starts the car's engine, he catches my eye in the rearview mirror.

I look away.

The ride to McLean is made in silence.

Now is not the time to tell Jack and Ryan that the President of the United States is a traitor.

When it is—say, within the next hour—it should make for an interesting topic of conversation.

21

Opposition

[Donna's horoscope today]

An "opposition" is when planets are exactly opposite each other in the astrological chart wheel.

As with the rest of life, oppositions create stress, anxiety, and heartache.

It can happen when your beloved lies to you.

And when your children disobey you.

And when you learn what horrible things your best friend has been saying about you behind your back.

Time to put things in perspective! And by that, I don't mean you should divorce your beloved. Or, disinherit your children.

And no need to ruin your former friend's life with a manifesto that quotes all of her other vicious remarks about others.

Instead, work to heal these rifts before slights and misunderstandings grow even more significant and ruin the universe you've worked so hard to create.

Can't we all just get along?

Let's make love, not war —
For the next twenty minutes, anyway.

"M<small>Y</small> <small>THANKS TO</small> A<small>CME FOR ITS SUCCESS IN ANNIHILATING</small> Horoscope," Marcus Branham says. "It was no easy feat, considering what you were up against."

Ryan smiles. "Arnie has informed me that the code modification to *Universal Peace* went undetected. Besides destroying all previous versions of Horoscope, now any further attempts to modify the code will lead to a net-worm infiltration, providing us with a back door to the servers involved."

"Brilliant," Branham murmurs. "And the perfect finale to my career."

I frown. "I beg your pardon, sir?"

"You heard correctly. In fact, you're the first to hear the news." Branham shrugs. "POTUS has requested that I come to the Oval, which I'll do immediately after this meeting. I have it on good authority that he will ask for my resignation."

I'm sure the emotions playing out on my face mirror those on Jack and Ryan's: Shock. Despair. Anger.

Finally, Ryan nods. "You'll be sorely missed."

"Thank you." There is a heaviness in both men's voices.

"Then I guess we should fill you in as soon as possible about other recent developments," Jack says.

Branham shakes his head. "At this point, I'd rather you didn't. As with Horoscope and Flame, I'd have to forward a summary report with any additional intelligence to my successor—someone chosen because the president has his allegiance."

In other words, keep what we know to ourselves.

Even if it proves that POTUS is an enemy operative?

If Acme can't trust the next Director of Intelligence, who can we trust?

Hell, I've got to say something—to all of them—

But then Ryan's phone buzzes.

He glances at the screen. What he reads has him sitting up ramrod straight. He frowns. "I've just been asked to go to the White House."

We're all stunned into silence.

Edmonton is going to dissolve Acme.

He'll ask Congress to conduct a formal hearing, call for an investigation based on what he knows about Jack's rogue extermination, and then threaten to jail Acme's operatives for following through on Horoscope and Flame despite having sanctioned them.

In Jack's case, the deaths of two women—one an elected official—will earn him a death sentence before we can prove Elle was a foreign operative.

And we'll have to convince the world that Edmonton is the real foreign operative.

Ryan turns to Marcus. "Since we're going to the same place, mind if I hitch a ride?"

Marcus smiles weakly. "I'd welcome the company."

Ryan tosses the car keys to Jack. "Take Donna to an early happy hour."

He knows me all too well.

Hmmm. I should keep my wits about me. I may say something I'll later regret.

WE'RE CAMPED OUT ON THE LAST TWO STOOLS IN THE MORRIS American Bar on 7th Street. The place is known for its craft cocktails.

For some reason, Jack is abstaining.

He's also philosophic about this mission and our role in it. "We're the knights on some grand political chess board! We carry out missions—subterfuge, exterminations, sabotage—upon the whim of a few political grandmasters! But sometimes they make the wrong call. And who pays for it? We do!"

At first, I wasn't going to drink either. But his diatribe is depressing me. I wave to the bartender, a hipster with the chin scruff to prove it.

He nods and meanders over. "What can I get you?"

"Make it interesting," I mutter. "And make it potent."

"I've got just the thing."

A moment later he slides something in front of me.

I take a sip. It reeks of potent, alright. "What's it called?"

"It's a Backwards Point: Scotch, Cynar, and vermouth."

I nod. If I'm to get through Jack's discourse on the life of a spy, I'll need something to take the edge off my guilt.

By the time I've downed it, Jack has moved on to his wariness about Edmonton. "I never thought I'd say this, but I think we've got a president even more conflicted than Lee. Worse yet, he's conniving."

Oh, Jack—dear, sweet Jack: you don't know the half of it.

This time, when I wave the bartender over, it's to request something stronger: something called a "flu cocktail"—rye, cognac, lime, ginger, and soda.

I know I should take it slow, but then Jack adds, "Why would he have wanted Vera dead? Didn't he know Lilith was right there in front of him all that time?"

I want to shout at the top of my lungs: *Yes, he knew!*

But if I do, I'll lose Jack forever—if not to a bullet when he least expects it, then to a conviction rigged to make him Edmonton's fall guy.

And if neither of these takes him, his guilt over Vera might.

As the bartender walks by, I mumble, "Let me try one of those Polish Octobers." I point to it on the drink menu: Bison grass vodka, pear brandy, lemon, bitters, egg white, and soda.

My stomach rumbles at the thought.

Or maybe it's telling me it wants food.

At that thought, a wave of nausea washes over me.

As I gulp for air and calm, Jack adds, "You were right, Donna."

"About…what?"

Tenderly, Jack strokes my cheek. "About our lives now —that is, the *rest* of our lives. Maybe we should leave Acme and this whole crazy life of lies, murder, corruption—"

It's too late Jack. Edmonton saw to that.

In no time, I've guzzled down the new drink set in front of me.

It's no fun drinking alone. Seeing the glass of water in Jack's hand, I frown. "Still teetotaling?"

He shrugs. "One of us has to be the designated driver, and my guess is Ryan won't walk in whistling a happy tune." He grins. "Hey, considering how 'happy' you've been,

I'm surprised you haven't already blabbed about what was said in your meeting with Edmonton."

My loud burp offsets my attempt at nonchalance. "It's just that...well, I feel it's best that we noodle through it with Ryan. That way, all three of us are on the same page as to our next move."

To shut Jack down from further nudging, I wave at the bartender, as if he's a rescue plane in the middle of the South Pacific. "Sir...*Oh, sir!* One of those!" I point to the drink he's about to serve to the woman on the stool behind Jack's.

The bartender winks. "A Banana Republic? Sure, I'm on it."

"He wants one too!" I point to Jack, who shakes his head adamantly.

"Bourbon, vermouth, banana, allspice, bitters? I'll take a pass," he says firmly. "I refuse to join your unfettered bacchanal." Suddenly, he nods toward the door. "Speak of the devil."

Who...Edmonton? Here?

I follow his gaze to the front door. Ryan has just walked in. He isn't smiling.

On the upside, he isn't frowning either.

Spotting us, Ryan makes his way over, bobbing and weaving through the bar's happy hour crowd.

Jack stands. "Take my stool."

Ryan doesn't hesitate. He eyes the Banana Republic that has just been placed in front of him and mutters, "This looks putrid."

"Considering Donna's intake of numerous and varied spirits, the term is apt," Jack warns him.

Ryan slides the drink as far away as possible. Noting the

bartender's raised brow, he growls, "Scotch. Neat. Make it a double."

Ah, it's going to be that kind of night.

Hearing Ryan's tone, I sober up enough to mumble, "Let me guess. POTUS canceled all of Acme's contracts."

"On the contrary. Acme is safe." Ryan leans in. "As long as I do POTUS's bidding."

"And what is that?" Jack asks.

"Take Branham's place as Director of Intelligence."

It's now Jack's turn to signal the bartender. When Hipster Dude sidles over, Jack points to Ryan's tumbler. "I'll have what he's having."

No need to let the extra Banana Republic go to waste. As I sip it, I ask, "Ryan, are you seriously considering the offer?"

"Yes, for a variety of reasons—one of which is that it safeguards Acme."

Jack frowns. "Then, who will run Acme?"

"I haven't decided yet," Ryan admits. "In the meantime, let's not mention anything to the other operatives until I've made up my mind."

Jack and I nod.

Then we down our drinks.

I need to tell Ryan that Edmonton is Scorpio.

But now that he's in POTUS's confidence, protocol dictates that he'd have to disclose the conversation.

Doing so would also put Jack in jail. Worse yet, it may get him killed.

It may get me killed too.

Ryan gives me a sidelong gaze. "Hey, since Branham shut

us down before you had a chance to tell us how your meeting went with POTUS, let's hear it."

Okay sure, let me regale you with Edmonton's offer—blackmail, really—to work at his side. Let me divulge his threat should I turn him down: that he'll ruin Jack's life—our lives—if I don't do his bidding...

All of it.

Jack nods toward Ryan. "You promised, Mrs. Craig. Well, our fearless leader is here now, so spill your guts."

Suddenly, I do just that—

Onto Jack's feet.

Ryan stares down at the mess before him: Jack's shoes and my life.

"Craigs, we have a long plane ride ahead of us. I'll take care of the bill while you go clean up."

DC's RUSH HOUR TRAFFIC GIVES ME PLENTY OF TIME TO TELL them the god-awful truth.

Instead, I opt for an embellished half-truth: "POTUS offered me a job too—that of 'Senior Security Advisor to the President.'"

Hearing this Jack stops short. The truck behind us startles us with an indignant blare of its horn. When we're once again a safe distance in front of it, Jack growls, "Just when were you going to tell me about this, Donna?"

"I told you! I wanted to wait until the three of us were together."

"Did you commit to taking the job?" Ryan turns around

so that he can look me in the eye: a downward angle since my hangover headache has me prostrate on the back seat.

I'm too ashamed to look him in the face, so I close my eyes as I murmur, "Yes."

"You told POTUS you'd take it without speaking to me first? Well, so much for 'the three of us noodling through any dilemma'." Jack retorts. "Let alone the two of us! And, what about the kids?"

"I...I don't feel any need to uproot them! Not now, anyway."

"How considerate."

I flinch at Jack's sarcasm.

No one talks during the rest of the drive.

When we get to the airport, security peruses our credentials and waves us through onto the tarmac.

Ryan gets out quickly. He walks over to George Taylor, Acme's pilot, who is doing an exterior inspection.

As I open the door, Jack says, "You can still say no." Through the rearview mirror, his eyes catch mine.

"Jack...I...I can't."

Oh, how I wish I could...

He closes his eyes.

JACK SITS UP IN THE COCKPIT WITH GEORGE. A PILOT HIMSELF, Jack enjoys any opportunity to discuss flight patterns, coordinates, and equipment.

In this case, it also gives him a reason to avoid me.

Now that my husband is out of earshot, Ryan asks, "Why did you say yes to Edmonton?"

"I'm sorry, Ryan. *I can't tell you.*"

"You did it because POTUS has something on Jack," Ryan insists.

I nod. "But...that's not all."

"He's got something on you too," he guesses.

"No! You see...I've got something on *him.*"

Ryan lets that sink in. Then: "You're right. This is not a conversation to have with me—or with Jack. At least, not now. But you should have it with someone as soon as possible." He places his hand on top of mine. "Lee."

I nod.

He's right. Lee will know what to do.

22

Grand Trine

[Donna's horoscope today]

In astrology, a "grand trine" occurs when three planets form a triangle.

This is a period of harmony. Creativity flows freely. Confidence is at its strongest.

Take a moment to study your astrological chart. Is there a grand trine in your future?

If so, take time to recognize and appreciate those who support and inspire you. Two in particular will play important roles during your grand trine.

You may ask yourself: "Wouldn't it be wonderful if my life were always in a grand trine?"

If only!

If only we were never faced with adversity.

If only conflict didn't put us and those we hold dearly in peril.

Ironically, to live a full life, we must be challenged. We must survive the tribulations put in our path.

All the more reason to choose your friends wisely.

"YOUR MOTHER HAS IMPORTANT NEWS!" JACK'S DECLARATION IS made to the children and Aunt Phyllis just as the family sits down to breakfast.

Somehow he's been able to sustain the bland look that's been on his face since we left Washington.

On the car ride back to Dulles and on the plane ride home, he didn't utter a word to either Ryan or me.

Ryan kept mute too. Maybe it's for the best. Soon Ryan may not be my boss, but he's still my friend. As such, I will follow his wise words and seek out Lee.

While in transit, I texted Lee with Ryan's suggestion:

I'd love to stop by for a chat tomorrow. You available, oneish?

HE WROTE BACK:

Always at your beck and call.

Before, I'd laugh whenever Lee used that phrase. Now I shudder. It's how Edmonton sees my role in our new relationship.

When Acme's plane landed in LA, Jack kept up the silent treatment.

With Aunt Phyllis camped out in the guest room, he had no alternative but to sleep in Evan's bedroom.

I wonder if his night was as sleepless as mine. For hours, I paced the floor, working out what I should say to him;

Deciding what I'd say to our children.

Well, now the time has come.

Jack's exclamation has put my children on high alert. When they turn to me, their faces reflect their anticipation. Mary seems intrigued. Jeff, wary, winces. Only Trisha greets the news with a smile—

Which quickly fades when I say, "I've been asked by the President to take a position in his administration. I think it is best that I do so."

Otherwise, we may lose your father.

I can't go through that again. I know you can't either.

All mouths drop open.

Aunt Phyllis chokes on her coffee.

"Mom—we can't move! Not now!" Mary is adamant. "This is my senior year! I can't just get up and leave!"

"I didn't say I was moving the family across the country. I said *I'd* be going." The words stick in my throat.

"But...when will we see you?" The anguish in Trisha's question brings tears to my eyes.

"I'll be home as often as possible—on weekends."

Jeff shifts his gaze to Jack. "Are you going too?"

"No," Jack says firmly. He does his best to smile. "You're stuck with me."

Trisha jumps up to hug Jack. "Not to worry, Mom. If Janie can look after her father, I can take care of Dad."

"Hey, that's my job!" Phyllis insists. "I'm here—and always will be—for all of you."

Hearing this, Trisha's eyes open wide. Jeff chokes down a snicker with a gulp of juice, whereas Mary closes her eyes in silent prayer.

Jack kisses Aunt Phyllis's forehead. Then he leaves the table.

A moment later, I hear his car pulling out of the garage.

He's headed to Acme without me.

Ryan will be making his big announcement today.

Despite Aunt Phyllis's help in dropping off Mary and Jeff, my detour to Trisha's school makes me later to Acme than I'd hoped.

When I walk in, the whole staff is already gathered in the handler pit. The crowd is thick enough that I don't see Jack.

Maybe that's for the best. No one else needs to see him give me the silent treatment.

All talk stops as Ryan's office door opens. He steps out, followed by Jack, who strides to one side of the wall behind Ryan. The tension that doesn't appear on Jack's face can be seen in his clenched fist. If he attempted to talk Ryan out of his decision to leave Acme, he must have failed.

"Now that we're all here, people, I have some important news. Good news—for Acme, and I hope, for the country too." Ryan scans the room. Catching my eye, he attempts a smile. "I've been offered the position of US Director of Intelligence."

The silence that seems to last a lifetime is finally broken by a thunderclap of applause.

Above it all, I hear Arnie whoop, "ALRIGHT! YES! GOODNESS PREVAILS!"

If only that were true...

"But I leave you in good hands. Replacing me as Acme's Director and Chief Intelligence Officer is Jack Craig."

No...

Can't be! Jack doesn't want it! He wants to leave it all behind...

At least, he did when I was willing to go with him...

FUCK!

This announcement is met with a second round of applause. Jack moves forward. By now he's actually permitted himself to smile. "I'm honored and humbled by your reaction. Here at Acme, Ryan has built more than a team. He's made us a family." He nods as he scans the room. "And as such we will keep to the prime objective as he has always stated it: We will only work for those who seek to strengthen democracy in our world. Our missions aren't the result of an agenda, but a vision to right grievous wrongs. We have each other's back. And above all, we trust each other."

Jack is telling me he no longer trusts me.

Why should he? He knows I'm lying to him.

All of Acme surges forward to shake his hand.

Not me. I push my way to the exit.

I've got to get out of here.

LEE LAUGHS AS HE GREETS ME AT THE DOOR. HE MAKES AN exaggerated attempt to look at his watch: "Are you still on

Greenwich Mean Time? You do know you're a couple of hours early, right?"

"If only I could set back my *life*!" I grumble.

Seeing my scowl, Lee puts an arm around my shoulder. "It's a bit early—heck, it's not even lunchtime, but you look as if you could use a drink."

After yesterday, the thought of anything that smells of alcohol or fruit—or worse yet, alcohol *and* fruit—makes me want to heave. "That's the last thing I want!" I shrug. "Are you up for a walk?"

He smiles. "I'd love that. Hey, do you mind if I take Harrison along?"

"Not at all."

He leaves me in the foyer while he trots to the nursery. A few minutes later, he's got the toddler in a chest carrier. In his jeans, sleeveless vest jacket, sunglasses and beanie, he could be any father on his way to a local park.

Sadly, we won't leave his twenty-acre estate, and his Secret Service detail will follow a few discreet yards behind us.

Just another way in which Lee is held captive by the position that changed his life forever.

Maybe what I tell him will allow him to appreciate the fact he got out with any life at all.

As we walk, I talk.

I tell him everything:

How Elle, embedded stateside decades ago by Russia,

built an identity that allowed her to rise to the height of power.

And how her compatriot, Bradley Edmonton, did the same.

I explain how Operation Flame was a diversion obscuring a bigger agenda: the launch of Horoscope, the laser weapon Lee killed when he was our president.

Hearing this, Lee's face loses all color. "From what you're telling me, it would have been built and launched anyway."

I nod.

"And since it was being launched covertly, it violates the Outer Space Treaty," he realizes. "The whole world—not to mention its target, our closest ally—would have every reason to believe it was a deliberate act of war."

"And Russia would come off as a benevolent ally," I add.

I also describe how Acme was able to track down the others whom Elle and Arthur turned into traitors.

Then, with a deep breath, I remind him of Edmonton's private meeting with Jack, here at Lion's Lair. "He tasked Jack with tracking down Lilith, but he knowingly led him to the wrong person."

"So Lilith is still at large?" Lee asks.

"No." I sigh. With what I say next, I put Jack's life in Lee's hands: "When Jack discovered this travesty, he took the law into his own hands. Lee, Elle Grisham was Lilith. Jack killed her."

Lee stops moving. From his gasp, he has stopped breathing too. Finally, he exclaims, "We have to get back to the house —now! Ryan and Branham are meeting us there—with Jack."

"What? But, why?"

"I'll tell you when we get there."

He's practically running.

I do what I can to keep up.

Only Harrison finds this funny. He squeals happily all the way to the house.

I RECOGNIZE RYAN'S CAR IN THE DRIVEWAY. THE RENTAL CAR must belong to Marcus Branham.

An au pair waits patiently in the foyer. Lee kisses Harrison's cheek before handing him off to her.

I follow him into the elevator that will take us to the mansion's top floor, where Lee's office is located.

Eve sits behind her desk. Jack, Ryan, and Marcus are there too, making small talk.

Seeing them, Lee, relaxes a bit. He actually smiles when he sees that his office door is shut.

The men nod their greetings to us.

Lee quickly shakes their hands, but then adds, "Bear with me a moment while I do something very important!"

He trots to his office door, opens it, and goes inside, leaving the door slightly ajar.

The next thing we hear is a large *CRACK*.

Then another, and another.

Alarmed, Jack rises from his chair. "Should I…"

At that point, Lee opens his door. He's carrying the antique golf club—the gift from Elle. Its wooden shaft is now broken in half. From the look of it, about three inches of the shaft had been hollowed out. A tiny metal square is buried in the hole.

Lee pulls it out and drops it in the water pitcher sitting on the corner of Eve's desk.

"A gift from Lilith," he explains.

I imagine Lee is searching his memory as to what he's said since he put it on his shelf.

I suspect we'll soon find out.

AS WE TAKE OUR SEATS IN LEE'S OFFICE, RYAN FACES OUR HOST. "I'm wracking my brain as to what we might have said since Elle gave that damn thing to you."

Lee rolls his eyes. "When I don't have important guests, I hang out in the library on the first floor. I can still work there, and it's closer to the nursery."

Marcus sighs with mock relief. "I guess we're lucky that you're such an involved father."

Lee shrugs off the compliment. "I'll always be playing catch-up with my children. The same can be said about intelligence issues since I left office"—he scowls—"after agreeing to be replaced by an embedded Russian operative."

It's better that Branham, Ryan, and Jack hear it from Lee than from me.

"What are you saying?" Jack asks.

"Tell him, Donna," Lee commands.

Oh, great. Okay, here goes everything: "Jack, Edmonton is Scorpio."

Jack says nothing for too long. Finally, he asks, "How do you know?"

"He told me himself. It's how he coerced me into

accepting the position as his security advisor. He knows you killed Vera Gantry…and Elle Grisham."

He stares at me. "You told him about Elle?"

No more lies. "Edmonton suspected it. He tricked me into confirming it. He then told me he'd have you investigated and tried for treason. It's the only reason why I agreed to—to work for him."

"You came here to tell this to Lee." It's a statement, not a question. Involuntarily, Jack glances my way. His steely gaze speaks volumes: *You told him because you trusted him. But you didn't tell me.*

"Yesterday, after I accepted Edmonton's offer, I asked Donna to confide in Lee," Ryan explains. Noting Jack's wariness at this new bit of information, he adds, "If you remember, Marcus was called into the Oval Office just before I was also asked to meet with POTUS. We rode together to the White House. I didn't know for sure he'd gotten sacked until after I accepted POTUS's offer to be his replacement. On the way to meet with you, we again rode over together. I immediately told Marcus I'd be taking the job. I then called Lee and told him."

"You did this before knowing Edmonton is Scorpio?" Jack asks.

Ryan grins. "Not exactly." He turns to Lee. "Why don't you explain?"

As with most of the awful things in my life, this also starts with my now deceased ex-husband: Carl Stone.

"I remember how shocked you were, Donna, when you

learned I'd made Carl my Director of Intelligence. Knowing his triple-agent status with the Quorum, you—and Jack and Ryan—had good reason to be upset." Lee shrugs. "What you didn't know is that I'd asked then CIA Director Branham to install a surveillance system in Carl's office, the Oval Office, and"—he pauses before adding—"Babette's office too."

Jack's eye catches mine. We must be thinking the same thing: *Lee wasn't so blind after all.*

And yet, he was still willing to take the fall for her. Go figure.

Noting our shock and awe, Lee admits, "Yes, Donna, your warnings these past few years did sink in about my not so dear departed wife... Still, I needed proof, I finally got it." He frowns. "Well, at least, enough of it to do the right thing for our country." He rises. "That's still my agenda. But I'll need your help—especially now that you'll be working from inside the viper's nest."

"The surveillance system is still active?" I ask.

"No. In fact, I had it deactivated after Carl's death."

"At least, the project was formally shut down," Marcus explains. "But what no one realized at the time was that the kill switch on the secure cloud had never been immobilized."

"So, everything seen and heard in those offices has been archived?"

Branham nods. "Imagine my surprise when I learned this! It happened a few weeks after the Quorum set up the investigation against Lee so that Edmonton could take his place." Marcus shudders at the thought.

"How did you learn about it?" Jack asks.

"For reasons which weren't revealed to us, one of our

closest allies hacked the cloud and came across the cache. After reviewing it, they backchanneled their findings to Ryan. In turn, he gave it to me."

"What was it, exactly?" I ask.

"An Oval Office meeting between Scorpio and Taurus."

"So, that's how you knew Edmonton was setting up Jack," I exclaim.

"Yes. But we had to let it play it out to have the evidence to present to the Attorney General and Congress."

"And Acme provided the evidence," Jack reasons, "But now we can't give it to you because you've been fired."

"That's not entirely true. Now that Acme's *new* director—you—has been briefed by its *former* director—Ryan—you'll soon be able to meet with the new DI on the issue—again, Ryan," Marcus explains.

"You'll just have to wait until I've been vetted by Congress and sworn in by the President," Ryan cautions. "In the meantime, Jack, Edmonton thinks he has you over a barrel. He's knows you killed an innocent woman and a congresswoman."

"And with Donna at his side, he thinks I'm under his control too," Jack reasons.

"Which is why Donna must accept Edmonton's offer," Ryan explains. "It's the only way we can get what we need to take him down."

Jack nods. "This is a lot to take in." He looks over at me. "We should talk."

No argument there.

"It's been a hell of a week, Craigs," Ryan agrees. "Take the day off. You've earned it."

Before I walk out, I give each of our three friends a hug.

I know they have our backs. And we've got theirs.

"I'M SORRY." JACK TAKES MY HAND AND LAYS IT ACROSS HIS cheek.

We didn't discuss where we'd end up. Apparently, like me, he hadn't wanted to go back to Hilldale. Our home is our sanctuary. It would have been a blasphemy to sully it with talk of the foul deeds that inevitably lay ahead.

Instead, we're sitting out on the ocean-view deck of our favorite restaurant, the Sand Dollar. Jack took me here on our very first date.

Back then, our relationship had serious issues. We'd been thrown together on a mission that was important to us, but in different ways. I wanted to avenge what I thought was Carl's murder. Unbeknownst to me, Jack wanted to catch my very much alive husband in the act of treason. We each had our own reasons for fighting the attraction we felt for each other. I knew that Jack's role as my children's father was temporary one. I hated the thought that they'd be losing their dad a second time. As for Jack, if he were right and Carl was now a Quorum operative, he'd be the one to put him behind bars.

Not the best way to sustain a relationship.

Now, five years later, we've survived, emotionally as well as physically.

Jack waited until the waitress had taken our order before breathing a word of his thoughts on all he'd just heard. Now he watches me closely for my reaction to his apology.

"I can't say I forgive you—" I begin.

His face falls.

"—Because there is nothing to forgive, Jack. Your reaction was natural in light of what you didn't know—and, as it turns out, what I hadn't been told either." I take his hand in mine. "I never congratulated you on your promotion."

"It's a hollow victory if I can't share it with you."

I chuckle. "If Ryan's scheme goes as planned, I'll have resigned long before I can be swept out with some new president's administration."

"In the meantime, we'll be a bi-coastal couple," Jack points out.

That puts a sly grin on my lips. "You know what they say: absence makes the heart grow fonder."

My comment has the opposite effect on Jack. His smile disappears. "Donna, what is Edmonton expecting from you?"

The truth. Always. Even when it hurts.

I sigh. "Besides reporting back to him on anything of interest to Russia? Maybe a black op? An extermination or two? Jack, I think we both know the answer to that. It could be…anything."

Jack nods. He knows what I'm not saying:

Sex.

In silence, we listen to the waves lapping the pier below us. Off in the distance, surfers in wetsuits slick as seals, calmly wait for the wave worth riding to shore.

If only life were that simple for us.

"Donna, darling, promise me one thing."

"Anything."

"When this is over, we're out."

"I promise." I say it without hesitation.

His eyes widen at the realization that very soon he may get what he wants.

If all goes as planned.

As his smile fades, I know it just hit him:

Nothing ever does.

—*The End*—

Next Up for Donna!

The Housewife Assassin's White House Keeping Seal of Approval

(Book 19)

In order to save Jack from being branded a traitor, Donna Craig uses her position as a senior security advisor to the President of the United States to expose the White House-embedded foreign saboteur from decimating the country's intelligence agencies.

Other Books by Josie Brown

The Extracurricular Series

Books 1, 2, and 3

The Totlandia Series

The Onesies - Book 1 (Fall)

The Onesies - Book 2 (Winter)

The Onesies - Book 3 (Spring)

The Onesies - Book 4 (Summer)

The Twosies - Book 5 (Fall)

The Twosies – Book 6 (Winter)

The Twosies - Book 7 (Spring)

The Twosies - Book 8 (Summer)

The True Hollywood Lies Series

Hollywood Hunk

Hollywood Whore

More Josie Brown Novels

The Candidate

Secret Lives of Husbands and Wives

The Baby Planner

How to Reach Josie

To write Josie, go to:
mailfromjosie@gmail.com

To find out more about Josie, or to get on her eLetter list for
book launch announcements, go to her website:
www.JosieBrown.com

You can also find her at:

www.AuthorProvocateur.com

twitter.com / JosieBrownCA

facebook.com / josiebrownauthor

pinterest.com / josiebrownca

instagram.com / josiebrownnovels